BLUE BLOOD

**By Kevin P. Wollenweber
and
HR Abajian**

Maybe you've heard, or been told, that human blood is blue in our veins because when headed back to the lungs, it lacks oxygen. But this is wrong; human blood is never blue. The bluish color is only an optical illusion.

Dolion Cozbi – Scientist

PROLOGUE

Final computer entry by Dolion Cozbi.
Environmental scientist and humanitarian.

MY TIME ON THIS PLANET is coming to an end. Am I sad to leave? Yes, I've some regrets. I wish I could've done more. Tried harder to save what is human and what we used to be.

If you read this, my last journal entry, I understand that I had many friends and supporters of my work. They knew what I was trying to accomplish. Unfortunately, I did not have enough of those people that believed. Believed in me and my research. Now, I have resigned myself to the truth. The truth that this planet is dying, and with it, all life that inhabits it. Plant, animal, reptile, insect, and yes, human.

Having conceded myself to this fact, I have decided to take my own life. Yes, this decision is perhaps premature, but it is my decision. I have grown tired. Too tired to continue the fight against ignorance and this has caused me to realize it was only a matter of time before the menace of ignorance that pursued me, found me.

My fate could've been different. My research had discovered and proved a solution to this planet's inhabitants. I've recorded, in my personal journal, this blueprint on how to create, and construct, *my* sphere. It is my hope and prayer that my personal journal will never be found. Only harm can come to whoever finds it. You might ask why I named *my* creation the Sphere? The answer is because it has no beginning or end. It is infinite and finite. Many of you would ask me to explain, but the very ignorance of humans would have taken my knowledge and used it for perverse and deceitful things.

I have built a prototype of the Sphere and it was successful. I believe, with every fiber of my soul, that I could have produced it on a much larger scale. A scale large enough to surround our entire planet. My research created an artificial ozone that could protect this entire globe from the effects of what humans have done to ruin that natural barrier that God made for us. God knew we were a fragile species. He also knew our planet was a fragile world.

It has been impossible for me to continue my life knowing this truth. Having the answer. Knowing I could have saved everyone, and everything, but now I have lost faith. I no longer believe in humanity. You will suffer what you must, and your world will die, and with it, all of humanity. Will God determine a new natural order, a prime species? Well, we will never know because it is too late for us.

My eyes grow heavy and my ability to type this final entry has become laborious. Should someone discover this entry after I am gone, know that the fate of the human species did not need to be extinction. Life for our species could have been magnificent, if only those in power would have listened. Leaders and politicians could've dropped their petty differences and struggles for power. They could have had the vision to see a future that was different than our past. If only they had believed me.

I have inserted an injection of poison into my body that will make my heart stop and my lifeforce end. With the last ounce of strength I have, I am walking out of my laboratory and onto the observation deck that overlooks the magnificent ocean three hundred feet below me.

My lifeless body will fall from this deck, plummeting down to the ocean that rages its battle against the rock that has formed the foundation on which I built my laboratory. I have dedicated my life, research, and work to the human experience. I have tried to redeem our species. Redeem us in God's eyes and have him believe, once again, that we are worthy to have dominion over this planet. Once my broken and deformed body is swept out into the ocean, my eternity will be revealed to me, at the mercy of the deep *blue* sea.

Dolion Cozbi, June 12, 2672

Three years later

Hendricks Vesper raised the glasses off the bridge of his nose and removed them, placing them on the table next to where he was sitting. His partner, Benjamin Tolmie, glanced over at his boss, stating, "You look very tired, Hendricks. I understand the need to absorb everything we've discovered here at Dr. Cozbi's lab, but maybe you should try to get some rest."

As he rubbed his eyes to gain relief from the strain of the computer glare, Hendricks responded to Benjamin like a father would who was trying to impart some parental wisdom on a young child, "Ben, I wish we had time to rest. Unfortunately, those in power should have listened to Dr. Cozbi. Now, our time is running out."

Benjamin turned in his chair to face Hendricks and quizzed his associate, "Did you follow Dr. Cozbi's work? You know, I mean, before his death."

Considering the question that had been asked of him, Hendricks carefully considered his reply, "No, not *all* of his work. Don't get me wrong, I think he was a brilliant scientist, but perhaps, he was misguided in his approach."

Hendricks stood up from the stool he had been sitting on and stretched his arms upward with clasped fingers and palms reaching towards the roof. Returning his arms to his side he reached up with one hand and with two fingers pushed back the long, nearly white hair that had fallen across his forehead. His slender, but muscular, frame revealed the ravages of a planet that had not been kind to humans, or any other living species. At forty-six years old, he looked, and was considered to be, an old man. Life expectancy on the planet had been reduced to only fifty-two years.

Benjamin returned his focus to the work he was conducting but continued his dialogue with Hendricks. "Dr. Cozbi and yourself would be close to the same age if he were still alive, wouldn't you, Dr. Vesper?"

Taken back by the question he was asked by his assistant, Hendricks chose to ignore it. Ben left his question unpursued as he noticed his boss was deep in thought and probably had not heard the question. He saw Hendricks reading a black leather-bound book. The cover was tattered, and it appeared to be very old, or at least used a lot. He would witness Hendricks pulling this same book from his coat pocket several times daily. Tolmie had always been curious about the book and what information it might contain on the pages inside. It was obviously a frequent source of reference for Hendricks. He had thought about asking him about what the source of fascination was regarding the book. But with the secretive way in which Hendricks handled the book, he thought better than to ask him.

Ben walked over to the portion of the lab that contained the centrifuge machine. He placed several vials of liquid into the machine, and then looked at Dr. Vesper, seeking his approval to start the machine. Hendricks nodded his head with approval and then returned to reading the tattered book he had pulled from his coat.

The transcription at the top of page six hundred read:

Cell Alteration and Purification. Hypothesis for altering human DNA to survive and thrive with harmful UV-B radiation from the sun.

Hendricks ran his index finger over the heading as if stroking a small child's hair and then closed the book, placing it back into his coat. He closed his eyes and tilted his head upwards towards the ceiling of the lab.

As the centrifuge began to spin, Hendricks felt an unusual confidence surge deep inside his body and soul, that this was going to be the right formula. This batch would be the answer. Hendricks whispered to himself so as not to alert Tolmie that he had mumbled anything, "Cozbi, my old friend, let us hope you were wrong, and blue blood is not an illusion."

TABLE OF CONTENTS

PART 1:
RETRIBUTION

There's a place I know of
Not far from here
Where the clean water flows
And salvation is near

CHAPTER 1: THE SHOT

THE LIGHTS IN THE TELEVISION STUDIO were hot, which made it extremely uncomfortable for everyone there as they prepared for the broadcast. Ben Tolmie stood in the background of the studio watching the makeup artist apply the tools of her trade to enhance the face of his associate, Hendricks Vesper.

"Is he almost ready?" An impatient Producer called out to the makeup artist.

Abruptly closing the kit that held the makeup, she turned, irritated, towards the Producer and responded, "He's ready. He's as good as he's gonna get." Her response was not well received by Hendricks. Despite being younger than him, he felt it was disrespectful and an insult directed at the man who most likely was going to save her life. An assistant to the producer showed Hendricks to a chair that sat adjacent to another chair which was currently void of an occupant. As instructed, Hendricks sat down in the chair while various other staff members adjusted the lighting to reflect the best light for the cameras.

Hendricks adjusted his black collarless shirt at the neck and brushed down the sleeves of the gray, tweed sportscoat that he had chosen to wear for this interview. When he was confident that his wardrobe was in order, he settled into his chair with one leg folded over the other.

An attractive blonde woman entered the room. Hendricks could see she had a good abundance of makeup applied to her face, but it wasn't necessary. Underneath the makeup, she had nothing to hide. He could tell her skin was smooth and unblemished. She reached out her hand towards him as he accepted the gesture and shook her hand. The woman's scent emitted the essence of an expensive perfume. "Hello, Dr. Vesper. I'm Antonetta Valde. I will be interviewing you today."

Hendricks attempted to stand to greet her, but she promptly instructed him to stay seated. She quickly adjusted her posture as another makeup person hurried in at the last-minute to adjust Antonetta's makeup. The smile she portrayed for Henricks displayed her perfect teeth. White and even. Obviously the byproduct of a good oral surgeon as women of today's world rarely displayed good teeth, let alone all their teeth. "Sorry to keep you waiting, Dr. Vesper. These lights are so hot and uncomfortable, but I can't get my producer to spring for better air conditioning," Antonetta quietly confided to her guest as if she was revealing a secret she didn't want anyone else to hear.

In the back of the studio Hendricks heard a voice call out, "Starting in five, four, three…" The camera zoomed in on Antonetta and she spoke to it like it was a long-lost friend.

"Good evening. I'm Antonetta Valde, and this is World Perspective Tonight. We have a very special guest this evening, the renowned doctor and scientist, Hendricks Vesper. Welcome, Dr. Vesper."

Infatuated with this woman, Vesper could barely squeak out a reply, "Thank you, Antonetta," he spoke with a slight stammer in his voice. Her eyes were green. A subtle green, but undeniably green. Her hair displayed highlights of brunette but not so much to distract from the blonde prominence. He was smitten by this woman.

Leaning towards her guest, she postured for the first question. "Dr. Vesper, your name has come to prominence in recent months on the heels of the announcement that you have made a remarkable discovery. A discovery that the leaders of the Territories say will alter our lives, dramatically. Alter them for the future of humanity."

Her eyes pierced his. For a moment he was certain she could see right through him, and she knew his secrets. Shaking off this feeling, Vesper forced a return to the moment with the demeaner of the genius he was versus a lovestruck schoolboy. "Well, Ms. Valde, first, please call me Hendricks. Dr. Vesper seems so formal, and I am not a formal person."

Valde gleamed her broad smile at him and reached out to touch his hand that was resting on his leg. "Good, then, please call me Antonetta. I prefer discussions where we're friends. Good friends, don't you, Hendricks?" He smiled a strained smile back at his host. Her hand on his had, once again, led to him to being distracted.

"Before I get into the details of your fantastic discovery, which you will unveil for our audience, tell me a little bit about your background. Where were you born, and how did you come to be a scientist and doctor?"

Hendricks delayed his response. He was obviously still uncomfortable. He gained his composure and spoke, "England. I was born in Manchester, England."

"Ah, I was certain I detected an accent," she interrupted him.

"Well, my accent has diminished a bit since I've been in the Territories. It does come back though, quite strongly I am told, when I talk with mates from across the pond," he responded with a nervous chuckle in his voice.

Antonetta returned his attempt at humor with a reciprocal laugh and returned the interview to a more serious tone, "Were you always interested in science and medicine, Hendricks?"

Feeling more at ease now, he answered, "Oh gosh, no. I always wanted to be a professional soccer player."

Antonetta was instructed to face the center camera, and she looked directly into it and spoke, "We're going to take a quick break. Stay with us as we're going to explore and learn more about our extremely funny and down-to-earth guest, Hendricks Vesper."

The mysterious voice in the back of the studio yelled "CUT."

Antonetta once again placed her hand on Hendricks leg. She leaned in close to his left ear and proclaimed, "I just love a man with a sense of humor. I believe our audience is surprised by your charisma. Keep it up!"

The man that was being interviewed was far different than Ben Tolmie had ever witnessed. This same man that he had spent every waking hour for the last five years with, was not the same man he was watching today. Ben was shocked by the casual chit-chat he witnessed with this woman. The man he knew never engaged in any idol chit-chat with anybody. The man he knew was intense and could be unpleasant.

The studio darkened, and the lights shone directly on the couple sitting across from each other. A voice called out, "Five, four…" Antonetta spoke directly to the camera, "We are back with the delightful, Hendricks Vesper. I am curious Hendricks, what made you get into the field you're in today?"

Positioning himself as if he were a camera savvy veteran that had been interviewed hundreds of times before, he looked directly into the camera and spoke to the audience watching on the airwaves, "Dr. Cozbi led me to environmental science. My main field is in Hematology."

"Were you an associate of Dr. Cozbi? Did you know him well?" Then, Antonetta, for the benefit of the audience, interrupted and took control of the interview to fill in the audience about Dolion Cozbi. "For our audience's benefit, who might not know about, or who was, Dolion Cozbi. He was a scientist known for his research in solving the effects of our depleting ozone. He was also known to be an eccentric that was extremely alarming about the future of humanity. Dr Cozbi's work was overwhelmingly debunked by the scientific community for not being physically possible, therefore he was never taken seriously and, eventually and sadly, wound up taking his own life."

Hendricks was clearly irritated. He didn't appreciate Antonetta's diatribe about Dolion Cozbi's contribution. With that same irritation emitting from his voice, he continued in his response to the television audience, "To answer your original question, Antonetta, I didn't know Dr. Cozbi. I studied his research and read his scientific publications while I was a medical student in Manchester. Even though he might have been considered a bit eccentric, and many thought of him as an alarmist, Cozbi's body of research had some merit. His research on creating an artificial ozone was genius."

For the first time since the interview began, Antonetta was speechless. She believed she might have hit a nerve with her guest and had offended him. His humorous demeaner had disappeared, and she was certain she might have lost his trust.

Without acknowledging the concern that Antonetta displayed on her face, Hendricks continued, "I became interested in Cozbi's sphere research. In theory, taking sphere technology to a planetary scale to artificially create a stable ozone was a novel concept. He was successful in creating sphere technology, but on a smaller level. His mistake was believing it could be produced on a scale to encircle our entire planet. Perhaps I shouldn't say it was *his* mistake. Maybe it is better to refer to it as *man's* mistake."

With caution, Antonetta proceeded on with this line of questioning. The journalist in her couldn't resist doing so. "Can you tell us how you know Dr. Cozbi's research, on sphere technology was feasible?"

Hendricks' attention seemed to move towards one of distraction, or perhaps he had simply grown tired of the interview, but he seemed reluctant to answer her question. He regained his composure and, for the sake of not having the audience consider him a quack, he replied, "*We* found Dolion Cozbi's laboratory. It was no secret that Cozbi was a recluse and worked alone. We discovered his lab, but first, I must interject about my statement, *we*. My associate and partner, Benjamin Tolmie and I, together, found Cozbi's lab."

The camera panned to the back of the studio where Ben was standing. Ben's embarrassment showed through as the tall man with the long dark hair, pulled back into a ponytail, gave a slight wave towards the camera. He was relieved when the camera panned away from him to return to Hendricks and Antonetta. "Ben and I came to know each other while at a government agency we were employed with. It became very evident to both of us that we shared a common belief. An idea that wouldn't be considered to justify giving research money to us. I shared with Ben that I had seen photos in scientific magazines that showed Cozbi's laboratory. We knew it had been abandoned upon his death, and if we could find it, perhaps this lab could provide the resources we needed to pursue *our* research. Those magazines provided the hints of where the laboratory might be, and Ben and I started our search."

Antonetta, was slightly timid in chiming in with yet another question, but she blurted out, "And you found it?"

"It had been abandoned for quite a while, but with some elbow grease and the fact that Ben had received an inheritance from his family to secure us financially, we brought Cozbi's lab back to life. It was there that we were able to access and resurrect Cozbi's research logs to review videos and read data on his experiments. This is how we learned and recreated his experiments on sphere technology."

Antonetta stared deeply at her guest, asking, "So, is this the discovery you have come to reveal to our audience tonight? You have rediscovered a technology that some former outcast scientist couldn't get anybody to accept years before? A planetary *bubble*, so to speak."

Hendricks began to laugh uncontrollably. Once he regained his composure enough to speak to his interviewer, he answered with a haunting tone, "No, no, Ms. Valde. Dolion Cozbi's sphere will never be an answer for the *entire* planet, but it *will* be the answer for a fragment of it. This technology is almost complete and being deployed in a secure and private area. Funded entirely by a private corporation. The sphere, once built, will begin a transformation. A transformation that will regenerate plant, animal and, most importantly, human life."

Fascinated and shocked, Antonetta continued her pursuit of extracting information from Hendricks, "So, this is the answer for humanity? Get inside the sphere and all will be fine?"

"No, no, no! This will never be the solution! Dr. Cozbi didn't realize it, but *I* do. Ben and I were successful in creating Cozbi's sphere on a large enough scale to begin building a series of connected spheres that will save food sources like plants and vegetables. Animals, reptiles, birds, every fundamental thing that is now dying on this planet."

"And what about us? It is widely reported that human's time on this planet is in jeopardy," Antonetta asked like a selfish child wanting their afternoon snack.

"These spheres could never be big enough to house humans along with everything else. They can't be used like the Ark of Noah," Henricks spoke like a preacher at the pulpit.

"Then your discovery, your revelation for humanity is something else, isn't it, Hendricks?"

Dr. Hendricks Vesper bowed his head and looked directly at the floor of the studio. He raised his head to stare directly at the camera and speak bluntly to those that had tuned in to see this interview, "Yes, it is. You see, Dolion Cozbi was an environmental scientist. A *brilliant* environmental scientist. Ben and I didn't create sphere technology, we made it work better. We are hematologists. We are *blood* scientists. We used Dr. Cozbi's lab to find a way to adapt human DNA to coordinate and adapt to the current predicament we humans have been forced into. If you wish to thrive as a human being, you can accept our solution. You can learn more about our discovery at our website, blue.com. For those that wish to visit the website, you will find information about our answer for humanity."

"And then what, Dr. Vesper?" Antonetta pressed on.

"You will learn how you can be altered forever. You will learn how to become the *new* humanity. A human that is immune to the radiation damage caused by our ozone."

"And just how will this alteration happen?" Antonetta pleaded.

"By taking the shot, Ms. Valde. By taking the shot," Henricks replied without expression. The studio went silent, and Antonetta was forced to terminate the interview due to time being up. Antonetta knew the audience wanted more answers. It was her job to get those answers for them.

Hendricks stood up and removed the microphone that had been clipped to the collar of his shirt. He walked over to where Ben was standing, placed his arm around Ben's shoulder and both men walked out of the studio. Antonetta, for the first time in her professional life was speechless and took an eternity to get up from her chair.

CHAPTER 2:
BEGINNINGS

STANDING IN FRONT OF THE BATHROOM MIRROR, Elijah Price ran the hairbrush through his receding hair line. He called out for his wife, Lark, to come join him in the bathroom. She arrived at the bathroom door and poked her head in to see her husband pulling strands of his hair from the brush. "Honey, do you think I should just shave it all off? I know several guys who've faced the fact that their hair is on its way out and have succumbed to the realization that bald is better," Elijah pleaded in earnest, knowing full well that Lark wouldn't approve his plan.

Turning away from the bathroom, Lark left her husband standing there without an answer. "Well then, I guess that answers my question," he smirked to himself as he put the hairbrush on the counter and exited the bathroom to put on his work clothes.

A short time later, Elijah walked out of the bedroom in his one-piece taupe colored jumpsuit. On the suit, just above the breast pocket, was a blue oval patch with white embroidery that read, Elijah Price. Right below his name read the words, Supervisor. On the opposite side of his uniform, was a patch with a yellow circle and a rendering that appeared similar to Leonardo DaVinci's 'Vitruvian Man' depicting the perfect man, embroidered in blue and inside a yellow circle. The name of his employer was incorporated into the logo. The name read; Spheretech, Inc.

He arrived at the modest kitchen that was just down the concrete tube that served as the hallway from the sleeping quarters. Elijah shuffled past Lark, placing his hand on her shoulder as her back was towards him. He removed a container of nutrition bars that supposedly supply at least half the daily nutrients needed for humans.

Removing one and taking a large bite, he practically gagged at the flavor that was bursting inside his mouth. "Man, you would think this company would want to keep its employees happier by providing food that we could actually eat," he spoke as he gulped down some liquid that tasted equally nasty but was provided to hydrate the human body.

Lark smiled at her husband and offered him the wisdom of the situation they were currently in, "We were starving and homeless not so long ago. You should be grateful you have this food, my dear."

"Ya know, you're absolutely right, my love. Having this chance to live in concrete tubes, underground, with this wonderful and appetizing…" Elijah held the remainder of the nourishment bar between two of his fingers, examining it, before closing his eyes and inserting the last bite into his mouth.

Coming to his side, Lark wrapped her arms around him and gave him a kiss on the lips. "Can you check the plants in the hydroponic garden before you go up, babe? I'm not sure but I think they might need more water."

"I sure hope this rationing water to grow plants will be worth it. I know gardening is your talent, my darling Lark, but it just seems weird to be growing vegetables underground," Elijah candidly spoke.

She gave him another kiss and responded to his statement like a parent telling their children to be patient about opening their presents on Christmas morning. "Once you get to eat a salad from the vegetables we harvest, you'll think it was all worth it." She helped her husband place a scarf over his face and head, wrapping it to make Elijah take on the resemblance of a desert nomad. He patted his front pocket to make sure his sunglasses were there. A person that didn't wear protective glasses while on the surface could face irreparable damage to their eyes.

Touching the soil around the plants in the hydroponic garden, he was confident it was moist enough. Elijah was pleased to see several sprouts beginning to form above the surface of the dirt. "That's my girl,' he muttered under his breath with pride at his wife's achievement. He left the cylinder that housed the garden and proceeded to a metal door. Twisting the handle, Elijah pushed the door open, placed his sunglasses over his eyes, and proceeded up the seven steps to the surface.

He was pleased to see a friend sitting in an open trailer with bench seats on either side. The truck to which the trailer was hitched displayed the same Spheretech logo that was stitched to his jumpsuit. Climbing up and onto the trailer, Elijah sat down next to Braden Samuleson, who not only was a close friend, but also worked for him. He assumed Braden was smiling at him although it was almost impossible to recognize any facial expressions through the scarves they wore. "Good morning, boss," Braden exclaimed.

Elijah responded to his friend with a cynical response, "I don't know why, if I'm the boss, I have to ride in this trailer with you slackers." Both men laughed at the comment, but it was of short duration. As the trailer began to move, the mood became sullener as the men viewed the surrounding landscape rolling out before their eyes. What was once lush with grass, flowers, and critters of various species living on the land, was now desolate. An occasional leafy weed was the only living thing trying to hang on for dear life.

The truck and trailer made a left turn and came to a stop in front of a building that was constructed of what Elijah believed was some sort of plastic material. The men that were passengers on the trailer exited down and off the trailer. Elijah looked up at a sign that hung from large wood pillars that were embedded in the ground in front of the entrance to the building.

The sign, painted in simple black letters, read: Spheretech, Inc. Extrusion Plant.

CHAPTER 3:
THE BOARD

THE SEVEN BOARD MEMBERS of Spheretech, Inc. sat quietly around a large mahogany table. They sat in black highbacked leather chairs that swiveled. The backs of these chairs engulfed the men and made them look like small children attending their first day of school.

Theopolis Clyborn, the Chairman of the Board, opened the door and strutted into the Boardroom. He sat in his opulent chair at the head of the table facing the other board members.

He was a man of short stature. Bald and with a pudgy build, he sported a handlebar mustache which he stroked incessantly. Looking out over the top of black framed reading glasses, Clyborn addressed the other board members with a question. "How do you think our boy did last night?"

There was general agreement amongst the board members that Hendricks Vesper served the purpose they had intended for him. Jonathan Simon, the Board member that was second in charge, chimed in on the discussion, "I was a little worried in the beginning of the interview. Still, I think he recovered well and did exactly what we wanted him to do, and that was to *sell* the shot. That's our cash cow, by God!"

One of the lesser Board members, Byron Johnson, blurted out, "What about spheres? Isn't that what this company is all about? I understand Vesper created this injection, but exactly how are we going to make money on *his* shot? The only way we can make money on this injection is if we get the governments to mandate it and pay for it!"

Clyborn let out an uncharacteristic bellow that made his belly jiggle like he was Santa Claus. The Boardroom became eerily silent. Then he became very serious. He removed his glasses, and holding them in his right hand, stood and walked over to the glass panes that encircled the Boardroom that sat on the thirteenth floor of the only concrete building that overlooked a landscape that was harsh and unforgiving.

Without turning around to face the other Board members, Clyborn spoke in a very loud and affirming voice so that all of them could hear, "Johnson, what you just said about getting the government to pay for the injection, well that is just *genius*! That is exactly what we are going to do." Then he added, "Cozbi's silly spheres, that is only a rouse. A necessary rouse, but a rouse none the less."

Down below the building that housed the headquarters of Spheretech, Inc., Elijah Price scanned his key card which gave him and his crew entrance to the Extrusion facility. As he walked in, he removed his sunglasses as they weren't needed inside the facility. His gawking revealed that this was the first time he had witnessed exactly what he was hired to do. And it was magnificent.

CHAPTER 4:
FIRST

AFTER A LONG FLIGHT, Hendricks and Ben arrived back at the laboratory that also served as their residence. Hendricks opened the door that provided entrance into the living quarters. Placing his suitcase next to his bedroom door, Hendricks walked into the kitchen and proceeded directly to an upper cabinet and withdrew a bottle of brandy. Reaching over to another cabinet, he grabbed two glasses and motioned to Ben, who had just appeared in the kitchen. "Don't know about you, Ben, but I am wound tight as a drum after today. I'm going to have some brandy. Maybe, a few brandies."

"Oh, definitely count me in, Hendricks," Ben replied like a dog waiting for his daily meal.

With glasses filled, both men retired to the living room and plopped down on their usual chairs of choice on the rare occasion they afforded themselves a moment of relaxation. Hendricks brought the brandy to his lips and took a large gulp. Much larger than normal, for a liquor that was designed for sipping. Neither man chose to speak. The comfort of silence was attractive, and both men decided to invite it into their living room.

It was at least ten minutes before the peace of the moment was broken by Ben. "Do you think the Board is happy with the interview?"

Hendricks managed a slight chuckle in his reply before answering, "Well, based on both of our phones ringing non-stop with every media station in the land wanting to interview me, or you, about my last comment in tonight's interview, I would say I executed their plan to perfection."

Ben smiled as he brought his glass up to his lips to drink. "What now? What's the plan now?" Ben asked in earnest, due to being in the dark about their future.

"We'll leave here to go to the Sphere1 location. The land is excavated, and the extrusion facility's ready to go online. Spheretech will send a limo for us the day after tomorrow. We'll be flying out of a private airfield near Monroe. I need to be at the Sphere1 site when the first piece of the sphere panels are installed."

Ben studied Vesper's face before drilling deeper into his boss's revelation that they would be heading to Sphere1. "You've been successful in finding the right person to lead the first extrusion?"

"Yes, I believe so. We found a man who has a vast amount of experience with polymer extrusion. He's been down on his luck since plastic's virtually outlawed in most of the Territories. When we found him, he was more than willing and eager to join us," Hendricks answered.

"Who is he?" Ben continued the questioning.

Hendricks thought for a moment before answering. "I think his name is Rice. Edward Rice." Slapping his head with an open palm, he recanted his answer and said, "Price. Yeah, that's it. Price is his last name. Lots of experience in managing plastic extrusion machines."

"But sphere technology isn't plastic. It's organic. It's a living organism," Ben added to the conversation.

Hendricks affirmed his colleague's analysis. "That's correct, but before the organism is activated, when it's in its dormant state, it behaves, and looks, almost like liquid plastic. That's the reason I need to be there when we start. We both know that after it's activated is when the magic starts. These people that are building Sphere1 will need someone there to push their jaws closed, because they will be open and in awe."

Ben laughed in affirmation of what Hendricks just said. Both men finished their brandies and, realizing that the day had moved into early morning of the next day, stood up from their chairs to begin the movement to retire to bed. Hendricks reached his bedroom first but before entering, turned to face Ben and spoke. "Hey, Ben, a thought just occurred to me. We have tomorrow to recover from the events of today, so before we get thrown back into the fire, perhaps we should take the injection."

Ben was caught slightly off guard and replied, "You have some serum here at the lab?"

"Yep. I kept two injections here. One for you, and one for me."

"Is that a wise thing to do? I mean, with the Corporation backing this whole thing. Is that part of their *plan*. For the two scientists that engineered the serum to get the injection before they have a chance to, you know, sell it," Ben asked in the manner of an accomplice in a crime objecting before succumbing to peer pressure.

"I don't care, Ben. This is our time! Our opportunity to be the two greatest scientists that ever lived."

Ben stood, looking at Hendricks Vesper. His stare immolated both a feeling of apprehension and a feeling of exhilaration. "Go get 'em, Hendricks. I'm game."

Like a schoolboy getting let out for recess, Hendricks bounded up the staircase that led to the research lab. He walked over to a refrigerator with a glass front and opened it. Inside, on the top shelf, sat two lone vials of serum. One vial was labeled with a black marker with the initials, HV. The other vial matched the first but read, BT.

Hendricks removed the vials from the refrigerator and closed it gently. Holding them like they were precious, fragile treasures, Hendricks grabbed two syringes from a drawer and proceeded back down the steps.

Upon returning from the lab, Hendricks found that Ben had sat back down in his chair. Ben glared at the vials being held tightly by Hendricks.

"You ready, Ben? You get to go first. I mean just in case this injection turns you into a monster, like Dr. Jekyll and Mr. Hyde, I can kill you!" Hendricks let out a bellowing laugh which caused Ben to feel a slight cringe.

Agreeing to get the injection first, Ben rolled up the sleeve of his left arm. Hendricks carefully transferred the serum from the vial and into the syringe. Squirting a small amount of the liquid out of the hypodermic needle to ensure there was an unobstructed flow, Hendricks swabbed alcohol on Ben's arm at the bicep. Just prior to Hendricks inserting the needle, Ben asked the question, "Why are the vials labeled with our initials? Aren't they the same?"

Not taking time to answer Ben before inserting the needle, Hendricks pushed the plunger of the syringe containing the serum, emptying the contents into Ben's bloodstream. He extracted the needle and placed a protective cap over the needle. "You're younger than I am, Ben. Your dose is slightly higher than mine due to that. This is what the research from the serum development lab shows. They use our formula, but they decide the dose for each person. Females get less than males of the same age."

Ben felt somewhat relieved by Hendricks' answer. It seemed to make sense. Then Hendricks sat down and eagerly rolled up the sleeve on his right arm. Ben reciprocated the event he had just received from Hendricks. After following the precise CCs of serum that were recommended for a man of Vesper's age, the blue serum had been successfully administered into both men's bloodstreams.

After completing the task of taking the injection, both men sat staring at each other. Hendricks broke the silence by explaining, "I doubt anything's going to be different, Ben. We aren't going to feel much of anything different. Probably best we retire to bed and we can check each other tomorrow. Sleep will most likely do us good at this time."

"No doubt," Ben agreed.

Hendricks pulled back the comforter on his bed and fluffed the pillow before crawling in. It was dark in his room. He always needed it dark in order to get his mind to quit racing and get the few hours of precious sleep he could manage each night. He knew the light of day was right around the corner so he knew he must try and fall asleep before any streak of daylight invaded his room.

Earlier, having fast-forwarded through the excessive number of voicemails from various members of the media looking to expand their careers by getting the next interview with him, Hendricks had deleted all of them, except one. His phone was the only light that shone in the darkness. He had to listen one more time to that one message. He hit the play-again button on his phone. The voice of Antonetta Valde echoed through his phone, filling his room and his soul. "Hello, Hendricks, this is Antonetta. Antonetta Valde from World Perspective Tonight. Uhm…I'm reaching out to you and leaving this message. I'm not making this call to see if you will let me interview you again, although that would be sweet if you would want to talk with me, you know, as friends. I guess I'm calling you because I find you different. I mean as a man. Oh crap, why am I bothering you with this nonsense I've been spewing. What I'm trying to say is…I want to see you again. Can you reach out to me and let me know if you want to see me too?"

The message ended with the sound of Antonetta hanging up. Hendricks shut off his phone and let the dark engulf his room along with the echo of her voice.

CHAPTER 5: ORIENTATION

THE INSIDE OF THE EXTRUSION FACILITY was much larger than it looked from the outside. Elijah couldn't even speculate how big this facility was from what he could glimpse through the wall of small windows that provided a barrier to the plant's interior. Once his entire group of ten men and two women were inside the building, a figure emerged via a metal door that was controlled pneumatically.

A black man with a broad and pleasing smile that displayed a front upper tooth that had been capped with a silver crown hurried to greet the group. "Hello there, Team A," the man motioned everyone to gather around him. "My name is Silver James. Well, it's Jon James actually, but everybody calls me Silver. If I must explain why, well, then I'm sorry for you." Elijah and the other members of Team A chuckled at the jovial greeting they just received from the man.

Gathering everybody closer to him, he continued his greeting, "I will explain later the significance in the designation of y'all as Team A. For now, I want to give y'all the lay of the land and orientate you to this facility, and exactly the job you'll be doing for all of humanity." Elijah liked this guy. His accent was clearly southern Territory. He found comfort in him and that brought some peace to his apprehension about being here and coming to work for Spheretech.

Dressed in a clean room white suit, sans the hood covering, Silver pointed towards the wall of windows that framed the lobby of the facility and spoke. "As you can see, there is no direct access to the plant. The reason for that is because this facility is a clean room which explains this fancy suit I'm wearing." Elijah found this statement from him strange. He had been an Extrusion Specialist for most of his adult life, and none of the plants he had worked at had ever been a 'clean room' facility. There was never a reason for it to be, from what he could recall.

"I suppose you're asking yourself why a clean room?" Silver asked simultaneously as the question had popped into Elijah's head. "That question will be answered for you soon enough. I'm sorry for all the mystery, Team A, it's just, to answer all those questions now would be putting the cart before the horse." Wishing that explanation had made him less apprehensive, Elijah had to put his questions on hold knowing, or hoping, they would eventually be answered.

Silver placed his index finger over a small dark screen that read his fingerprint. Once affirmative identification had been made, the door popped open, and Team A followed Silver through it. They were in a long hallway adorned with white porcelain tile that emulated a sterile atmosphere. Silver pointed to the left, where a sign beside a door read 'Women's Locker Room', and to a door on the right labeled 'Men's Locker Room'. He said, "Each of you will gain access to this area the same way you just witnessed that I did. You will be fingerprinted, and that fingerprint will become your access key to this part of the facility. Every time you come into this facility, you are required to enter the locker room of your gender, undress, and shower. Do not worry about hygiene products, Spheretech supplies everything you will require."

"This is definitely different than any orientation I've ever had," Elijah thought to himself. Once inside the locker room, the men of Team A muddled about, admiring the cleanliness of it. Each man had an assigned locker in which to hang their uniform, scarves and sunglasses. Silver requested that each man disrobe and move to the shower areas. Elijah watched as Silver himself proceeded to disrobe. Curious about the event, Elijah raised his hand to ask a question.

"Yes, Mr. Price. Can I help you?" Silver responded to the raised hand.

"You're taking a shower too?" Elijah quizzed.

Silver let out a small laugh as he continued to disrobe and replied, "As I said, every time you come through that big metal door that we all just came through, you gots to take a shower. No alternative."

As the men in their nakedness entered into the shower area, Silver showed them the dispensers that contained shampoo, conditioner and body soap. Each shower stall contained a digital monitor that would control water temperature and pressure.

Elijah looked around at the men in the shower area and could see the delight etched on their faces. As he dipped his head under the running water, Elijah felt the ecstasy of hot, steaming water. The water itself smelled delightful. There was no chemical sanitation smell like the excessive chlorine that permeated their subterranean showers. Even the shampoo and soap had an aroma that was pleasant without being harsh.

"I would suggest you shower here, instead of at home, if you happen to be a morning shower person. Here you have no rationing. Stand here, under this fresh, hot waterfall for as long as you want. For those of you that shower at night, y'all might want to change your hygiene schedule," Silver laughed. Elijah considered this a major perk of the job, considering how much water consumption that would save for Lark to expand her garden.

Elijah stood before a warm, hard burst of air that dried his entire body. Once dry, he exited the shower area and into another locker room containing various products like lotions, gels, and a comb and hairbrush. Each member of Team A had their own 'clean' locker with their name posted above it. Inside each locker was a clean room suit adorning the same name and title patch as their *outside* uniforms. Except this suit contained a patch, located on the upper arm of the right sleeve, which displayed the same corporate logo but this one had the words 'Sphere1'. The suit fit perfectly. It amazed Elijah that this company placed so much emphasis on detail.

Motioning everybody to join him, Silver advanced beyond the second locker room and out into the main facility. Heads moved back and forth as the members of Team A eventually moved out and onto the main floor of the facility. Elijah could see the looks of wonder in each of their eyes.

Silver smiled at the group, making no effort to hide the appliance that adorned his front tooth. "What you think of those showers, ladies?", he jokingly addressed the female members. Both bobbed their heads in affirmation that they hadn't recently enjoyed anything as much.

Glancing around the facility, Elijah guessed the building was at least twenty thousand square feet. It was difficult for him to gauge as he was having trouble seeing all the way to the rear of the building. He assumed it was the rear of the building as he detected there were several large doors that probably moved from floor to ceiling. He wondered if those same doors, when extended upward, were adjacent to, or perhaps even close to, the excavated area. An excavated area that was bowl shaped and, from what he was told by the men that hired him, was close to one hundred and seventy acers in circumference.

CHAPTER 6:
BLUE

THE SUN CREPT AROUND THE EDGES of the drawn blinds like a cat burglar gaining entrance to their next job. Hendricks rolled over in his bed seeking to continue the sleep he so desperately needed. Unfortunately, he glimpsed the light, and this forced his desire to look at the illuminated alarm clock on the nightstand next to the bed. He grumbled, "Ten thirty, crap!" Realizing the time of day indicated he had only had five and a half hours of rest, he tossed the bed covers off from around his body and, placing his legs on the floor, he pushed his feet into slippers that had been placed neatly on the floor.

His mind was already racing with all the items he needed to get accomplished today. The focus of his thoughts was on the journey that he and Ben would be undertaking tomorrow. His excitement about finally getting Sphere1 underway was abounding. He wondered if Ben was as restless as he was. Sphere technology didn't seem to inspire the same excited emotions with Ben as it did with him. Regardless, it was the first step, and it needed to be done.

Hendricks shuffled from his bedroom and into the bathroom. Turning on the light he grabbed his towel and hung it on a hook next to the shower. Peeling off his pajamas, he turned the handle that started the water pouring from the shower head. He placed the handle in the spot that he always did that ensured the temperature of the water was how he liked it, which was almost at a scalding temperature.

After allowing a short time for the water to reach the desired temperature, Hendricks stepped into the shower. Almost immediately, he jumped like a frog on a lily pad, out of the shower and back onto the bathroom floor. He reached an arm into the shower to feel the water. He was curious as to why the water felt so cold to him because he clearly saw steam rising up from the shower floor. He was stumped as to why the water felt so cold.

Turning the handle much farther than he ever had to increase the flow of hot water, he, once again, reached a hand into the shower. Although it felt warmer than before, it still wasn't at the temperature he preferred. He decided it was best to just hurry his bathing versus trying to investigate why his hot water seemed so luke- warm today. He finished his shower and grabbed his towel from the hook he had placed it upon and, after drying himself, he stepped over to the mirror. He thought it odd that the mirror was completely steamed over. The water just didn't seem that hot today.

Hendricks took his towel and wiped the fog that had formed on the mirror. Looking into the mirror he was startled, so much so that he pushed back from the counter, almost tripping. He moved forward to the mirror, and in disbelief, he blinked his eyes at what he saw. Moving even closer to the mirror and switching his face from left to right, he moved slightly back from the mirror.

Up to this point in time, and for his entire life, Hendrick's eye color had been hazel. Staring back at him from the mirror appeared a man whose iris color was now ocean blue. As blue as you would find in seas of the Caribbean. "I didn't see this coming," Hendricks pondered to himself as a man that had just seen a ghost.

He stood in front of the mirror for what seemed like an eternity before he finally pulled himself away to move back into the bedroom. Dressed casually in blue jeans, a tee shirt and continuing to wear his slippers, Hendricks walked into the kitchen to begin the morning ritual of brewing coffee. In fact, with the pace of their recent lives, both he and Ben brewed several pots every day.

Hendricks was rinsing the coffee pot when he was suddenly startled by Ben's voice calling out from his own bedroom in an excited manner. "Holy Cow, Holy Cow, Holy Cow," Ben, clearly exasperated, repeated over and over. Hendricks set down the coffee pot and hurried to Ben's bedroom door to investigate. Ben swung open the door just as Hendricks arrived. Ben stood before Hendricks pointing furiously at his eyes, eyes that had once been brown in color but now were the same ocean blue color as his partners.

"Look, Hendricks. Look!" said Ben, who was clearly agitated. Then, he seemed to calm down as he stared at Hendricks. "Wait, you too?" Ben offered in a stupefied manner.

"Yes, Ben. Me too."

Hendricks instructed Ben to come into the kitchen and sit down. Ben, who was still breathing heavily from an accelerated heartbeat, quizzed Hendricks, "Did you know about this? That this was a side effect?"

"No, Ben, I didn't. None of the clinical tests conducted by the lab reported that a subject's iris color changed after injection."

"Should we be concerned about this development?" Ben inquired, hoping to get an answer that might calm him.

Hendricks stepped up to Ben and placed a hand gently on his face and inquired. "How is your vision, Ben?"

"I don't see a difference."

"Me either, Ben. Let's be diligent. Remember, we're scientists. We need to draw blood on each other and do our diligence to this occurrence. Perhaps it's temporary. We just don't know," Hendricks replied like a father calming his child that had just fallen from a swing set.

Ben felt compelled to add the following question, "Should we alert the lab? After all, if they haven't shown this side effect in their trials, they might want to know."

Hendricks pretended to ponder Ben's question before answering, "Let's not jump the gun, Ben. We need to do our diligence. We need to calm down and have some coffee and something to eat. You know how you get when you're 'hangry'."

Neither man spoke much as they ate their morning meal. Hendricks suggested they go upstairs to the lab and get started on drawing blood. He offered his arm first, to get Ben preoccupied with *busy* tasks to relieve his anxiety. Ben carefully inserted the needle into Hendrick's left arm and began to draw blood. As his blood filled the vial, Hendricks was elated and found it hard to control his emotions. Inside the vial was exactly what both men had devoted several years of their lives to see. His blood was a deep color of blue.

CHAPTER 7:
NEW BEGINNING

A VOICE CAME OVER THE INTERCOM of Silver's radio requesting that he come to Extrusion Platform Number Seven. Excusing himself from the members of Team A, he stated he would be right back and for them to feel free to walk around the immediate area where they presently were. "Just don't touch anything," Silver exclaimed in a half humorous way as he walked away. The other half of his statement struck Elijah that he was being totally serious.

Elijah was mesmerized by the extrusion equipment. The size was simply much larger than he had ever seen or operated. A large, red number '1' was painted on the side of the machine just above a panel that contained several controls. It certainly explained that platform number seven, where Silver had gone, meant that this facility had at least seven extrusion machines.

Looking upwards to the ceiling, he saw five hoppers that most likely contained the base material that fed into the machine. Every machine that he had ever operated before had only one hopper, which was manually filled by the operator, and the filler usually consisted of pellets of solid polypropylene. These five hoppers were huge, and moved on a conveyor system that appeared to stop at a pneumatic pressure tube while the hopper was filled with whatever material they would be working with. He was curious as to why there were five hoppers because extrusion machines generally moved very slowly, and a hopper could very easily be filled whenever it was running low on base material.

Elijah's curiosity peaked even more when it didn't appear that the machine's water tank was connected to a heating unit. Extruded material must flow through extremely hot water to become pliable when it reached the dye unit. Well, at least that's the way every extruding machine he had worked on operated.

These were questions he needed to ask, along with noting the size of the extrusion die which was the flattest and largest he had ever seen. He suspected that this machine would be extruding sheets. Large, flat sheets. From a short distance he could see Silver approaching the group. Walking straight up to Elijah, he reached out his hand and placed it on Elijah's shoulder. "Impressive, isn't it?" Silver spoke, with his shiny tooth showing brilliantly.

Gathering the members of Team A around him, Silver announced, "Sorry for my short absence Team A, but the wait is going to be worth it." Just then, sirens began blaring, and lights began flashing. "Time to follow me towards the large doors at the back of the facility. We gonna get a show today."

Elijah, along with the other group members, followed their guide to the back of the facility. As they walked, they witnessed the large door begin to rise from its closed position, and with an accordion movement, move up towards the ceiling. As he walked past other machines that were similar and as equally impressive as Number One, Elijah reached the back of the building. He looked up to see the door reach its open position and stop.

Silver instructed the group to move through the doorway and stand clear of where the door had sat when it was fully closed. Elijah could feel cool air being blown towards the doorway they had just come through. Once everyone was at a safe distance, the sirens and lights flashed once again, and the door began to close. Once the door was fully closed, the group found themselves in a large open room void of any machinery. At the very back of the building was another large door, but this one moved horizontally and disappeared into the wall of the building.

Elijah stood in amazement as the door opened and he began to catch a glimpse of the landscape as it came into view behind the building. At approximately three hundred feet to the rear, and another three hundred feet below the floor of the extrusion plant, he was looking out upon a concrete surface formed to fit the inside of a bowl that had been excavated from the earth. A ramp descended from the back of the facility and joined the concrete bowl with a series of roads surrounding the circumference of it.

Even at an elevated level, Elijah couldn't see where the concrete bowl ended. It reached out much further than he had been told or could imagine. Silver called out for the group to follow him, interrupting Elijah, who did not want to take his eyes off the wonder before him. He led them through a metal door which read, 'Not An Exit'. Once through the door, Elijah found himself in a stadium sized auditorium. At the front was a huge white screen that extended fully across the auditorium.

Silver walked to the front and addressed Team A once they had all been seated. "Okay, Team, you're going to have a chance to relax and watch a short movie presented by our Chairman of the Board of Spheretech, Mr. Theopolis Clyborn. After the film, I'll answer any questions that you have, and then we'll move to another part of the facility in order to take your fingerprints, that will allow security entrance for you to do the valuable work you've been so fortunate to be chosen for."

The lights dimmed and the film started with Clyborn introducing himself to Team A. Elijah carefully listened as the 'Big Guy' conveyed to them that they were the *first* Extrusion Specialist Team, and they would be embarking on history, with their mission being to extrude what he referred to as, *panels*. These panels, along with others of different sizes, would be used to build the very first sphere of its size. When completed, the sphere would extend across two hundred and fifty acres and reach a height of twenty thousand feet. With that statement, Elijah and most of his team, he was sure, found themselves gasping for oxygen.

The rest of the film went largely ignored after the thunderous explanation about the duty that was laid before them. The lights of the auditorium came on and Silver could see the stupefied stares on the faces before him. He displayed his platinum smile and calmly asked, "Any questions before we go for fingerprinting?"

Unable to let the mysteries of what his team had just seen and heard go unanswered, Elijah adjusted his posture and sat up in his chair. "Yes, I have a few questions, just curiosities I suppose, but I'll ask them anyway. First, I didn't notice heat units attached to any of the extrusion machines we saw. Will they be installed by the time we start production?"

Silver replied with a prompt answer that was equally compelling to any extrusion specialist. "Our water will not be heated, Elijah. On the contrary, our water will be *chilled*. This operation will be very much the same as what you have done in your past, except, we...you...will be conducting *cold* extrusion."

A mumble transcended around the group that was seated in the auditorium. Elijah was equally confused by what Silver had just said. "Okay, I'll let that answer go for now because I'm probably equally as confused as my Team. My second question is, when we followed you to the back of the building, when the large door was raised and then lowered, I felt a significant amount of air blowing my suit. Why was that?"

Silver gave a brief chuckle before supplying a respective answer, "Our facility is a clean room, Mr. Price. The air you felt was to keep any pathogens from the outside from penetrating into the production facility."

Elijah stroked his chin after receiving the answer he had just been given. "Okay then, I guess that is my next question, I'm not sure exactly what we are going to be extruding, but those hopper bins were huge, and there seemed to be a lot of them. What, exactly, will we be extruding, and why do we need to be concerned with pathogens?"

Silver's manner turned quite serious with his answer. "Elijah, we live in a new world. Science has risen to provide the tools needed to combat and conquer this new world. I do not feel that I can adequately answer your question right now. But, to not ignore your valid question, I would ask you to be patient."

"Patient? How in the heck can we do our job if we don't know what we are going to be working with?"

"Hendricks Vesper will be here in two days. He will be working directly with you, Elijah. Overseeing our beginning. I suggest you become familiar with your machine over the next couple of days, then ask Dr. Vesper," Silver answered, knowing he could not divulge any more information today.

CHAPTER 8:
LARK

WRAPPING HER LINEN SCARF AROUND HER NECK and up around her face to cover it, Lark almost forgot her sunglasses before stepping out onto the surface. She quickly ran back down the stairs and grabbed the glasses. Putting them on, she hurriedly ran back up the stairs. The sun was bright today, and she could immediately feel the heat it produced. The stark landscape of the surface surrounded her and, as with every time she came up to the surface, it made her sigh.

Off in the distance she detected dust that was being churned up by a vehicle approaching her. When the truck pulling the trailer that carried her husband came to a stop twenty feet from where she was standing, her heart was beating rapidly. She was excited to see her husband and to hear all about his first day working for Spheretech.

Jumping off the trailer, Elijah waved at the members of his team that remained on the trailer and were heading towards their subterranean homes. He headed towards his wife who was running towards him. Wrapping her arms around him, he felt the embrace of a woman that had endured so much in this treacherous world. He welcomed her arms around him and he reciprocated by holding her tight, as if he might never let go.

Grabbing Lark's hand in his, he led her towards the entrance of the staircase that descended to their underground home. As they reached the bottom of the stairs, both had already removed the protective nomad coverings from their faces. Throwing open the door to their barren home constructed of concrete tubes, Elijah took Lark into his arms and kissed her lips with passion. He loved this woman with every fiber of his soul.

Walking arm in arm down the pathway to their kitchen, Lark questioned him, "Your uniform is clean. I expected it to be, you know, dirty."

Elijah smiled with amusement at her perception. "Today was just orientation. Albeit a very interesting orientation. I don't wear my uniform in the facility, so it doesn't get 'dirty'.

Lark tilted her head in confusion at her husband's revelation. "Then what do you wear? Do you work in the nude?" She playfully responded.

Elijah sat down in one of the two kitchen chairs that had been supplied for them. Patting his lap, he invited Lark to come sit with him. "I have so much to tell you, sweetheart. It's amazing. The reason I don't wear this uniform inside the facility is because we're supplied clean room uniforms."

"Clean room?" She exclaimed.

"Yes, clean room. Can we eat first, before I tell my story? I'm starving."

Not wanting to push her husband into telling her everything about his day yet, Lark got up from his lap and walked to the oven where she removed a dish that contained what Elijah guessed was meatloaf. Without the meat, of course. He watched as his wife prepared the evening meal, admiring the woman who had her back to him. Even with the company issued jumpsuits they were provided, Lark's five-foot frame revealed a woman whose body was put together in all the right places.

They had met when Lark was a student at Colorado State University and Elijah was working at an extrusion plant that was nearby. She was studying to get a degree in Agricultural Science and was highly regarded as a genius in that field by her professors. Elijah would see her walking from her class to her car every Monday, Wednesday, and Friday. He couldn't help but notice her auburn hair, brown eyes, and, of course, her body.

One Friday afternoon, Elijah noticed her car wouldn't start. It had been very cold that day in Northern Colorado and Elijah figured the extreme cold had taken its toll on an otherwise weak battery. He was hesitant to approach her, but she had already moved from the car and had popped open the hood to the engine. With other students around the parking lot, Elijah guessed she wouldn't feel uncomfortable with his approach.

She was shy at first, when he addressed her car not starting, but she accepted his offer to assist. As he explained the possibilities that might cause her car to not start, Elijah couldn't help but notice her fair skin that produced small, but evident, freckles. Her lips and nose were almost the same shade of red. It was very cold.

Even after all these years, and the damage the sun had caused to humans that remained on earth, Elijah could still see the freckles showing through. As the couple ate their supper, and Elijah filled Lark in on all the events of his day, he told her that Hendricks Vesper would be coming to oversee the start up. As he told his story, the astonishment on Lark's face continued to grow.

"*The* Dr. Vesper?" Lark replied like a rock star fan at the stage door waiting to see their idol.

Elijah had never paid much attention to Vesper, but he acknowledged that Lark must have. "Yep, the same guy we watched on the broadcast the other night with that hottie, Antonetta Valde."

Lark walked over to her husband and gave him a playful shove after hearing his comment. "Well, I don't think she has anything on me." She unzipped her jumpsuit to reveal her naked body to Elijah.

"She's got *nothing* on you, baby," as he picked her up in his arms and carried her to the bedroom.

CHAPTER 9: CHANGES

BEN TOLMIE SAT WITH HIS RIGHT EYE PRESSED to the eyepiece of the ocular tube of the microscope. "Simply amazing," he exclaimed with total fascination. Adjusting the objective lens from one stage to the other, Ben turned the brightness level from high to low.

Hendricks had already spent the last hour reviewing the specimen slides. His findings where precisely what Ben was now seeing and realizing. The slides containing the blood samples taken from each man revealed that the lymphocytes that produce the antibodies to fight infection were still white in color. The basophils were also present and remained unaffected, but the monocytes, which are normally kidney shaped, were now totally round.

Ben was obviously fixated on the erythrocytes from his blood sample. Prior to the injections they took, his sample showed a deep predominant red color, but now his blood was a dark color of blue and, instead of the various sizes and shapes of normal red erythrocytes, his blue blood sample revealed sizes and shapes that were consistent and perfectly round.

Switching the blood slides over to those taken from Hendricks, everything appeared the same as his, except for the erythrocytes. Hendricks' were not round or consistent in size. Ben was greatly puzzled at the difference between the two of them. Ben looked up from the microscope and called out to Hendricks who was busy logging data into the computer. "Did you see the difference between your erythrocytes and mine, Hendricks?"

Turning his chair to face Ben, Hendricks replied, "Yes, I certainly did. I just don't know what to think about it."

"Do you feel it's a reason to be alarmed? I mean, maybe one of us is having a reaction to the serum," Ben offered in speculation.

Hendricks pondered just how he would address Ben's concerns. After a brief pause, Hendricks spoke, "I believe it warrants additional research, Ben. It may be significant, or it could be that each person's erythrocytes react differently. I've documented it in the research log. I just don't think the equipment here at our lab is advanced enough to get us any answers. Good news is we're heading to Sphere1 tomorrow, and the lab there is state-of-the-art."

Ben resigned himself to the fact that Hendricks was right. Then, Hendricks questioned Ben, "How do you feel? I guess we should be very concerned if your answer is 'not well'."

Ben thought for a moment and smiled. He replied, "I feel better than I have in years. My mind is clear, and I don't feel fatigued."

Hendricks nodded his affirmation and turned to face his computer. Bringing the cursor to hover over "My Itinerary," Hendricks opened the attachment and reviewed the document. It read:

6:00 am   Limousine will arrive for pickup of Vesper and Tolmie and drive directly to Spheretech private air strip.

8:30 am   Flight will depart for Centennial Airport in Colorado Territory.

10:45 am   Arrival at Centennial Airport. Limo will meet passengers in front of the airport, transporting them to Sphere1 location.

12:30 pm   Lunch with Board of Directors

Hendricks closed the document and logged out of his computer. In what was a normal action for him, he reached up to remove his glasses and place them into their case. What was different on this occasion was that he had never put his glasses on. Despite having always required glasses when he worked on the computer, this time he didn't need them. His vision was perfect.

Ben had already retired to his bedroom when Hendricks decided that he had better also. Crawling into his bed, Hendricks couldn't help but marvel about what had occurred earlier. "Hmm, no glasses. What a surprise." Pulling the covers of his bedding up and around him, he discovered another product of the blue serum. The evening had not yet turned to night and glimpses of the light from it being dusk still penetrated his room and he was still able to close his eyes and he immediately fell asleep. For the first time in many years, he slept like the dead.

CHAPTER 10: REUNION

IT WAS QUICKLY APPROACHING SIX O'CLOCK in the morning, and Ben walked out of his bedroom rolling a large suitcase. Hendricks acknowledged him and commented, "Geesh, Ben, I don't think it's going to be that large of a jet. They might charge you extra for your baggage."

Ben let out a sarcastic chuckle, replying, "Well then, I hope you can spot me the extra, because my partner bilked me out of my life savings in a scheme to save humanity."

Laughing, Hendricks rose to help his friend roll the suitcase towards the front door just as the limo arrived precisely on time. "Six o'clock straight up. Leave it to the Board to do everything precisely on time."

"I thought you Brit's loved preciseness," Ben replied.

Not quite understanding Ben's comment, it finally sank in, and Hendricks confirmed, "I guess I've lived in the Territories so long that I've adopted the habit of procrastination." With that answer, Hendricks opened the door that led to a gravel driveway where the limo was parked. A neatly dressed man hurried up to both men, grabbing their suitcases from them, and escorted them to the rear passenger door of the limo. "I got your bags, gentlemen," the driver announced. "Just climb in and enjoy the ride."

Once positioned in the back of the opulent limo, Ben quizzed Hendricks as if he were a young boy sitting in the seat of a moving truck headed for a new home, "Do you think we'll ever return here?"

Hendricks looked longingly out of the window of the limo, out and up, towards the laboratory and the home that had provided for them for the last few years. "No, I don't believe we ever will, Ben. Cozbi served us well in so many ways, but our time and usefulness here has run out its string. I believe that is what you Yanks say, isn't it, Ben?"

"Yeah, something like that," Ben replied as the limo turned to drive down and away from the lab. Two hours later the men arrived at the private airstrip and boarded the Lear Jet that would shuttle them to Colorado. In another two plus hours, they disembarked from the jet and set foot on the ground in the territory of Colorado. Looking to the west, Hendricks was in awe of the Rocky Mountains that jutted up above the landscape. The mountains produced a blue tint to them, and he found it pleasing.

A man in a black suit, who was obviously an employee of Spheretech, walked with Ben and Hendricks pointing out that, at one time, the mountain peaks showed white snow caps on the higher elevations. He sadly said, "Those are gone now. Haven't been there for several years. I used to go snow skiing when I was a boy. I would go with my father. Of course, he's dead now. Died from the radiation." Ben felt a twinge of sympathy for the man, but it only lasted a moment. He wished he could tell the man that he need not suffer the same fate as his father.

With other employees rolling their luggage after them, both men walked through a terminal that handled commercial flights for wealthy corporations. The airport didn't seem too busy, which indicated to Hendricks that the number of wealthy corporations had been reduced to only a few.

Ben and Hendricks were directed to a long limousine that was parked at the front of the terminal. Hendricks wasn't sure how long the trip to Sphere1 would take and hoped he might be able to shut his eyes and get in a quick nap before meeting with the Board. That idea was quickly trashed when he ducked down to enter the limo and he immediately caught a scent of perfume, a fragrance that he had found it hard to get out of his mind and senses.

Sitting in the back of the limo was an additional passenger he had not expected to see nor had been told about. In a divinely fitted red knee-length skirt and matching blazer sat the one distraction to his quest he had faced ever since their first meeting. She smiled her ruby-lipped smile at him and softly spoke, "Hendricks, my dear friend. So nice to see you again." In all her seductiveness and glamour sat no other than Antonetta Valde.

CHAPTER 11:
TEST

ELIJAH WAS EXTREMELY NERVOUS. He wondered if he had enough time in training to seem competent on Extrusion Machine, Number One. After all, Hendricks Vesper himself was coming to watch him, and he wanted to impress him that the Board of Spheretech had made the right choice to have him lead this team.

As the test was coming to an end, he looked up at a skybox which hovered high above him. The darkened windows no doubt hid the watchful eyes of whoever might be watching. He knew for sure that a pair of those eyes belonged to Silver James. The test ended and Elijah gathered each member of Team A around him. He placed his hands on his hips and spoke, "I think that went well. All of you communicated with each other and…"

Silver approached the group clapping. Elijah marveled at just how fast he must have come down from the perch above them. "I don't think that test went well, I think it went *great!*" He continued to clap as his boisterous voice had interrupted Elijah in mid-sentence. Elated at the praise that was being dealt out, Elijah breathed a sigh of relief.

"So, Team A, I'm thinking it went so well that the team has earned the rest of the day off. Go home, get some rest, because tomorrow you're going to need it." Not wanting to cast away the reward that was being offered to them, Elijah became extremely curious about the last words Silver had said.

Pointing at the large hoppers above them, Silver provided the answer to Elijah's curiosity. "Tomorrow, we, I mean you and Team A, will go live. You will be making history by extruding the very first panel that will be used to build Sphere1!" With that announcement the group became very excited, hugging and patting each other on the back. Elijah wished he could feel the same exhilaration. He was nervous but did his best to hide it from Silver and his Team.

As Team A began to filter towards the locker room to begin their much-earned shortened day, Elijah held back. The team motioned for him to come join them and Elijah waved and called out, "I'll be with you all in a minute." Silver came up to him, asking, "What's the matter? Go celebrate with your team. You've earned it!"

Elijah glanced around at his environment before returning his focus to Silver and asking, "Do you really think so? Do you really think we're ready?"

"You and the team are as ready as you will ever be. Have confidence my man, have confidence," Silver replied like a coach ready to send his team out onto the gridiron for a championship game.

Walking together towards the rest of the group that was far ahead of them, Elijah decided it was as good of a time as any to ask Silver a question that had been on his mind for some time. "Silver, how did you come to be here? You know a lot about *everything* that is going on at this facility. I was wondering if you're an Extrusion Artist yourself?"

Silver acknowledged Elijah's curiosity and figured it wouldn't hurt anything to fill in his supervisor of Team A on his background. "No, I've never run an extrusion machine. In fact, I'm an engineer."

"An engineer? You mean, like, you design the machines? Something like that?" Elijah replied with a flabbergasted tone.

"Yep, something like that. These machines, and their controls, are all my design," Silver responded, but not in a boastful manner.

"Have you always designed machines? Production machines like these?" Elijah continued to ask in an attempt to satisfy his curiosity.

Silver paused for just a moment. He stopped walking and turned to face Elijah. "Actually, my background and specialty are in artificial intelligence. I create machines, so to speak, that can *think* and *feel*."

Elijah was suddenly silent. This revelation by Silver was beyond his wildest imagination. He felt it best not to continue to drill Silver for additional information. He had probably been told more than he should have, but he liked Silver, and didn't want to defile the trust that this man had placed in him.

As the two men reached the entrance to the locker room, Elijah thanked Silver for the information and opened the door. "Are you coming, Silver?" he asked.

"Not today, Elijah. You go and enjoy yourself. I have a lot to do to prepare for tomorrow. After all, we will be hosting the infamous Dr. Vesper."

CHAPTER 12:
THE PORTRAIT OF DORIAN GRAY

ANTONETTA STARED INTENTLY at Hendricks as the limo travelled the roadway between the airport and the site of the construction of Sphere1. Ben couldn't see her eyes behind the dark, shielding sunglasses she wore, but he was certain she had picked up on the color of *their* eyes. Since joining her in the limo, Hendricks had said nothing to her. Feeling the need to break the uneasy silence, she spoke. "Guess you gentlemen are wondering why I'm here?"

Hendricks turned from looking out the window and gave a sharp reply to her question, "Yes, Antonetta, just exactly why are you here?"

"Glad you asked, Hendricks. You see, I was invited to join you by *our* employer," she stated with a hint of smugness.

Hendricks stared intently at her as he responded, "*Our* employer?"

Antonetta smiled, revealing the perfection of her teeth before continuing the conversation, "Yes, our employer. You see, I have joined Spheretech as their Public Relations Officer. I said goodbye to World Perspective Tonight. We shall be seeing each other quite often now, dearest."

Ben felt it necessary to chime in, "And just exactly *what* will the Public Relations Officer do?"

"Well, Mr. Tomlie, I will be placing all of you men in the very best light possible as we unveil that *the shot* is going to be available to everyone who wants it."

Hendricks couldn't help but pry deeper at the explanation she had just provided to them. "This is what Corporate has told you? That the shot will be available to everybody that wants it? How is that possible? The research alone to bring the shot to this point cost the company billions. How could the population, even if they want the shot, afford to get it?"

Antonetta laughed at Hendricks. "Oh, my dear, wonderful, Dr. Vesper. You and Dr. Tolmie need to get out of the lab more often. Haven't you heard?"

"Heard what?" Ben quizzically asked.

"The President of the Territories of North America has committed to purchase the injections from Spheretech. It's a deal worth more money than you can imagine. Foreign governments are expected to follow. Our company is very rich!" She barked out with amusement.

The ride to Sphere1 was filled with silence for the remainder of the journey. Hendricks' mind was in overdrive regarding what Antonetta had just told them. As the limo headed east into northeastern Colorado, it became evident to Hendricks why this area had been selected for the site for Sphere1. Land was abundant here and stretched out for as far as the eye could see. He also knew that if you were going to test the effectiveness of sphere technology, what better place to do it than a mile from sea level where the ozone's depletion was even more prominent.

The limo stopped at a heavily guarded gate and, after a short discussion between the driver and the guard, was allowed to pass through. Soon, the limo came to a stop and the driver opened the door for his passengers to get out. Hendricks stepped out first and upon doing so he recognized that this area was elevated above the construction site.

Surveying the area, Hendricks could see outcroppings of various buildings, one being quite tall. He immediately recognized that it must be the Corporate building. He marveled at the size of the excavated bowl that would be the foundation of the sphere. Ben, being the better gentleman of the group, offered his hand to Antonetta to assist in her departure from the limo. She glanced around at the landscape laid out before them and was as equally impressed as Hendricks.

Ben inserted an uncharacteristic bit of humor just then, "Well, Toto, we're not in Kansas anymore."

Hendricks, Antonetta, and Ben received directions to walk towards a majestic log cabin just behind them.

"We'll get all your belongings. This is where you'll be staying. I'm sure you'll find these accommodations quite satisfactory. I'll be back to pick you up, Dr. Vesper, at 12:15. As you can see, the Corporate office is a short trip, but too far to walk," said the dark suited driver.

"Don't you mean you'll be picking up all three of us?" Vesper quizzed.

"I'm sorry, Doctor, but there's been a change of plans. Only you will be meeting with Theopolis Clyborn for lunch today. The two of you will be meeting alone. Dr. Tolmie and Ms. Valde will have lunch prepared for them in the retreat,"

Hendricks was surprised by the change, but today had been a series of surprises. "Well then, guess I'd better go freshen up," he replied to the driver.

"Very good, Dr. Vesper. We'll be departing in approximately thirty minutes."

The three new arrivals entered the home and gathered in all the opulence and splendor it offered. The home had all the appearances of a mountain chalet but was out here in the middle of nowhere. Still, Hendricks found it appropriate for the setting. As he walked up a staircase with railings carved from solid pine, he stopped to select which bedroom he would occupy.

Antonetta followed close behind him and stopped Hendricks just before he entered his chosen room. She softly grabbed his left arm, causing him to stop and face her. Piercing him with her deep, green eyes and freezing his ability to move, she spoke softly to him in order not to be heard by Ben who was still downstairs. "Hendricks, I know my being here has come as a shock to you. I'm sorry for that." Stumbling for the right words to say, she continued, "It's just...I...was offered the job. I wasn't unhappy where I was at. In fact, I was quite comfortable. I just knew this was my chance to be closer to you."

Hendricks wasn't sure how to respond. Secretly, he was pleased she was there. It's just that he had so much to accomplish now, and Antonetta could be a distraction. She reached up to gently caress the bangs of his hair that had fallen across his brows. She had a look on her face that puzzled him. "What is it?" he inquired.

"Your hair. Have you started dyeing it?" she asked, carefully moving her fingers through his hair like they were a comb.

Hendricks thought her question was quite odd and replied, "No, I've never dyed my hair. Why do you ask?"

"It's not totally gray anymore. In fact, I would call it salt and pepper. More pepper than salt. And your eyes, I don't recall them being this deep color of blue."

"I traded my soul to become young again. Just like the portrait of Dorian Gray." He mocked her.

"Also, did you and Ben always have the same color of eyes? I could have sworn he had brown eyes when I met him at the interview," she said, challenging his sarcastic answer.

Hendricks, knowing he might have been insensitive to her perceptions, gave her a slight kiss on the cheek and turned to retreat to his bedroom to prepare for his lunch meeting with Theo Clyborn. Antonetta, just as she had felt after their last interview, stood speechless in the hallway, unable to move.

CHAPTER 13: MEETING

THE CORPORATE BUILDING was magnificent beyond description. Hendricks walked off the elevator on the thirteenth floor into a room that was, in its purest description, decadent. The top floor was circular in shape with windows that served as walls, providing a 360-degree view of the terrain below.

Theopolis Clyborn walked over to greet Hendricks as he walked into the Boardroom. Sticking out his small, sweaty hand to shake Vesper's, he welcomed him and directed Hendricks to sit down at a small table that had been set up for the men to dine at.

"So glad you came, my boy," Theo expressed with gratitude.

"We wouldn't miss it for the world, sir," Hendricks replied, despite feeling some disdain for his lunch partner.

Clyborn smiled as servants began lunch service. The afternoon meal consisted of Caesar salad, fresh salmon and sautéed vegetables. Hendricks couldn't recall the last time he had eaten fresh fish. Along with other species of animals on earth, fish were rare, and very expensive. He was quite hungry after the travels of the day and kept the conversation light.

Clyborn folded his napkin and placed it on the table, signaling the servants to come and collect the lunch plates. "You know, Hendricks, I am quite sorry for the surprise this morning. I'm sure the extra passenger today caught you off guard. I thought it best to meet with you alone today."

Seeing it as an opportunity to get some answers about Antonetta's appearance, Hendricks placed his napkin on the table and asked his host, point blank, "Exactly why is she here, sir?"

Getting up from the table, Clyborn moved to a window to further observe the world below. He motioned for Hendricks to join him. "Hendricks, she is the most connected and capable person I know of to arrange for our broadcast the day after tomorrow."

"Broadcast?" Hendricks asked, being totally oblivious to any plan to broadcast anything.

"The entire Board, including myself, are going to take the *blue* injection during a public broadcast on Friday. We want to show the people of the Territories that this injection is safe, and more than that, it's necessary." Hendricks was speechless. "Antonetta will kick off our campaign after the broadcast by informing everybody just where, how, and why they should get the shot."

"Are we ready to go to that extreme?" Hendricks asked.

Clyborn laughed at Hendricks question, "Extreme? My boy, this is our survival. The Government of the Territories has purchased enough serum to make sure every human in the Northern Territory can get the shot! We were just contacted by the Chinese government. They want to buy one million doses!"

"So, Antonetta is here to take us global?" Hendricks chimed in.

"Yes, Hendricks, global! I brought you here, alone today, to advise you of the plan and to let you know you and...what's his name..."

"Ben Tolmie," Hendricks replied in an irritated manner.

"Yes, that's him, Tolmie. We expected both of you to be part of the broadcast and receive your injections along with the Board. You know, to show solidarity for its safety, but I noticed, when you first stepped off the elevator, that you've jumped the gun." Clyborn explained like a disappointed father might.

"How did you know I had taken the shot?" Hendricks asked.

Twisting his mustache, Clyborn offered the answer, "The blue eyes, my boy. The blue eyes."

Puzzled at Clyborn's answer, Hendricks felt it necessary to prod Clyborn further, "You're aware of the transformation to the iris color of those that take the injection?"

Clyborn answered with an almost cynical tone, "The lab that did the clinical trials reported that it occurred in 100% of the test subjects. It had no residual impact on the patient's health, it was simply a by-product of the injection."

Hendricks was amazed at what Clyborn had just revealed to him. Upon hearing this, he decided it was best not to expose that his nearsightedness had been reversed since taking the injection.

"Well, no matter. You shall still be the face of Spheretech. Antonetta has assured the Board that you *must* be the person the public connects with the company. She has faith in you, and so does the Board. I assume Tolmie has also been injected?" Clyborn asked.

"Yes, we injected each other," Hendricks answered.

"Well, no problem. Antonetta doesn't feel he connects with the common folk. I know he's been your assistant for many years, but Tolmie will need to be assigned elsewhere. She finds him, you understand, boring."

Hendricks was perplexed at everything that had been revealed to him at this meeting. If it weren't for his *plan* and everything falling into place, he might be angry, or even offended.

Clyborn continued to twist the ends of his handlebar mustache which Hendricks found extremely irritating. "I will let you go, my boy. I understand you have a big day tomorrow. The first panels will be produced and installed in Cozbi's sphere."

Having stomached just about all he could of this man, Hendricks decided it was best to just leave. Taking one last glance at the terrain below, he could see his future laid out before him. "Thank you, sir. I'm sure I'll be seeing you soon." With that farewell, he entered the elevator that was open and waiting for him and departed for the guest residence.

Ben was very inquisitive about the events of the meeting, but Hendricks decided to keep the conversation general and centered on the construction of the sphere. Deep down, he sensed that Ben saw right through his deception. The men had a light meal together as Antonetta had been called away to do whatever she had been asked to do.

Hendricks excused himself, citing that he was extremely fatigued. "It's been a long day, Ben. Tomorrow will be even longer for us so I'm going to retire."

After reaching his room, Hendricks shut the door and opened the carafe containing the rarest of fine bourbon he had ever seen. Dropping an ice cube into a glass, he sat in a chair that had a small table next to it. He wasn't fatigued at all. In fact, his energy level was extremely high. He sipped a couple of tastes of the bourbon and set his glass down. Hearing a slight tap on his door, he called out to the person on the other side of the door. Fully expecting it to be Ben wanting to impart some additional intuitions about almost every subject, Hendricks called out, "Come in."

The door slowly opened, and Hendricks was surprised to see Antonetta's face peaking around the door. "Can I come in?" she sheepishly asked.

Hendricks motioned for her to enter. It would be early in the morning before Antonetta would return to her room and her own bed.

CHAPTER 14:
GOD, DON'T LET ME LET HIM DOWN

HE ROLLED OVER IN BED, finding the warm body of his wife sleeping with her back towards him. Moving closer to her and cradling her next to him, her body shifted to accommodate his embrace. Lark placed her arm over Elijah's to accept his embrace. She understood he needed her warmth, her feeling of love and security. Her husband was about to have the biggest day of his life.

Without saying much to each other this morning, Elijah kissed Lark on the cheek and walked down the concrete, subterranean hallway where he exited through the metal door and up to the surface. Lark allowed his quietness. She knew he was deep in thought.

After taking his shower and putting on his clean room suit, Elijah, along with his crew, found themselves at Extrusion Machine Number One. It was humming. A sound that signaled there were no more tests, no more delays. Today, a panel was going to be extruded and he was the one person responsible for it being a perfect panel.

Looking up towards the observation room that was high above him, Elijah knew that Silver James was certainly there, watching like a father who was seeing his son walk up to the plate at his first baseball game. Elijah sensed that Silver was not alone. Somehow, he knew that

Dr. Hendricks Vesper was standing beside Silver in anticipation of his research and work being made real. "God, don't let me let him down," Elijah mumbled a short prayer to himself.

Elijah raised his arm above his head and, with his index finger outstretched, gave a circular motion, signaling to his team that it was time to start. Braden Samuleson nodded his head in affirmation of Elijah's command and hit a button on the main control panel which caused the base material to begin pumping into the hopper.

The hours Team A spent drilling for this moment proved successful. The material flowed through the extrusion machine, and much to Elijah's astonishment, the cold extrusion forced the flow through the dye and delivered a white, almost translucent sheet onto a conveyor belt where his team placed it into a refrigerated container that would hold the other twenty-nine sheets that would follow.

Elijah was fascinated by the panels. He expected them to be much thicker than they were. He estimated each panel to be no thicker than one inch and 12' X 12' square. He wasn't sure how panels of this dimension could possibly hold up being used for construction. He also pondered just how each of these panels would be attached to each other. He wasn't versed in building construction, but simple physics told him there was more to these panels than meets the eye.

After three hours of extruding these mystery panels, his team had filled more than twelve containers and moved them into a refrigerated area near the back of the facility.

Elijah signaled his team to shut the machine down and take a break. Braden walked up to him and patted him on the back and spoke, "I don't know what these are boss, but let's hope they're what the big bosses wanted." With those words, Braden walked off to join the rest of the team.

Elijah went to the main computer to check the readings on all the systems and upon doing so turned and let out a gasp of air like someone would do when surprised or scared. Standing there was Silver and none other than Hendricks Vesper. Reaching out his hand to embrace Elijah's hand, Hendricks spoke, "I believe that went well." Silver interrupted and introduced the two men to each other. Elijah was impressed that Vesper seemed so calm and collected. He, himself, was a mess.

"I went to the *finishing* section to inspect your panels, Elijah. They're perfect. They had to be perfect, since your panels are the first and the base pieces of Sphere1 construction." Hendricks commented like a proud father.

Elijah felt a twinge of relief after hearing this praise.

"Thank you, Dr. Vesper. We appreciate this opportunity."

Hendricks smiled at Elijah, and placed his arm across his shoulder and replied, "Glad to have you here. So, will your team be okay without you for a while? I want you to join me outside. It's time for you to see the fruits of your labor in action."

Elijah was speechless, but managed to squeak out a response, "Yes, of course, they'll be fine. It will be an honor to join you." Hendricks and Elijah climbed into an electric powered ATV that had been parked near Extrusion Machine Number Two. With Hendricks driving the distance towards the back of the facility, the large doors began to move to the ceiling. Elijah could feel the cool blasts of air behind him keeping the integrity of the clean room behind them intact. He recognized the containers next to them as being the ones that held the panels that his team had produced.

As the overhead doors closed behind them, the sliding doors in front of them opened, revealing the terrain that held the concrete bowl. Hendricks could tell this sight amazed his companion. "Awfully impressive isn't it, Elijah."

"More than you can imagine, Dr. Vesper," he replied.

"Now, now, since we are going to be lifelong friends, you better just call me Hendricks," he offered.

Even though he did not feel totally comfortable with what Hendricks had just offered, Elijah felt it would be in his best interest to comply with the request. As the containers that held the panels were being loaded onto trailers that were being pulled by small tractors, they began their journey towards the bowl. Elijah was surprised to see Hendricks peel off his clean room suit, revealing normal street clothes underneath. Hendricks placed the clean room suit in the back of their ATV and returned to the driver's seat. He smiled at Elijah, revealing his deep ocean blue eyes and spoke. "I can do this, ya know. This not wearing any protective clothing. I don't even need sunglasses, but you, my friend, had better wear these." Hendricks produced a pair of sunglasses from a compartment in the ATV.

"We can just sit here, Elijah, and watch the show just fine. I promise, you will be amazed."

As the two men sat watching the containers pull up near the center and west edge of the concrete bowl, Elijah hoped he wouldn't be stepping on the toes of his new found friend, but he was compelled to ask questions. That was his nature, and he couldn't resist. "Dr. Vesper, uhm, I mean Hendricks, how is it you don't need any protective gear? Isn't that dangerous for you?"

Hendricks laughed at the question. "I was wondering if you would be astute enough to ask me. There is a reason I don't require the protection you do, my friend. I have received the *shot*. In fact, sitting here in the back of the facility, watching the show, I feel a little bit uncomfortable. It's almost too cold for me."

Astounded, Elijah continued to pry, "This is the shot you referenced in your interview with that gal from World Perspective?"

"I'm impressed you watched, Elijah. Yes, that's the shot. You see, ah well, probably best to not let the cat out of the bag, I encourage you to watch the broadcast tomorrow. Everything will be explained then."

Elijah decided not to prod Hendricks any further on this subject. "Can I ask what you are going to do with the panels we produced? I'm confused just how they will be used in the sphere construction. They don't have the bulk to be used as any support, plus I'm curious just how they will be joined together."

Hendricks reached out his left arm and pointed towards the bowl. Workers had just removed the first thirty panels from the containers and placed them side by side forming a larger square at the base of the concrete bowl. "Just watch."

Once the panels were laid next to each other, Elijah noticed that they weren't touching but had a separation of approximately thirty inches. As the hot sun beat down vigorously on the panels, Elijah noticed a strange occurrence. The panels began to pulsate. It was almost as if they were alive. What was even more astounding is Elijah was convinced they had begun to grow.

Then, these individual panels seemed to join together, forming one conjoined shape that appeared to now be as large as an acre. Elijah was certain his mouth was hanging wide open at the sight unfolding below him. Not only was there one solid panel now existing within the concrete bowl, but the panel had taken on the shape, or curvature, of the bowl.

"How is this possible?" Elijah exclaimed, wanting to remove his sunglasses to get a clearer view but thinking better of it.

Hendricks laughed with amusement. "My dear friend, Elijah. Your panels aren't plastic. They aren't made of polymers. These panels are living organisms. This sphere, once complete, will feed and survive off the radiation of the sun. We had total faith in you, and your team, to achieve this feat. Silver has spoken so highly of you."

Still unable to fathom what was unfolding below him, Elijah sat and watched as if paralyzed. The radio that Hendricks was carrying chirped with Silvers voice. "Hendricks, we have a problem at Extrusion Machine Number Two."

"We're on our way," Hendricks replied grabbing his clean room suit from the back of the ATV and putting it on. Once back inside the facility, Hendricks and Elijah exited the ATV and met Silver.

"The panels from Team B aren't surviving. They come through the dye but begin to warp and disintegrate." Silver excitedly explained.

Elijah walked over to where Germain Tomilison, the supervisor for Team B, stood. Elijah could tell Germain was nervous and hesitant on how to correct the issue. Looking up and down Machine Two, Elijah walked over to a sensor near the water containment that was before the dye. "Germain, the water temperature is too hot. Believe me, it must be between 33 and 40 degrees."

Germain glanced at the temperature reading which read 50 degrees and responded, "This just doesn't make sense to me. How can colder water make any difference?"

Elijah reached over to the control panel and adjusted the temperature down to 33 degrees. Within minutes, he had the members of Team B start the extrusion process again. The material coming off the conveyor, despite being smaller in dimension than the panels he was making, were firm, translucent, and flat. "Trust me, Germain, if you had seen what I saw, you would know this is the way it has to be."

Elijah continued to instruct Team B through the process. He knew he was stepping onto Germain's territory, but it had to be done.

Off in the distance, Hendricks conferred with Silver. "It's time my friend. Price is our man. It's time for you to devote your time to *our* project."

Silver nodded in agreement. A short time later, Silver advised Elijah that Hendricks had to depart for meetings, but he would be seeing him again soon. "Quite the man," Elijah responded as he started to walk back towards his team.

Before Elijah could get out of ear shot, Silver called out to him, "Hey, Price, Hendricks wants you to take my job. You interested?"

CHAPTER 15:
ANTONETTA'S SHOW

LOOKING AROUND THE STUDIO that had been built for her at Sphere1, Antonetta was astounded by it. It was professionally done and contained all the state-of-the-art technology you could need or want. The crew that would do the broadcasts was hand-picked. Many of them were harvested from her former employer.

She smiled at the production crew as she stepped into a room adjacent to the studio where the Board of Directors for Spheretech had gathered. "Okay, gentlemen, this is how this broadcast is going to go down. I am going to start the broadcast sitting with, and interviewing, Hendricks Vesper." Theopolis Clyborn interrupted her instructions by asking, "Is that the best way to start? Won't our audience be confused, thinking that you work for World Perspective instead of us, and this is just a continuation of your previous interview?"

Antonetta glared at Clyborn with green eyes that could turn red at any moment and shoot a deadly laser right through his skull. She calmed the resentment of his interruption in her voice and replied, "Mr. Clyborn, first, please do not twirl your mustache when you are on camera. The viewing audience doesn't care about the magnificence of your stash!" Clyborn stopped twirling his mustache immediately and dropped his eyes to keep from meeting hers. "Secondly, the audience doesn't care about me and where *I* came from. They care about Hendricks Vesper.

The audience wants to know more about the shot. What it is, what it does to protect humans, and most importantly, is it safe? Once Dr. Vesper gives them that information, they will want to know where to get it! That is where you come in, Mr. Clyborn."

Antonetta explained to the Board that they will be ushered into the studio and each will receive the injection. The viewers will be told that the Territory Government has made it available for every citizen that wants it. They can and will get it for free. The locations of the mobile injection sites will be posted across the Territories. Dr. Vesper will then be interviewed about Sphere1 to wrap up the broadcast.

Antonetta confirmed with each of the Board members that they understood her instructions. Upon having secured that confirmation, she reentered the studio and walked to where Hendricks and Ben were standing. "Will I be required to be on camera?" Ben inquired.

"Not tonight, Ben. I do appreciate you being here though," she said as she gently touched his arm. Antonetta placed her arm around Hendricks to guide him to the chair he would be sitting in. Once seated, she informed him that once the injections of the Board were complete, she would question him about Sphere1. As those questions are being asked, footage of the start of the construction of Sphere1, and what had been completed so far, will be shown. She continued to explain that the completed computer models of Sphere1, and all the plants and animals being moved in would be shown to the viewers.

"This will cause a frenzy with those watching in the Territories," she whispered to Hendricks. Before he could question her revelation, the lights dimmed, and the program was being broadcast.

Everything that Antonetta planned for the broadcast was proceeding perfectly. Hendricks explained in lay terms everything about the shot. She was so proud of him that she almost couldn't contain herself. The Board members received their injections and were escorted off camera, leaving Theo Clyborn to speak to the audience about the mobilization of the Territory Government to administer the shot.

The broadcast returned to footage of Sphere1 now, and also the computer model showing it completed. Hendricks was quietly anticipating what was going to be said to bring about the *frenzy*. The camera's red light came on, displaying to Hendricks that he and Antonetta were live. Antonetta took on the posture of a seasoned interviewer and posed a question to Hendricks, "Once the landscape, plants and animals are safely inside Sphere1, will it be sealed, or will a portion of it be open to the elements? That seems a bit counterproductive doesn't it, Hendricks?"

Shifting uncomfortably in his chair, Hendricks knew he would have to answer the question. "The Sphere will be entirely sealed once everything we require is contained inside."

"And just how will all the plants and animals be cared for and protected?" she asked. Hendricks knew he was being led by her. He also knew that these were answers she already knew, answers that he had provided during intimate, late-night sessions, but he didn't care. This was *his* plan, and she was actually falling right into it.

"Sphere1, and each sphere that will come after it, will have ways to enter and exit." He chuckled slightly. "Of course, those entrances and exits are secret and known only to a select few of us. What I can tell you for sure is, we will need humans inside the spheres. Only humans that have received the injection will be able to enter the sphere environment. It will be mandatory to preserve the integrity and safety of the other living creatures."

Antonetta smiled a sinister smile as she asked her next question. "For those that want to come to Sphere1 and be part of the *new humanity* that have received the injection, how should they do that?"

Hendricks glowed deep inside at her question. He thought, "Good girl! Not only are you beautiful, but you're smart." He paused a moment before answering her question. "Go to 'blue.com' to apply." The broadcast ended with that revelation and Antonetta and Hendricks were informed that the website was blowing up.

"See, *frenzy!*" She smugly commented.

The studio had gone almost dark and Hendricks and Antonetta, alone in the studio, embraced. He kissed her on the lips and then, grabbing her shoulders with both hands in a firm but intentional manner, spoke, "You were magnificent tonight, Netta."

Accepting the pet name he had given her, she jokingly replied, "You too, Hen." Unaware to both of them, Ben had entered the studio and had seen the show of affection. He walked towards them, and in order not to alert them to what he had just seen, Ben smiled and called out to them as they quickly separated from each other.

"Ben, you surprised us," Antonetta responded.

"Sorry, my friends, I didn't mean to startle you."

"What's up, Ben?" Hendricks asked in an innocent manner, still not convinced Ben hadn't seen them embrace and kiss.

Holding a syringe in one of his hands, Ben sheepishly shrugged his shoulders and replied, "I just figured it was a good night, Ms. Valde, to turn those green eyes blue."

CHAPTER 16: MANIPULATION

LARK LOOKED OVER AT HER HUSBAND with her mouth open in astonishment at what they had just watched. She picked up the empty cups from the tea they had drunk during the broadcast and carried them to the kitchen to place inside the sink. "I just don't know, Elijah. Everything seems so fishy to me." Lark exclaimed as she placed the cups in the sink.

"What is it about what we watched tonight that bothers you so much?" Elijah queried.

Lark turned away from the sink and faced towards her husband. Needing to contemplate his question before replying to it, Lark continued to think about her answer carefully. She finally blurted out her answer, "I just think…Oh, I don't know, it seemed manipulative."

Elijah was surprised by her statement. "Well, it is *their* sphere. I guess they can demand whatever they want," he said.

"It's not just the demand that all who would want to come here would be required to take the injection, it was the way it was said. It seemed authoritarian." Lark responded.

Elijah considered her response and replied, "Yeah, I guess you're right." Then, Lark posed a question that made him a bit nervous. "Will we have to take the shot, Elijah? We live near Sphere1, and you work there, building it. Will the shot be mandated for us, or will we be forced back out

69

to wander in the wilderness?" He really didn't know the answer to her question. He walked over and gave her a tender embrace. "Whatever happens, sweetheart, we will go through it together."

Lark appreciated the hug from her husband. She revealed to him that she didn't trust the people that developed these injections. "You know me, Elijah. I'm a naturalist. As you have enjoyed recently, my hydroponic garden is doing quite well. Those things from my garden are the only things I trust to go into our bodies."

The herbal tea that they had enjoyed this evening was proof of Lark's expertise and abilities.

CHAPTER 17:
BLUE COMPLIANCE

HENDRICKS STEPPED OFF THE ELEVATOR. Standing there to greet him in the conference room was Theo Clyborn. "Thank you for joining me this morning, my boy." Clyborn expressed with a sense of glee. Hendricks was surprised that Clyborn was not twirling his mustache.

"I told the rest of the Board not to worry about attending the meeting this morning. I just wanted to visit with you again, alone. Just the two of us, my boy," Clyborn spoke as a father would that was going on a father-son fishing outing.

"Glad to be here, sir." Hendricks said, even though it was a lie.

Clyborn went back to twirling his mustache like a drug addict who had gone without a fix. "So, last night was a major success. Lots of people want to be part of this. We just closed the deal with the Chinese this morning for one million doses. Looks like we're going to need to start the additions to Sphere1."

Hendricks acknowledged what Clyborn had just told him. "My concern is with everybody that we accept to come work at Sphere1, and you understand we can be very selective on who we accept. I'm concerned that other, less desirable people, will come. The word will get out!" Clyborn said in an arrogant way.

"Less desirable?" Hendricks questioned.

Theo smiled and responded, "You know, those who have not received the injection." Hendricks took notice of the deep ocean blue color of Clyborn's eyes.

"I understand, sir. Rest assured, with what I am working on, having 'undesirables' won't be an issue."

Clyborn, as he twirled his mustache and with a fervor that indicated he was perturbed, replied, "Listen, Vesper, in the future you will need to pass anything you are *working* on by me."

Hendricks, in an apologetic and subordinate manner, responded to Theo, "It's just a little project that I've had Tolmie and James involved with."

Clyborn let out a bellow that sounded like "Harrumph"!

Hendricks held out his hands towards Clyborn, and in an apologetic manner like a Mafia Boss ordering a hit on a rival said, "Don't worry. After tonight, you'll be gone and have nothing to worry about." Then Hendricks spoke in a voice that sounded like an actor on an instructional video. "I want you to excuse yourself from this meeting and go to your residence. In your bedroom closet, hanging from a hook, you will find a long rope. One end you will tie to the stair banister on the second floor. The other end of the rope has a noose that is already tied for you. Slip that noose around your neck and pull it tight. Then, you fat pudgy imbecile, I want you to crawl over that banister and jump."

Clyborn stared at Hendricks like a dog that had been requisitioned to go for a walk by his master. "I'm sorry, my boy. I forgot that I have something I have to do and I must end our little get together. Please, excuse me." Clyborn dismissed himself and walked to the open elevator. Hendricks, with a broad smile watched as the elevator door closed, and Clyborn disappeared from his sight.

Later that evening, Hendricks' champagne glass clinked the glass that was held by Antonetta. He stared into her deep blue eyes as he took a drink of his champagne. Just as he was ready to move in to steal the first kiss of the evening, the phone rang.

"Vesper here," he answered.

On the other end of the line there was a slight pause. Then a tentative voice came on the line and spoke. "Dr. Vesper, this is Sphere1 Security. Sir, we've had an incident at Theopolis Clyborn's residence."

As Hendricks listened to the voice on the other end of the phone, he already knew the details. The difference in the blue serum that Ben Tolmie saw in his blood and had been so inquisitive about the day after they took their injections was working to perfection. He knew that humanity had finally taken a turn. And that turn would lead to their total submission, and dominance over them by one man. Antonetta watched as he hung up the receiver and placed it back on the cradle of the phone. She was impatient to learn the reason for the call, as her deep, ocean blue eyes, intently studied him.

PART 2:
THE FIRST GENERATION
WAR

Oh, who knows how long this will last

Now we've come so far, so fast

But somewhere back there in the dust

That same small town in each of us

I need to remember this So baby, give me just one kiss

And let me take a long last look

Before we say goodbye

CHAPTER 18:
CONTAMINATION

Eighteen months later

STARING AT THE MAGNIFICENCE BELOW, Hendricks paced along the windows that surrounded the thirteenth-floor conference room of Spheretech. He marveled at the sheer size of Sphere1 as it was nearing completion. He was equally impressed by how the construction of Sphere2 was moving along and on schedule. He understood that he had Elijah Price to thank for that.

Since the last remaining Board member of Spheretech had resigned to live a simpler life, Hendricks Vesper was anointed as the leader of Spheretech. This anointing was declared by a democratic vote of the residents and employees of Sphere1. They considered him to be a *savior* so to speak. Many referred to him as a Messiah. The one who had saved humanity from destruction.

The acceptance of the injection by the populace brought glee to Hendricks. With the administration of the blue injection proceeding along, the number of workers, not to mention citizens, of the Sphere community was multiplying. Perhaps multiplying too fast, he considered. He had decided that those that received the injection should live within the Spheres. Even though they could survive and thrive very well on the surface outside the sphere, he was concerned with the growing population that had yet to take the shot.

The risk of contamination between those who were injected and those who weren't was something he did not want to risk. He also knew this element would need to change. That decision about what to do was fast approaching. A decision that would alter the course of the world they lived in. Hendricks was disturbed that Elijah had yet to take the injection. He had discussed it with him several times. The response he would receive from Elijah was always, "Perhaps soon. We are still debating that subject." Hendricks knew very well that '*we*' was the resistance Elijah was getting from his wife, Lark.

Although his biggest asset in the building of his empire was resistant to becoming *his,* literally in body and mind, he needed Elijah. The leader of his extrusion facility had moved up in the company and was now the leader of the entire Sphere project. He was a natural leader. Blue bloods and red bloods alike trusted him, and more importantly, followed him. In many ways, this made Elijah Price a threat to him, but he had to push that thought out of his mind.

Picking up the radio that connected directly to Elijah's, Hendricks pressed the press-to-talk (PTT) button. On the other end, Elijah answered. "What's up, boss?" Elijah responded.

"Can you break away from what you're currently doing? I want to discuss your idea on how to join '1' and '2' together, since the two spheres seem to be resistant to doing that."

Elijah was pleased that Hendricks wanted to meet with him. Ever since the very first day that he began extruding the *living* panels that formed Sphere1, those panels had become like children to him. He wasn't a scientist like the genius that now led them, but he felt like he somehow *knew* these creatures. He knew how they thought because they were, indeed, intelligent.

Climbing into his own personal ATV, Elijah pressed the pedal downward which started the electric motor. As he exited the extrusion facility, high above him, Hendricks Vesper watched the vehicle moved towards the building that he now called his.

CHAPTER 19:
PI

SILVER JAMES WAS INTENSE as he pressed the button that would bring his creation to life. At first, nothing happened, and Antonetta appeared a bit impatient that her time was being wasted. Suddenly, two small blue lights appeared where the eyes of the being existed. Silver breathed a sigh of relief. A short time later, a voice came out of his creation and spoke, "Hello, Silver. I am pleased to see you again."

Antonetta was amazed. This creature was, in all appearances, human. If it weren't for his bronze skin tone and the fact that he wore no clothing and she could see he had no genitalia, this being immolated a human in every aspect. "Pi, I want to introduce you to Antonetta. She is the person I told you about," Silver said to his creation.

"Pleasure to meet you, Antonetta. I am looking forward to serving you and Dr. Vesper. I have been created to serve," Pi spoke with reverence to her.

"That is very nice, Pi. Serving Dr. Vesper is what we all must do."

Pi smiled. It was an eerie expression because it seemed so human. "I look forward to meeting Dr. Vesper" he replied.

Silver interrupted the bonding between Pi and Antonetta and interjected, "Pi, I remind you that Dr. Vesper will most likely prefer to be called Hendricks."

"I will leave that decision up to him. He is a great leader, and I am here to serve him," Pi responded.

Antonetta smiled at Silver with the affirmation that his work was a success. She knew Hendricks would be very pleased with the results of his work.

"Now, Pi, I will have you accompany me back to my lab. I have some minor adjustments to make before I take you home to live with Hendricks and Antonetta," Silver's tooth shone through as he spoke. The bronze, human-like being rose on command, and as both excused themselves from Antoneta's presence, walked out the door of the residence.

"Will I be put to sleep again as you make my adjustments, Silver?" Pi inquired.

"No, never again, Pi. You have been brought to life forever," Silver revealed. The two beings traveled swiftly to Silver's laboratory which was inside Sphere1, which had just been sealed permanently. Coming to a portion of the Sphere, Silver acknowledged the two guards standing outside the sphere. He could see the guards were Bluebloods by their eyes and the fact that they were clothed in tan jumpsuits, with no protection to their heads or skin.

One of the guards approached the sphere and withdrew a small, tubular device from a holster attached to his side. Pointing the tube at the sphere, the translucent gold tint that was characteristic of the sphere suddenly disappeared, leaving an opening for Silver to drive through.

Once through the wall of the sphere, it closed and the golden hue returned, as if nothing had breached it.

Silver and Pi travelled a short distance further. Pi was fascinated by the cattle and elk that grazed together in a meadow next to the laboratory. "Did you create those creatures?" he asked Silver with all the innocence of the new and learning intelligence he was.

"No, Pi. Those existed on this planet before. Hendricks has found a way to save them," Silver responded as he turned the vehicle into an area to park.

"Save them so they will live forever? Just like me?" Pi replied.

"Yes, forever, Pi."

As they entered the laboratory, Silver and Pi were greeted by Ben Tolmie. He walked out of his office greeting them, "How did it go?" Tolmie questioned of Silver.

"Better than we could have hoped for, Ben," Silver exclaimed.

Pi, not wanting to be left out of the conversation interjected, "I'm excited to live with Hendricks and Antonetta. She seems very nice."

Ben was hesitant to respond, but, understanding the youth of his and Silver's creation, responded, "Yes, she is very nice, Pi."

Silver instructed Pi to go to the portion of the lab where it had been assembled. As Pi complied and walked towards the lab, Silver asked Ben to step back into his office. Once inside, Silver closed the door to the office and spoke quietly, "It went so well that I know Hendricks will want us to activate the rest upon seeing how wonderful Pi is."

"I'm sure he will, but the rest aren't like Pi," Ben responded.

"No, they aren't, but they are what we were asked to create," Silver said, acknowledging the truth that Ben had spoken.

Both men walked to a large window on an interior wall of Ben's office. The window reflected as a mirror might, until Ben turned on a light next to the window. Lights came on in succession in a large room behind the office. After every row was illuminated, the two men looked at each other as hundreds of bronze-colored beings were revealed. Yet to be activated, these beings were just like Pi. Except, once activated, they would protect Hendricks and the Blueblood people against all enemies.

Chapter 20:
Subs

ELIJAH STEPPED OFF THE ELEVATOR and, for the first time ever, he entered the conference room at the top of the Spheretech Corporate Headquarters. Hendricks walked quickly up to him and proceeded to embrace him, which caused Elijah to be surprised. Laughing, Hendricks released him. Pointing towards a seat in an area where they could talk, he invited Elijah to sit. Once seated, Hendricks joined him and attempted to ease the tension that Elijah was clearly displaying.

"Don't worry, my friend. I understand just how intimidating this room can be. I've sat in the chair you now occupy. Trust me, our meeting today is totally because of the respect I have for you." Hendricks expressed with as much sincerity as he could.

Elijah's shoulders relaxed somewhat, and he replied, "Sorry, Hendricks, I don't mean to seem so tense. It isn't every day you get summoned to the top of Spheretech to meet with the Emperor."

Hendricks chuckled, "Emperor. I like that! Mind if I borrow it?"

Both men were feeling more at ease and the conversation continued with Hendricks asking Elijah questions. He seemed genuinely interested in how Elijah and his wife were getting along. He was particularly interested in their subterranean living. For instance, did they find it difficult to exist underground? How did they cope with the mental stress?

Hendricks soon discovered that Elijah was reluctant to answer him. Opting to discontinue this line of questioning, Hendricks turned the conversation towards the spheres.

"I'm perplexed, Elijah. With Sphere2 nearing completion, I don't want to have both Sphere1 and 2 to be separate. All our efforts to design a way for both Spheres to join have been without resolution. In theory, the two spheres should join naturally at their closest point, but they don't. I understand you might have a solution." Hendricks looked directly into Elijah's eyes like a cop interrogating someone that might have committed a crime.

Elijah moved nervously in his chair due to the apprehension he felt, and responded, "I guess my first question to you would be *why* do you require the spheres to join?"

Hendricks continued to stare at him. A stare that indicated that his guest might have stepped out of bounds. Considering whether or not he should answer Elijah's question, he thought quickly on his feet and provided an answer that was truthful. He wasn't sure if he would live to regret it. "Elijah, Spheretech's future is to not stop with just 1 and 2. We are planning on creating several more. As many as it takes to house all of humanity that wants to join us, living inside the spheres. We'll need the ability to connect. To join. We need to be a united community."

"And those that aren't injected, that live subterranean, what about us?" Elijah questioned.

In a weird way, Hendricks appreciated Elijah's candor but decided this was the proper time to lie. "The sphere communities will continue to care for those of humanity that wish to remain underground. The 'subs' as I like to call them. They have been instrumental in helping build this empire. They won't be forsaken."

Elijah accepted his answer as truth. After all, Hendricks had done so much for Elijah since he and Lark had come to Spheretech.

Smiling, Hendricks placed his hand over Elijah's. It was a technique he had learned from Antonetta. It provided a closeness, a trust between two people, and Hendrick's so desperately needed Elijah, and perhaps most importantly, Lark, to trust him. "I still haven't given up on you and your wife, Elijah. I want you to leave your subterranean home. I want you and Lark to take the shot. I want to build you a home beyond your wildest dreams. Inside the Spheres."

Elijah was speechless. This was an offer that *was* beyond his wildest dreams. He was certain that it could sway Lark to reconsider their present situation and take the injection. Still, his inquisitive nature forced him to inquire about something that confused him. "Do you remember your very first interview on World Perspective Tonight?"

"Yes, like it was yesterday. Why do you ask?"

Once again, Elijah felt uneasy at his boldness. "During that interview you said that Sphere1 would never be a home for humans. Humans would only be the caretakers for the animals, gardens, and such."

Hendricks stood up and walked towards the windows that looked out towards his empire. With his back to Elijah, he replied, "Things have changed, Elijah. With the Territory government collapsing, I'm becoming increasingly concerned for *our* safety. As the leader of this experience, I feel it's my duty to provide protection. It's time for the Bluebloods to come inside the protection of the Spheres."

With his mind racing at the explanation he had just been provided, his thoughts did not consider, or think to ask, if this protection would also be provided for the 'subs', as Hendricks had referred to them.

Turning in a hurried fashion to seize the moment of the revelation he had just given Elijah, Hendricks sat down again and pleaded with him. "So, as you can see, it is important for you to tell me what plan you might have for joining our spheres."

Unable to resist the hypnotic blue eyes of the leader of Spheretech, Elijah held out his plan no longer. "The problem you have, Hendricks, is the Spheres are the same size and mass. Sphere1 and 2 are also engineered to grow no larger than the bowl to which they are assigned. If they were to join, *they* know they would become one sphere and their intelligence tells them that it can't be done."

Hendricks sat with a stupefied look on his face. His mind wandered from the current conversation he was having and returned to the laboratory, high on the pillar made from centuries of the ocean pounding against it. "Cozbi was right. This could have been done in space. The sphere would have grown to encircle the entire planet since it wasn't encumbered to remain in a defined area. Cozbi, you were right ol' boy," Hendricks thought to himself. Realizing that Elijah was looking at him with an odd expression, his thoughts returned to the moment. "Sorry, Elijah, my mind wandered for a moment. So, tell me, what have you come up with?"

"Construct a smaller sphere. The smaller spheres will then join the larger spheres creating a passageway between them. Sphere1 and 2 will accept the smaller sphere thus providing a passage between the two. You see, Hendricks, the large Spheres of 1 and 2, well, they *compete* against each other like two older siblings. The smaller sphere is no threat to them. So, they accept it," Elijah imitated the bonding of the larger spheres to the smaller one with his hands clasped together.

Hendricks displayed deep thought at what Elijah had just presented. Several minutes went by before Hendricks responded. "And you can make this happen?"

"It will require new dyes to be made, but, yes, I can handle it," Elijah replied feeling anxiety at what he had just committed himself to.

"I will authorize anything you require, Elijah. Give me a timetable."

Elijah carefully weighed the question he was just presented with. "I'll have Sphere1 and 2 connected in one month."

Hendricks laughed uncontrollably, so much so that it made Elijah feel that what he had just said had been one big joke. Once Hendricks regained his composure, he brought both hands to be placed on Elijah's shoulders and spoke, "Please, say yes. Please say you and your lovely wife will join me for dinner, Elijah. A little surprise. I have built a new residence inside Sphere2. It will be completed in three weeks, and I want you and Lark to be my first guests! Please, say you will come to my Palace and join me. I call it my Palace. I'm sure you will agree when you see it."

Elijah produced a large smile but then it was rescinded. "But Hendricks, Lark and I have not been injected. We can't enter the Spheres," he stated with disappointment.

Hendricks acknowledged what Elijah had just said and answered, "Well, never say never. We have an entire month to correct that issue. But even if we don't, I'm the *Emperor* and can invite whomever I want. Even if my guests are 'subs'!"

CHAPTER 21:
THE WATER

ASCENDING THE STAIRWAY TO THE SURFACE, Lark swung open the door. She looked out upon the barren landscape that showed the ravages from the heat of the sun, unabated by an ozone to protect it. She needed to go to the surface. Despite the dangers of exposure for too long, she could not stay in her subterranean prison any longer. For the sake of her mental health, she needed to get out.

She decided she wouldn't hike too far from the sanctuary of her home. As she walked, she was astounded by the size and number of massive holes that had been excavated with the intent of having concrete tubes laid within them, then being covered over, to serve as housing for those that must live below. Those who would not accept the blueblood injection.

These holes in the ground had received no concrete tubes. There would be no more housing built for those who decided to live sans the blueblood injection. Most of the people that had occupied the subterranean housing had opted to take the injection. Looking out into the distance, Lark could see the translucent golden hue of the Spheres, knowing that was where the former sub residents now lived. Many of them her friends.

Coming to the edge of one of these trenches, Lark spied an opening deep down at the edge of the excavated area. She was curious, and determined to discover what the purpose of this opening could be. Carefully, she climbed down the edge and, with caution, neared the opening. At first glance it looked like a cave opening. She couldn't see very far into the opening as light ceased to penetrate far enough to see how deep it went.

This fascinated Lark because it was so out of place and so very odd, considering the area that had been excavated was flat terrain. She gazed about the opening, and it became clear to her that it was encased by rock. She was certain that the excavators had stumbled upon a rock formation. Perhaps the eroded remnant of an ancient mountain.

Lark reached inside a pack she wore across her chest. Luckily, she found a small flashlight that Subs used to traverse the surface at night when they gathered at the central meeting area of the residents of the underground. Knowing that it was probably not a wise decision, she turned on the flashlight and entered the opening to explore this anomaly.

Just a short distance inside the cave entrance, Lark moved the light to expose the walls of a cavern that appeared to get wider with every step as she moved forward. She removed the nomadic covering and sunglasses from her head.

Every step exposed a cooler and more comfortable temperature that brought a smile to her face. Seeing that the cavern walls seemed to be solid rock brought her some comfort that this cave would not collapse. Then it occurred to her, if the excavators knew that this cave existed, why was it abandoned, being less than two miles from Sphere1. She knew that underground dwellings were no longer being built due to the dwindling Sub population, but this was quite the archaeological find.

Suddenly, she heard a sound further into the cavern. She stopped walking to try and detect just what the source of the sound could be. She was determined to move further into the cave despite knowing that if anything happened to her, she might never be found. Then, the light emitting from her small flashlight caught a glimpse of something fantastic.

Her mouth was agape as she surveyed the ground and sides of the cavern. The cavern emptied into a scene that shook the very foundation of her imagination. She would have to return home and wait for Elijah before returning to this site. They would require additional light to adequately witness what she was seeing. The setting before her revealed an underground lake. Fresh water, as far as her meager light she could project. She knew of wells and underground streams existing in Colorado, but this was beyond comprehension.

She knew that the Spheres relied on deep underground wells for their water supply. The Subs water was reliant upon these wells, and it was piped into them. Reclaimed water was also a main source of the supply that they relied upon. This lake, this magnificent lake, could be a game changer. If they could tap this source, the subterranean dwellers would no longer be dependent on Spheretech.

Her ability to grow food underground, on a scale large enough to support her friends and community, could become a reality and Hendricks Vesper would no longer dictate their future.

CHAPTER 22:
FUTURE

STEPPING OFF THE TRAILER that carried him home, Elijah, as always, was grateful that Lark was there to greet him. Once inside their underground home, he could feel that Lark exuded an excitement that was more intense than he had witnessed from her lately. She was pacing back and forth with excitement and finding it hard to suppress her discovery.

"What in the heck is up with you today, Lark? I've never seen you this amped up!" He said in an effort to get her to start communicating about what had brought her this much excitement.

"Do you know if we have a generator? Oh yeah, and maybe some floodlights?" Lark echoed in a manner to only fuel more confusion from her husband.

"Sure, I happen to have those things in my bottom dresser drawer in the bedroom," Elijah sarcastically answered.

Looking at her husband with playful disgust she replied, "I know we don't have anything like that here at our home, but do you know where we can get something like that?"

More bewildered than ever, Elijah decided to appease her request with a legitimate answer. "I'm sure I can ask around and get that equipment, or something close, but why, my dear wife? Why would you need floodlights?"

Finally calm enough to give her husband a recap of the journey that she went on today, the excavated area, the large opening, and the cavern containing the subterranean lake, she waited for a response from Elijah. "I thought I asked you to never explore the surface alone," he barked at her.

Not deterred by her husband's angst about her journey, she added, "I know you don't like me to go to the surface on my own. I didn't plan on discovering an underground cavern and lake today, but you must admit, it's amazing. It can change everything!"

"Everything?" Elijah exclaimed out of confusion.

Clearly frustrated with his response, Lark decided the best direction for this conversation would be to just speak her mind. "There is ample room and water to begin teaching our *kind* how to grow our own food. How to become self-sufficient and dependent on only ourselves."

"What you are saying, depend on only ourselves, not the Sphere dwellers? Not on Hendricks Vesper?"

"Exactly!" Lark exclaimed.

Lowering his eyes to the ground to keep her from seeing that he was deeply considering his next response, Elijah answered, "Lark, I understand your disdain for the Sphere dwellers. I know you don't trust Hendricks Vesper's determination to have all of us take the injection, but maybe it isn't the worst thing. Maybe we should consider taking it. Today, Vesper offered to give us land, a home of our own. If we are injected, we could live on the surface once again. I know how you long for the surface."

Lark's stare pierced the very interior of his soul. She spoke with the effectiveness of a master debater, "Inside the Sphere? Is that where you really want to raise our child?"

"Maybe it wouldn't be the worst decision..." Then Elijah froze. He felt paralyzed and unable to respond. His mind swirled with wonder, and he felt that, for one brief moment, he had risen above this planet. It took an eternity for Elijah to collect his composure enough to squeak out one simple word of reply, "Child?"

Acting as if it were an everyday occurrence, Lark gleamed a huge smile and answered, "No injection for me. I'm pregnant."

Elijah embraced his wife for so long she felt like he might never let her go. "Do you know for certain? I mean, how do you know?"

"Lena Yung. She was a nurse practitioner before coming here. She examined me and did a blood test. She was as shocked as I was. It's been a long time since she has seen any woman pregnant. It appears that we have accomplished something fantastic here, my love."

Elijah couldn't contain himself. Tears were falling from his eyes. He was shaking his head in disbelief as he said, "A baby! I'm going to be a father!"

Lark kissed her husband deeply, and with tears of her own, spoke firmly to him. "And, there will be no injection! Lena told me that she's suspicious of it and encouraged me, us, to not take it! I will not subject our child to anything unnatural."

Embracing his wife again, Elijah now understood that this underground existence would be his future, Lark's future, and hopefully, a son's future.

CHAPTER 23: CREATION

HENDRICKS WAS BEYOND FASCINATED BY PI. From the very first moment Pi was introduced to him as their personal servant, he was astonished by this artificial being. In every way, Pi's mannerisms mirrored humans. He was attentive but knew when to leave the room. If not for his bronze skin color, like that of a statue depicting a famous ancestor of human history, Hendricks would swear he was human.

Antonetta entered the living area that had been designated to be the conversation and relaxation area of their new palace. She sat down on the sofa, snuggling up to Hendricks. She handed him a glass of wine that had been produced from the grapes grown in the vineyard in Sphere1. "Pi believes it is still young and it will be much better when it ages, but he believes it is ready to drink," she offered with her blue eyes wide open, indicating that she was surprised.

"Wow, so Silver created a wine sommelier!" Hendricks answered while laughing.

"I think our servant is charming. I have been a bit lonely lately. You've been working so hard and don't pay attention to me as much as you used to. At least Pi pays attention to me," Antonetta joked.

Taking the wine glass from her hand, Hendricks placed both glasses on the table in front of them. Kissing her passionately, he whispered affectionately in her ear, "He might pay attention to you, but can he do this?"

A while later, the couple lay next to each other. Antonetta, with her head on his chest, looked up into his eyes and revealed, "I can't have children. I knew that before I ever met you. I'm not sure how you feel about that?"

Hendricks hoisted himself up so that he could sit up with his back against the cushion of the couch. He turned towards her as she had also positioned herself into a sitting posture. He gazed upon her beauty. Every inch of her was perfect and she still inspired a yearning in him that he had never felt before. "I've thought about it often. I commissioned our scientists to research just how we can begin to populate our world again. I must admit, our research will be exclusive for the occupants of the Spheres, but we must find a way to create human children. Whether it be the old-fashioned way, or artificially."

"So, you're not disappointed that I can't get pregnant? I can see this is important to you," Antonetta's deep blue eyes seemed somewhat softer with her question.

"Life will find a way, Antonetta. Regardless, you are my love, and nothing will change that fact." One thing was evident to Antonetta, and that fact was that with every passing day, Hendricks appeared to be getting younger. It was also evident to her that he was acting as a younger man, as the love making returned for a sequel.

Pi greeted the couple, as their time alone had yielded to hunger pains, and they entered the dining area seeking sustenance. Antonetta gently touched Pi on his arm as she walked by him to sit at the dining table. As a created being, he had been programmed to enjoy human kindness and this brought him great enjoyment. He was genuinely fond of these humans.

As they began to eat their food, Hendricks stopped eating to ask Pi a question. "Pi, after we're done eating, would you like to accompany me to Dr. Tolmie's and Silver's laboratory?" Antonetta appeared slightly perturbed that Hendricks was going to abandon her this evening, but he reassured her that their visit to the lab would be very quick, and he would return to the palace, and her, shortly.

"There is nothing I would enjoy more. I have missed my creators. It would be wonderful to see them," Pi answered with all honesty, being the only way he could.

Hendricks watched as Antonetta continued to eat. He rose from the dinner table and walked around to where she was sitting, giving her a kiss on the cheek.

As Hendricks and Pi were driving to the laboratory, Pi asked a question that surprised Hendricks. "Dr. Vesper, I am curious about what you did to Antonetta during your carnal activity."

"You watched us, Pi?"

"I hope that I have not disappointed you, Dr. Vesper. I am here to serve you and Antonetta, and I cannot do your bidding if I am too far away from you. Have I stepped out of bounds?" Pi asked with the innocence of a child.

"I suppose not, Pi. Those moments when I share physical intimacy with Antonetta, well, let's just say those moments are private, and you should excuse yourself."

"I understand, Dr. Vesper," Pi responded.

"What are you curious about from what you saw?" Hendricks pressed on.

"Is that the manner in which humans are created?"

"We used to be created that way, Pi. It was done by coming together in the way that you saw me and Antonetta. Human procreation in this way ceased to be effective due to the manner that we humans destroyed the planet, and thusly brought death and suffering upon ourselves."

Hendricks explained as a father discussing the birds and the bees with their offspring.

"Then how are humans created now?" Pi asked in earnest curiosity.

Hendricks, with eyes straight forward as he drove to the laboratory, decided it was best not to provide this new creation with too much data and replied, "Humanity will continue, Pi. It must, and I will find it a way."

Pi didn't speak of it further, but Hendricks could tell that he was researching his data the same as a human would be exploring his thoughts. They pulled up in front of the laboratory and Hendricks stopped to admire the elk herd that was grazing in the meadow adjacent to the lab. They entered the lab to find Ben sitting at his desk in his office, along with Silver James.

Silver stood up from his chair to greet them. "Hendricks, glad you could come this evening. I didn't expect to see Pi with you."

Hendricks smiled and said, "Well, I believe it will be good for Pi to witness what we're going to do this evening. Plus, let's just say that Pi has shown a fascination about creation."

Ben pushed up from his chair and walked around the desk and said, "Well, Pi, tonight is your lucky night. You're going to meet a creation like yourself." Pi didn't seem to understand exactly what Ben Tolmie had just said, but he smiled a strained smile anyway. Ben swept his arm towards the office door in a manner to usher the three humans and the artificial intelligence named Pi out to the hallway, and moments later they stood in a section of the lab that displayed a sight that brought great amazement to Hendricks.

"Hendricks and Pi, I'd like you to meet Tremont." Silver said as though introducing a celebrity to a red-carpet event. Standing before them was a bronze statue. Silent and inanimate, Tremont's size eclipsed that of Pi by at least six inches. His mass was like that of an ancient gladiator, muscled and sculpted to show strength. But his physical features were very human.

Pi moved forward towards Tremont and examined the being as if he were examining a painting by a famous master. "He is quite large, Silver," Pi spoke.

Laughing, Silver replied, "Yes, quite large, Pi."

"Was he created this way to serve Dr. Vesper?", Pi asked.

"Yes, Pi. He was created this way to serve Dr. Vesper, but in a different way than yourself."

Pi could not peel his attention from the massive creation he was viewing. Hendricks stepped in and inquired, "Shall we activate him." It wasn't a question, instead it was more of a command.

A few moments later, with blue eyes glowing, Tremont spoke. "Is this one of the soldiers under my command?"

Silver answered him, "No, Tremont, this is Pi. He serves Dr. Vesper, but as a house companion."

Tremont looked Pi up and down with an indignant stare and replied, "I am pleased to learn that. He does not appear to be a soldier."

Pi, who at first was fascinated to meet a created being such as himself, found himself not liking Tremont. This emotion was foreign to him, and he would have to explore his data further to learn why he felt this way.

Hendricks slapped Silver and Ben on their backs and with an outburst of praise said, "Nicely done. Is he fully weaponized?"

Ben solemnly answered, "Yes, Hendricks. We are taking Tremont to the weapons range to test him and the weapons."

Hendricks motioned for Pi to join him as they left the room where Tremont had been activated. Without turning back, Hendricks spoke to Silver and Ben, "Make sure everything checks out and is under our control. Now that *it* has become activated."

Silver and Ben acknowledged his request even though Hendricks couldn't see them, and he knew they would comply. As he and Pi traveled the distance to the Palace, Hendricks found Pi to be unusually silent. Pi's attention was deep into searching his data for information on weapons. What he discovered revealed to him that if this was what Tremont would be equipped with, he was glad that Silver hadn't intended that for him.

Antonetta heard them enter the residence. She breathed a sigh of relief that Hendricks had told her the truth. They hadn't taken long. The day had been long, and despite having more energy than she could ever recall, she felt slightly fatigued.

As she welcomed Hendricks into their bed and she moved into his embrace, bringing comfort to her as she fell asleep, she was unaware that her Fallopian tubes, which had been scarred and closed for her adult life, had been repaired. The Blueblood injection, just as it had in restoring a vibrant youth to Hendricks, had performed this repair. Her egg, now fertilized, had divided and an embryo that was created in the old-fashioned way, was growing inside her.

CHAPTER 24:
A FAMILY IS JOINED

WATCHING AS THE FINAL PANEL WAS HOISTED INTO PLACE, Elijah felt like he would vomit. Every part of the construction of the joining sphere had gone according to plan but this panel would reveal either success or failure. The anticipation was overwhelming. Sitting alone in the ATV that had been provided for him by Hendricks, he was distracted by another vehicle pulling up next to him.

Elijah glanced over to see who the driver might be. It was Hendricks who exited his ATV with an intense focus on the event unfolding before them. Just like clockwork, the smaller sphere that was designed to create a bridge between Sphere1 and 2 completed its form. They both knew that most likely the smaller sphere would do exactly as it was designed. The big question was, would Sphere1 and 2 adopt their smaller sibling, thus joining the three to become one.

With the heat of the sun pounding on the three spheres, Elijah and Hendricks waited for something miraculous to happen. It didn't. The only thing they saw were two large spheres separated by one small sphere, each separate from the others. Hendricks, who had yet to acknowledge Elijah, finally spoke. "It was a novel idea, Elijah. Unfortunately, an idea that has failed." Elijah felt like his entire body was about to give up and he would simply collapse right then and there.

"I really thought this would work. I really, really, did," was all Elijah could answer.

"Time to get back to the drawing board," Hendricks said with soft spoken remorse that clearly showed he was disappointed. Elijah, who had not left his ATV, pressed the pedal that would propel the vehicle forward, wanting desperately to leave and return to the underground, to the hole from which he came.

Suddenly, Hendricks called out like a barker at a carnival, "Look! Something's happening!" Like two large dogs sniffing a smaller one, Sphere1 and 2 began to expand and investigate the smaller sphere. Elijah sat in wonder as both began to pulsate as they had when originally formed. A short time later, both 1 and 2 accepted their new younger sibling and joined together with the smaller sphere, creating a perfect passageway between them.

Elijah had never heard Hendricks laugh so hard and for so long. "It worked! It worked! It worked!" he exclaimed, pointing at the bonding of Sphere1 and 2.

Wanting to collapse, Elijah simply bowed his head to his chest and thanked whichever god had delivered him today. Hendricks ran over to Elijah's ATV, and like a soccer player that had just won the World Cup, hugged Elijah so hard that he thought he might pass out. "I guess we were too impatient," Elijah expressed, not knowing what else to say.

Hendricks beamed a broad smile and proclaimed, "What are you doing just sitting here? You're the Chief Operating Officer of the Sphere Empire. You're my right-hand man! You need to get started on construction of Sphere3!"

Elijah was speechless. He would need to question Hendricks to find out if he was in earnest about the promotion, but for right now, he would just enjoy the moment. "Six o'clock tomorrow evening at my Palace for dinner and a celebration of your new position. Right, Mr. Price? Oh yes, and I fully expect you to bring your wife, Lark."

Elijah assumed that his questioning if the promotion was real had just been answered. He was quite curious about how Hendricks knew his wife's name. "Yes, we are definitely looking forward to it," Elijah answered, not knowing if Lark would share his excitement.

"Come to the south road entrance of Sphere2 tomorrow. I will inform security that you're approved to pass. Oh, yes, and come casual." After the last reference about how to dress, Elijah thought to himself, "How else can we dress, we only have one outfit."

Elijah acknowledged that he understood the directions and returned to the Extrusion Facility tobcelebrate with the people that had made this vision come true.

Feeling unsure just how the evening would go, Elijah and Lark made the journey from the underground city to the south road entrance to Sphere2. Elijah pointed out the fruits of his labor that now formed the bridge between Sphere1 and 2. "How are you going to address the injection tonight, you know, if it comes up? I can't imagine Hendricks Vesper would allow an underground dweller to be his COO, and live in Sphere City, without being a Blueblood." Lark asked, knowing that she couldn't wait any longer to have a plan.

Elijah answered, "Maybe we have been ignorant of the dangers of taking the shot, Lark. Perhaps we should consult with Sphere doctors about what possible issues the injection could create for our child."

Lark demanded that Elijah stop the vehicle. Turning directly at her husband with a firm but empathetic voice she responded, "Elijah Price! I understand what your success here has meant. We were down and out! On the brink of not surviving, but please look at me," Lark pleaded as she reached up with both hands to grasp his face. "I will not risk our child. You have done the job, and done it extremely well, without taking the shot and you will continue to do it extremely well living with me in our underground home."

Elijah acknowledged his wife's words. He loved her more than anything and would never force her to accept anything she refused to accept. He decided that if the subject came up, he would be honest with Hendricks. Honest about everything.

They pulled up to the section of Sphere2 that allowed the south road to enter the sphere. Lark's curiosity peaked at seeing the outside road and how it continued inside Sphere2. Although the road continued, the exterior walls of the sphere, despite being translucent, were quite solid.

The couple watched as two figures approached the interior wall. They watched as one of the figures placed a tubular device on the wall and the wall began a metamorphosis. A breach formed creating an opening large enough for a vehicle to pass. As Elijah and Lark entered the sphere, they were startled to see that the sentries that created the opening, were large, human in appearance, with glowing blue eyes, and were totally bronze, like ancient statues.

As they drove up the road, Lark turned to see the breach repair itself. She turned to Elijah and asked, "What in the hell were those things?"

Elijah shook his head and replied, "I'm not sure I want to know." Once the initial shock of passing the bronze beings had subsided, they removed their sunglasses. Both marveled at the golden hue that the sphere reflected. It was beautiful beyond anything they had seen. Rolling hills with adult trees lined the road they traveled to reach the palace residence.

Lark felt nostalgic at the sights she was seeing. Her thoughts reminisced about her youth and the crops she tended. Growing up a farmer's daughter in the former State of Colorado taught her much about what she knew today, and that was growing things. Then turning up a winding road, they arrived at the Palace of Hendricks Vesper. "Oh my god, it's beautiful," Lark gasped.

CHAPTER 25:
THE VISIT

BELIEVING THAT THEY HAD SEEN ALL THE SURPRISES they might witness that evening, Elijah and Lark were once again astounded at the sight of another bronze being walking out to greet them. Even though this being was smaller in stature than the two creatures they met at the opening of the sphere, it was, none-the-less, just as impressive.

This being's blue eyes showed an expression of welcome that was different than what they had felt from the other two. "Hello, Mr. and Mrs. Price. My name is Pi. I serve Hendricks Vesper and this household. Welcome. Let me escort you to Hendricks so you may find comfort and pleasure in his home."

Elijah, not feeling quite sure how to answer Pi, simply said, "Thank you."

Taking turns looking at each other with astonishment, Elijah and Lark followed Pi up a staircase with banisters made from solid gold and into an expansive room complete with furniture upholstered with opulent fabrics and, of course, a grand piano.

Asking the couple to make themselves comfortable, Pi directed them to a sofa that, frankly, made Lark uncomfortable to sit upon. Pi excused himself as he made them aware that Hendricks would be with them shortly and he would return to take their refreshment order. Elijah joked as Pi disappeared, "Lark, I wonder if Vesper will give us one of those?"

With Antonetta by his side, Hendricks entered the room with a beaming smile and walked to where Elijah and Lark were now standing to greet them. After receiving a boisterous hug, Elijah introduced Lark. Extending her hand in greeting, Hendricks bowed to place a kiss upon the top of it. "Excuse my greeting, Lark. A civilized greeting, from a more civilized time," he smiled as he spoke.

Lark reciprocated the smile although it projected an uncomfortable appearance. Pointing towards Antonetta, Hendricks said, "I'm sure you both know who she is, but to be formal, this is Antonetta Valde." Once the greetings were concluded, Hendricks expressed just how glad he was that they had accepted his invitation and asked them to sit.

Pi returned with a bottle of wine from the sphere vintner and offered each a glass. "It's very good. Trust me," Hendricks offered like a salesman at a local fair. Lark declined and asked if she could just have a glass of water. Antonetta followed her female guest's example and declined the wine, optioning for a water also. "It has been so long since I've felt nauseous, but for some reason my stomach has been very unsettled today," Antonetta admitted.

The men took their glasses and toasted to the success of the bridge connecting the spheres. Suddenly, Antonetta lunged from her seat to run to the restroom. Hendricks excused himself to attend to her, leaving Elijah and Lark sitting alone. "I'm sorry she isn't feeling well but I had no idea we were here to be interviewed by Antonetta," Elijah proclaimed.

Lark smiled at her naïve husband and replied, "Oh, trust me, we aren't here to be interviewed by her. Hendricks and Antonetta are together."

With eyes extended wide open, Elijah responded, "Together, together?"

Lark smirked and mimicked him, "Yes, together, together, dear husband."

A short time later Hendricks and Antonetta returned to the room. Elijah offered that maybe it was best to call the evening off, but Antonetta would not hear of it. The couples engaged in idle chit-chat before Hendricks addressed Lark directly. "Lark, how do you like being inside the sphere and seeing all the things it offers? I understand you used to love to garden."

Not wanting to venture into the success with hydroponic gardening that she was having with subterranean growing, Lark responded, "It truly brought back pleasant memories of my past, Hendricks. Although I must admit, being inside the sphere has been much warmer than I anticipated."

Looking sympathetic, Antonetta answered, "I'm sorry, Lark. It's a by-product of the blue injection. It does cause a physiological transformation where we prefer it to be a bit warmer. Are you uncomfortable? I could have Pi retrieve a fan for you."

Lark smiled and replied with appreciation that she was just fine. Hendricks began to pry into Larks past, hoping to find an inroad to sway her reluctance to get the injection. "I understand your background is in crop production. Is that true?"

"Yes, corn primarily."

Hendricks gently slapped his legs with both hands and exclaimed, "Corn! That is the food crop that is giving our scientists the most problem! We sure could use somebody like you to help." Before Hendricks could deploy his arsenal of treats to convince Lark that taking the injection and moving inside the sphere would be a benefit to everyone, Pi announced that supper was prepared and ready.

As they moved to the dining area, Hendricks decided it was best to bide his time. It was difficult for Elijah and Lark to converse much with their hosts during the meal because the food was decadent. It had been a long time since they had tasted food this delicious. Glancing over at Antonetta, Lark discovered that she had barely touched her food. With the meal concluded, Hendricks invited Elijah to join him in his study as he wanted some input on the plans to begin construction of Sphere3. Elijah was reluctant to leave Lark alone with Antonetta knowing that she had manipulative skills equal to Hendricks', but he felt obliged to accept the invitation.

"I'm so sorry for earlier. I just haven't felt very good today. Since taking the injection, I have never felt better, until today. Perhaps viruses have made their way into our sanctuary inside the sphere," Antonetta confided.

"Yes, perhaps," was all Lark could say in reply. About an hour later Hendricks and Elijah emerged from the study and Elijah extended their appreciation for the invitation and the wonderful meal, stating that it was probably time for them to make the journey back to the underground city. Hendricks and Antonetta bid their farewell to the Prices and Pi escorted them out of the Palace and to their vehicle.

With their guests gone, Antonetta quizzed Hendricks about whether he had been successful in convincing Elijah that the injection was the best for them. Hendricks looked solemn in his response to her inquiry. "There is an underlying reason that he is resistant. I can't put my finger on it, but I'm not sure they will ever comply."

As Antonetta began to make her way towards the bedroom, Hendricks said he was going to have a nightcap of brandy. "Okay, don't be long. I need you next to me to sleep and it's been a rough day," Antonetta responded. Hendricks gave her a kiss on the cheek as he sent her off to bed. He was equally concerned about her stomach issues since illness had been almost nonexistent with Bluebloods.

He decided he would send the doctor to see her in the morning.

As Elijah and Lark traveled towards the sphere exit, they noticed that the bubble they were contained inside allowed the magnificence of the stars to shine through just as if they were outside. Their marveling soon came to an end as their vehicle approached the ominous bronze beings that guarded the exit. As they drove through the breached walls of the sphere, Lark asked Elijah, "I wonder what those white tubular things those creepy things push into the wall are? It seems to create an opening."

"They emit a beam, or ray, of cold. The organisms that make up the sphere walls become dormant when they are exposed to cold. A section can withstand a temporary dormancy without collapsing the sphere," Elijah answered as though he were a professor teaching a class.

"How do you know this?" She quizzed.

"Because these organisms are like my children. I know how they work," Elijah answered.

Finishing the last gulp of his brandy, Hendricks picked up the phone and a voice on the other end responded saying, "Yes, sir?"

"Cut off the water to the underground city. Starting tomorrow, no more food allotments are to be delivered. It's time for decisions," Hendricks spoke with a tone that indicated he knew full well the decision he was making.

The voice on the other end answered, "Consider it done."

Turning off the lamp that was positioned next to him, Hendricks stood up from his chair and retreated to the bedroom.

As they neared the underground city that was their home, Elijah offered in conversation, "I certainly hope nothing is seriously wrong with Antonetta."

Lark chuckled at her husband's question. Despite the fact that through his fortitude and experience he had ascended the ranks of Spheretech, he was still a novice at the human experience, and particularly when it came to females. "She's pregnant, silly."

He was astonished by the insight his wife constantly displayed and this proclamation was no exception.

CHAPTER 26:
SUSPICION

READING THE ELECTRONIC MESSAGE OVER AND OVER, Ben Tolmie sat in front of his computer, weighing the contents of the message:

Ben,

How nice it was to hear from you. I'm genuinely glad to learn that your research and experiments have yielded fruit and that humanity has perhaps been offered a reprieve. How I long to be there, watching the evolution of our species.

Here, in what is left of Europe, things are in shambles. Food is scarce and sickness is abundant. I fear that what is left of civilization on this side of the Atlantic Ocean is all but over. The relentless effects of ozone depletion have all but doomed us. I do pray that you and Vesper have found the answer.

I'm so sorry that I have taken so long to respond to your inquiry from long ago. It wasn't my intention to ignore you. You have been, and always will be, my friend. My silence has been due to just how poor communication has become, particularly here in what used to be England.

I was successful in reaching out to a colleague I knew who was on staff as a professor at the University of Manchester, and after some distance of time I finally heard back from him. His correspondence indicated that he was not familiar with a Hendricks Vesper ever having attended the University.

He did some research, and along with that information, he discovered there wasn't any residential detail that he was ever born or lived in Manchester. Now, as much as that might leave the imagination to conjecture, it could be that Vesper changed his name or something to that effect. It's obvious that he is a genius and had to learn his specialties somewhere. So, I am uncertain what your motivation might have been to ask me to investigate this for you.

I am truly sorry if this causes you any distress. It is my hope and desire that we might meet again, but with every passing day, I fear that won't occur. The Blueblood injection is not available to us. The short sightedness of our leaders to get into the game, so to speak, has left us crippled and I conjecture to believe that we will soon, all be gone.

I wish you well, my friend, and may God save you.

God speed,

Reginald Lewis

Ben closed the document on his computer. He proceeded to close an image of Dolion Cozbi that had been taken shortly before his demise. Ben had enlarged the photo and placed it side-by-side with an older image of Hendricks Vesper. He wondered to himself why he had ever done that. He had no suspicion that led him to place the images together. Still, it was uncanny that the nose, mouth, and general shape of the head were very similar.

Of course, the image of Cozbi featured a bald man, clean shaven where Hendricks Vesper's image displayed a man with a thick head of hair and a full beard. Although the older photo of Vesper showed a man whose hair had turned gray, that certainly wasn't the man who led the Sphere Empire now.

Turning off the computer, Ben stood and gazed out upon an empty room that was once filled with his and Silver James' creations. Artificial intelligence that was designed, programmed, and built to answer to one man, and one man only, Hendricks Vesper. He turned off the light to his office and just before he exited to leave the laboratory, spun around and went back into his office. He turned on the light and returned to his computer screen. Calling up the documents that contained the message from Reginald Lewis plus the side-by-side images of Cozbi and Vesper, Ben hesitated as he reached out his right index finger, but then, hitting the delete key on his keyboard, he turned off the power to his computer and left to go home.

CHAPTER 27:
SACRIFICE

KLAOUS ANSON MET ELIJAH AND LARK as they pulled their ATV into the center of the underground city. He was waving his arms in an excited fashion to attract their attention. His accent was clearly German and, despite having moved to the North American territories long before the chaos caused by global warming, he hadn't lost his accent. "Elijah! Ve has all lost our vater. It isn't flowing in none of our dwellings."

Elijah climbed out of the vehicle and, with as much calm in his voice as he could manage, called out to Klous, "It's probably just a temporary problem. Let me go check our house and see if we've lost water also." Lark and he descended the stairs, and a short time later Elijah came up to address the group that had continued to grow in the common area. "We don't have water either."

The group that had gathered there was becoming excessively anxious as more people came up to the common area to profess that they did not have water flowing to their dwellings. Elijah held his hands up towards the group in an effort to get their attention. "Look, folks, I'm sure there is a good explanation for our loss of water. I'm sure that those who are responsible for ensuring water flows to the underground city are aware of the problem and are diligently seeking a solution. Truth be known, the sphere cities are probably experiencing the same issue."

Tyler Mansfield, one of the men that was on Elijah's original team in the extrusion facility spoke up, proclaiming, "You know that isn't true, Elijah. Vesper and his thugs have been plotting against those of us that chose not to take the injection for some time now." Elijah acknowledged the angst that Tyler was professing but had a hard time believing him due to just becoming the COO of Spheretech.

Elijah did his best to keep the anxious group calm and pleaded with them to return to their dwellings for the night. He promised them that he would get them answers in the morning and get their water flowing again. Elijah was a leader and most of the residents of the underground city revered him as such. Calmer heads eventually prevailed, and everybody descended back to their dwellings.

Later, as Lark and Elijah lay in bed, he found it difficult to sleep. Deep down, he sensed that something had changed and perhaps nothing would ever be the same. After a night of fitful sleep, Elijah pushed himself up from the bed and prepared himself to head for the extrusion plant. The radiant sun had yet to rise in the east when Elijah arrived at the extrusion facility. He was early to arrive, far ahead of his team.

Knowing that Hendricks rarely slept, Elijah hoped he could reach him with the telephone line that fed from his office directly to Hendricks. As he placed his thumb on the screen that would provide admittance to the plant, a red light appeared on the console that displayed an error. He tried again, achieving the same negative results. Elijah was confused and after trying several times to gain admittance, he returned to sit in his ATV.

Elijah heard his team approaching in the trailer. Seeing his friend, Braden Samuleson, step off the trailer, he summoned him over to his ATV. He recapped with Braden the failed attempts to gain access to the facility. Braden walked over and placed his thumb on the console only to have the same red light come on indicating failed admittance. Each of Elijah's team attempted to gain entrance, but to no avail.

The members of Team A became quite frustrated by this new development. Many began to grumble that this was in connection with the loss of water. Elijah gained their attention and instructed everybody to return to the underground city and their homes. Despite their frustration with the situation, they complied because they were allegiant to Elijah.

Sitting alone in his ATV, Elijah decided the best course to follow would be to return to his home. If all of this was a simple malfunction, or mistake, Hendricks could reach him at home, and he could get this mess all sorted out. He turned his ATV around and headed for home.

Elijah descended the steps to find Lark surprised by his appearance. He told her what had occurred at the extrusion facility and she, with a concerned look on her face, explained what she had encountered earlier. "I went up soon after you left for work to get our food allotment. I like to get in line early. The truck that delivers the food never came. It never came, Elijah!"

"Get on the communication system that Klous built and let the other residents know we will have a community meeting tonight, just as soon as it is dusk," Elijah requested.

"Okay. Are you worried?" Lark questioned.

Elijah came up and embraced her and answered, "Extremely." Several times during the day, Elijah picked up the phone to try and reach Hendricks. No answer ever came.

As the sun disappeared into the western sky and twilight gained its foothold on the land, Elijah and Lark ascended to the surface to find a large group of residents already gathered. Elijah could sense they were anxious and even angry. Coming to the center of the group, Elijah addressed the residents. It had been a while since they had everybody attend a community meeting, and Elijah guessed they numbered approximately four hundred residents.

Elijah, in as strong a voice as he could manage spoke like a politician at a town hall meeting, "Folks, unfortunately, I know no more now than I knew last night."

A resident called out from behind Elijah, "I thought you had connections with these people. These...these blue eyes!" Turning, Elijah could see it was Tobias Krill. He moved forward towards Elijah displaying his muscular build. He was known as a hot head with a quick temper which was evident from the scar that ran from the bottom of his right ear and along his cheek to the corner of his mouth. Elijah always wondered if he had received the scar in a knife fight but hadn't the nerve to ask him.

Elijah did his best to temper the anger being shown by Tobias. He had respect for the man's abilities at the extrusion facility as a member of Team B. Elijah didn't want to jeopardize their working relationship. He noticed that Tobias was carrying a large stick with an abundance of cloth wrapped around the top. Looking around, Elijah noticed that several other residents were sporting the same.

"Elijah, we have given you long enough to get answers. We can wait no longer. We are going to Sphere2 tonight. We are going to demand that Vesper give us answers!" Tobias yelled partly at Elijah and partly to incite the crowd that had decided to join him.

Elijah feared for the people that were obviously siding with Tobias. "Sphere2 is almost ten miles from here. You can't expect to walk all the way there tonight. C'mon folks, you need to rethink this!"

Tobias would hear nothing that would sway him from leading this mission tonight. Waving at the other residents of the underground city to follow him, Tobias began moving away from the common area with the rest of the angry mob in tow. Calling back at Elijah, like one of the pro wrestlers he used to watch when he was a kid, he boasted, "We ain't walking, Elijah. The Blueblood that drives the trailer, well, let's just say he ain't in too good of shape tonight."

As Elijah watched the mob disappear into the night, he walked over to Lark. He was concerned for the stress this had caused her. He felt helpless. Coming to where she stood, he placed one of his arms around her shoulder. He could see she was crying. Standing next to Lark was Andrea Krill, Tobias's wife, whose face also showed tears had been flowing.

Lark looked up into the solemn eyes of her husband. Eyes that displayed a man who was confused and defeated. "Elijah, you have to follow them," she professed with an urgency that told Elijah she was serious.

"Follow them? Do you really think I can stop this?"

A small tear was falling from one of her eyes. Elijah looked over at Andrea whose face showed a look of terror.

Andrea spoke up with words that were barely audible through her quivering lips. "Elijah, I'm afraid for my husband. I need him here with me. I'm with child."

These words pierced Elijah to his soul. The joy he felt at Andrea's announcement was second only to when Lark had informed him of her own pregnancy. Two women from the underground city had conceived. They weren't sphere city women. Humans were finding a way without the injection and without the sphere.

Elijah knew what he must do. He hugged his wife and nodded his head at Andrea and walked towards the entrance to his underground home. He climbed into his ATV and, glancing back towards the people who remained congregated in the common area, he drove out into the darkness in the hopes of convincing an angry people that this was dangerous and futile.

Moving as fast as his ATV would let him, he followed the trail towards Sphere2. Elijah guessed he was nearly thirty minutes behind the group being led by Tobias. Approximately half a mile from an entrance to the sphere, Elijah could hear angry voices yelling. Stopping the ATV to hear better, Elijah jumped out of the ATV and climbed up a small dirt hill hoping to see what was causing the commotion.

Even though it was dark, the moon gave off enough of a reflection from the relentless sun to enable him to see. The sticks with cloth wrapped around the top had been lit on fire and the torches glowed against the darkness like fireflies remembered from Elijah's childhood.

Immediately, Elijah could discern a figure that was clearly Tobias. He was shaking his torch at another figure that, with each passing moment of his eyesight becoming better adjusted to the dark and the surroundings, Elijah recognized as one of four bronze men that they had encountered when he and Lark had visited Hendricks the night before.

He watched as Tobias approached the bronze being. He saw the bronze man reach down on his right side and in one fluid motion he extracted a long object and extended the arm that held it, pointing it directly at Tobias. A bright blue flame emitted from the tapered end. There was no sound, no explosion, and as quickly as the blue flame appeared, it disappeared. There was no doubt in Elijah's mind that the blue flame he had seen was the propellant that had sent a deadly projectile towards his friend. Tobias fell to the ground.

What happened then shook Elijah to his core. The other three bronze beings produced similar weapons from their sides and began to fire them on the group from the underground city. It was only a matter of minutes before all of them lay motionless on the ground. Fear and tears had come to Elijah. He couldn't move. The event that had just unfolded before him was beyond belief. Then, he could see that there were more bronze beings coming out from the sphere.

With their blue eyes casting an eerie light upon the landscape, they began dragging the dead back into the sphere. Elijah, though terrified, knew he needed to get back to the underground city. As his brain finally kicked in to tell him he needed to move, he could hear the bronze beings talking to one another. The command was for them to scour the immediate area to ensure there were no survivors.

Elijah knew he must move and move fast. Then, as if one of his own knew he needed to be saved, the beings were called back to the sphere. Elijah heard them call out that there was one who had survived. As the bronze men returned to the sight of the massacre, Elijah reached his ATV and quickly turned it in the direction of the underground city. As he maneuvered the ATV the best he could, with no lights to guide him, he turned to see a flash of light behind him.

The fears that Elijah had considered earlier had come true. He wasn't sure who had just given their life to save him, but he now realized that from here on out, nothing would be the same. Hendricks Vesper had drawn an evil line. A line that said you must take the blue injection. If not, the result would be that you weren't fit to be human. The result would be genocide.

CHAPTER 28: ASSUMPTION

HENDRICKS STOOD IN ASTONISHMENT and disbelief. Seeking a chair in which to sit down, he reached over to pour himself a drink of whatever the crystal server held inside it. Taking a large gulp, he calmed himself and proclaimed to Antonetta and the doctor standing nearby, "Pregnant? You're going to have a baby?"

Antonetta beamed a smile that could light up the darkest cavern, "Yes, my dear Hendricks, a baby. This is truly a miracle," she proclaimed.

The doctor spoke up at Antonetta's proclamation, "Yes, not only is the pregnancy quite miraculous, but it also seems we are having an epidemic."

Confused by the words that the doctor had just spoken, Hendricks had to delve further into its meaning. "Epidemic? Why are you calling a pregnancy an epidemic?"

Upon sensing that he had just expressed something that was not taken in jest, the doctor clarified his statement. "Sorry, Dr. Vesper. What I meant is, we have recently diagnosed several of our females *with child.*"

Standing up from his seat, Hendricks produced a broad grin directed at the doctor. "Well, isn't this tremendous news? Tremendous indeed!"

The doctor, realizing that it was best to leave the couple to their privacy, excused himself and left the room. Hendricks walked over to where Antonetta was seated and, kneeling to her level, placed an open hand on her stomach. Antonetta could see a small tear flowing from his eye. She began to cry herself, not only because of the news they would be having a child, but it had been a while since she had seen this depth of tenderness from him.

Despite being overwhelmed with the news of Antonetta's pregnancy, Hendricks couldn't help but let his thoughts venture to the wonder that perhaps, just perhaps, human fertility had been restored. Restored by the blue injection. This side effect was very unexpected. Males and females had become infertile. The human race was in jeopardy, but not now.

The injection could be the reason that dominion over this earth had been restored to its rightful owners. At least for those with blue blood running inside their veins.

Glasses filled with champagne clinked in celebration of the incredible news that Hendricks had just revealed to Ben Tolmie and Silver James. The three men shared in the astonishment of the news it brought. Handing out a cigar to each of his closest circle, they lit them and blew the smoke out as it engulfed the triumph of the moment. Then the conversation turned towards a more business-like tone.

"Ben, I am pleased with the work that you and Silver have accomplished here with our artificial intelligence. But…" Hendricks spoke as if he were guarding a deep secret that he was about to reveal.

"But?" Ben replied, hoping to propel Hendricks to reveal what was on his mind.

Hendricks smiled and shrugged as he puffed on his cigar, "Oh don't fret, Tolmie, my ol' friend. I want you to suspend your work here on our bronze friends. I feel we've achieved enough in their development for the time being. I want you to focus on finding out if our blue injection could be the source of restoring human fertility. I need you to begin research on the blood of those women that have become pregnant. I need to know if our *blue* is the reason, and I don't know of anybody better than you to start the blood analysis."

Ben smiled at Vesper and answered, "Of course, Hendricks. I'll get started right away."

Feeling a little uneasy about the interchange he had just observed between Ben and Hendricks, Silver became concerned that if Ben were to focus on a project other than A.I., what did that mean for him? Then his answer came. "Silver, we couldn't have done all this without you. Please understand that."

"Thank you, Hendricks," Silver reluctantly offered.

Hendricks focused his entire attention upon Silver and spoke, "While we suspend our A.I. research and development, I'm going to need you to return to the extrusion facility. We've got to keep our panel production on schedule for when Sphere3 is ready to build."

Silver stared intently at Hendricks before replying. "I have no problem doing that for you, Hendricks, but what about Elijah? He is knee deep in that facility and knows our material better than even me."

Hendricks took another draw on his cigar and blew the smoke out into the room. "Let's just say that Mr. Price has made a very poor decision and is no longer going to be involved with our mission."

Staring at each other, Silver and Ben had nothing to say, but their blue eyes indicated that they understood exactly what Hendricks meant.

Silver's ATV traveled through the connecting sphere between the larger ones on his way to his home in Sphere1. His thoughts couldn't help wandering into memories of his life before Spheretech. As top of his class at MIT, he was recruited to join a prestigious company that was heavily invested in the development of artificial intelligence. When it came to writing code for machines that would become self-aware, there wasn't anybody better. He had a special gift.

He had ascended the ranks of that company and was highly considered one of the best A.I. minds in the Territories. His research and development in the arena of A.I. was highly coveted, and it sometimes involved people with malicious intent. His success led to riches and prestige. Then it all came crashing down.

The Government of the Territories became suspicious of just how fast A.I. was advancing. It was concerned that it could be used militarily and shut down any companies that were engaging in the development of A.I. With the pressure that had been placed on his company by the Government, Silver lost not only his job, but he lost his passion and reason for living.

He considered ending his life then, and tonight, hearing Hendricks shut down his A.I. development here at Spheretech, he was considering ending his life now. As he pulled up to the meager living quarters which were nothing compared to what he should have been provided, especially due to the contribution he had made to Hendricks, he exited the ATV and walked in the front door.

A prototype of the very first human-like A.I. he had created sat on a table. Just the head, with several wires connected to a large processing unit. It spoke, "Good evening, Silver, so nice to see you again. It has been a long day with no stimulus. I enjoy human interaction."

Silver moved over to where the head was sitting on the table and pulled up a chair in front of it. Silver smiled and responded, "Well, I'm here now, Primus. What would you like to talk about?"

Primus' eyelids closed slowly and then opened. Silver was upset that he hadn't been able to speed up the facial reactions on him. His time and efforts had been spent advancing the development of the bronze humanoids of Hendrick's army.

Primus was his creation at his former company. At the time, he was truly a marvel and was well on the way to becoming a fully functional A.I. Just like a first child, Silver had a soft spot in his heart for Primus. Primus was fully self-aware. Even though he had no torso in which to move, he had senses and thoughts. He slept, dreamed, and was curious.

"I sense you are not yourself tonight," Primus offered as an analyst would of a patient laying on a couch in a psychiatrist's office.

"No, I'm not, Primus. Very observant of you to notice. My work at my lab has been suspended. I have been ordered to return to the extrusion plant," Silver responded.

"Do you have to obey that order?" Primus intuitively asked.

Silver paused for a moment before answering, "Yes. I question why this decision has been made, but I must comply with the order."

"Please explain 'comply'," Primus asked like a student seeking direction.

"It's like being forced to do something," Silver answered.

Primus's eyes indicated he was processing what Silver had just told him. "So, forced means against your will, correct, Silver?" Primus offered in interpretation.

"That is correct, Primus. I cannot disobey this order. Plus, it would be rude for me to do so. Spheretech and Dr. Vesper brought me here to build the extrusion plant. I helped them to develop the machines that would produce the panel for the spheres. Because of my hard work, I was allowed to follow my dreams, and create Pi and the others."

"Is Pi doing well?" Primus asked.

"Yes, quite well. But enough of me, what would you like to talk about?" Silver indulged Primus.

"When will I be made whole?" Primus asked in total innocence of his current state.

Silver stumbled for the words to answer him. All he could offer his creation was the truth. "I'm not sure if you will ever be a complete being. Primus, I brought you here when my former position was eliminated. I did so at great peril. The world was not as fond of your kind as I was."

"I'm happy that nobody forced you to abandon me. If this is my future, to exist as I am now, I consider myself whole," Primus admitted.

Totally overwhelmed by just how far his creation had come, despite not having all the superior technology of Pi and Tremont, Silver sighed and turned from Primus to avoid having to explain the tears streaming from his eyes. Deep inside him, Silver preferred the company of these symbiont creations.

Knowing at the heart of his soul that what Hendricks Vesper was planning was wrong, it was with these words spoken by a machine that was only just becoming self-aware, that Silver Jon Jones became aware himself, that somehow, he must fight to stop Hendricks.

Pi hovered close to Antonetta as she reclined, reading a book. Looking up from her reading, she noticed the expression on Pi's face which indicated that he was perplexed. "Troubled tonight, Pi?" she inquired.

"Yes, Antonetta. I am curious. Will I ever be able to create a child inside me, like you?" Pi asked with total innocence.

Antonetta couldn't help but laugh, but she brought a seriousness to her face so as not to offend Pi. "No, Pi. The child that is growing inside me is reserved for humans. Your kind will never create children, but please rest assured that you will be very valuable to me. I will need your help after my child is born, to be his friend, his protector, his companion."

Pi smiled at the answer he had been provided. "I have been made whole by what you have just told me. I desire to learn what love is because that emotion is foreign to me. I yearn to help care for the child and learn what love is."

Antonetta smiled her affirmation of Pi's proclamation and returned to the novel she was reading.

CHAPTER 29:
PERILOUS

ELIJAH ACKNOWLEDGED LARK as she gently closed the door of their bedroom where he sat quietly. "Is she finally asleep?" Elijah softly asked, as if he were sitting in church.

"For the time being. I can't fathom how Andrea is feeling right now. I can't imagine how any of these families are feeling," Lark admitted.

Elijah stood up and began to pace the room in deep thought. "I'm going to have to try and calm these people. This has gone too far. Get a message to everybody that we will have a meeting tonight. Can you do that for me Lark, please?"

"Just what do you think you can do, Elijah? What happened was deliberate. We've made the choice to not take the injection, and now, Vesper will see to it that we are dead, one way or the other," Lark barked at her husband as quietly as she could so as not to wake their house guest. Afraid to answer his wife, Elijah tempered the conversation by alerting her that he needed time to think.

As the sun disappeared, bringing the safety of darkness to the inhabitants of the underground city, Elijah, Lark, and Andrea climbed the stairs to the surface. Elijah wasn't surprised to see that everybody that dwelled in the city was in attendance. The crowd moved closer to Elijah, almost smothering him in humanity. He held up both arms with his fingers extended upwards and called out to the gathered group with as loud of a voice as he could offer. "Everybody, I know that the events of last night have caused all of you to question everything. I wish I could answer those questions, but I can't."

"What are we to do, Elijah?" A voice called out from the crowd.

Elijah bowed his head in defeat but raised it back up to answer the multitude. "I recommend that all of you surrender to the shot. Don't fight this any longer."

Lark, who was assisting a tired and distraught woman in Andrea Krill, gasped. She had difficulty believing what her husband had just professed to the crowd. Lena Yung hurried to Lark and Andrea's side. As the only person in the underground city that resembled anything close to a physician, she grew concerned with her patients who were pregnant. Klous Anson followed her to join the three women.

The crowd began to chant their displeasure in what Elijah had just proclaimed. "WE MUST FIGHT! WE MUST FIGHT!" echoed from the crowd.

Elijah, frustrated, pleaded with them that they had no idea what he had seen the night before. These beings had much more firepower than they could ever hope to combat. Braden Samuleson and his wife approached Elijah. With a defeated look on his face, he professed to him, "Look, Elijah, we have decided to accept the blue injection. We are so sorry, but we just don't have this fight in us. We have suffered so much already and it's time to suffer no more."

Feeling no sense of betrayal, Elijah gave his best friend since coming to Spheretech a sympathetic look. Moving forward and hugging Braden's neck, he kissed his cheek. No words needed to be spoken. Elijah released his friend from his embrace and turned back towards the gathered multitude. A muscular man came forward signaling the attention of the crowd.

Elijah recognized him as Hector Gonzalez. Hector was part of the excavation crew that moved earth to accommodate the curvature of the spheres. Elijah also knew he was former Territory military before coming to join Spheretech. Hector asked Elijah for permission to address the crowd to which Elijah agreed.

"Look, folks, I understand your desire to fight these things that Elijah has described, but he is right, we don't have the weapons or the means to fight them."

Voices from the crowd spoke up, "Then what are we to do, Hector? Just wait here until they murder us all?"

Hector turned to face Elijah and with an intenseness in his eyes replied, "I believe I know where there are weapons. Weapons and ammunition that were abandoned when the Government collapsed. If we could get to them somehow, and we could find a vehicle that could carry them, we would at least stand a fighting chance."

"How far, and how do we travel there?" Elijah questioned with an air of disbelief.

Hector pointed directly at Elijah's ATV. "That's how we go. You and me."

Elijah, who was still struggling to accept any part of Hector's plan, offered, "That ATV is electric! We have maybe three hundred miles on a full charge. Even if that will get us to where you believe there are weapons, and we can find a vehicle that still has diesel fuel, which was outlawed long before we came here, how do we get a vehicle that size to start and run?"

Grabbing Elijah's head in his cupped hands, Hector smiled and reassured him, "Because, I am a mechanic like you have never seen before, my extrusion friend."

Somehow, Elijah believed him. It was a risky journey they would be undertaking, but deep down, Elijah believed it was one they would have to take.

Packing the duffel bag that Elijah had brought with him from his and Lark's journey from the wasteland to this place, he could see the look of sadness in his wife's eyes. "I need you to come back alive! Do you hear me, Elijah Price?" Lark proclaimed. Bringing his wife close to him and kissing her on the lips, Elijah acknowledged with his actions that he would return to her.

Elijah looked over at Hector who was sitting next to him in the ATV and asked, "You up for this?"

Hector pointed at the barren landscape that canvased out before them and responded, "I don't think we have a choice my friend."

With the morning sun beginning to rise and with all the food and hydration drink that they could collect from the meager contributions of the underground community, the men drove forward on their perilous mission.

CHAPTER 30: NEW HOME

LENA YUNG, KLOUS ANSON, AND ADREA had joined Lark in her home at Elijah's request. He told them he would just feel more comfortable having them stay with Lark while he was gone, especially since she was carrying some special cargo in the way of his child. Secretly, he asked them to stay with her in case his mission with Hector went the wrong way.

Klous exited the garden section and came into the living quarters where Lark and Lena were sitting. "My oh my, zat is vun amazing garden you have planted there!" Klous excitedly exclaimed to Lark.

"It has been a huge undertaking, but thank you for your kind comments, Klous. I am concerned though. With the water getting shut off, all the vegetables will surely perish," Lark responded.

Klous, who was not wanting to make Lena worried or upset, asked Lark if she could join him in the garden area. He told her that he had a question about one particular plant, which was really a fib to get her to join him. Once inside the garden and certain they were out of earshot of Lena, Klous admitted that he just wanted to get Lark alone to discuss their present situation.

"Lark, I know zat you understand just how desperate zat our situation is becoming. Zis entire community only has enough water to last a few days. Even if ve had da water, our food supply may only last ten days or so, and dat is if ve ration our food to the fullest. Your vonderful garden here von't last vithout water," Klous confided with her even though it was like preaching to the choir.

Lark walked over to where a small crop of tomatoes was growing actively on the vine. Pulling one of the ripe tomatoes from its stalk, Lark held it up to Klous and responded to his soliloquy of doom. "Klous, what if I told you I know where there is water. Enough water for all of us left here. Enough water to last us many years into our future!"

Carefully descending the hill created by the excavating crew that had been preparing the area for additional subterranean residences, the group, consisting of Klous, Lena, Lark, and Andrea, approached the entrance to the cavern that Lark knew existed beyond their sight.

Directing her friends through the opening, Lark asked them to turn on their flashlights. Once she had found the generator that Elijah had procured and brought to the site, she asked Klous if he would start the generator. After several tugs at the cord that would propel the motor, he accomplished the feat, and the generator began to roar loudly. Then, Lark flipped the switch that would ignite the lamps that Elijah had hung on the cavern walls.

With her hands on her hips with accomplishment, Lark studied the astonished faces of her friends that had accompanied her to their future home.

The sun had become unbearable, and Elijah and Hector determined that they must find shelter in the wasteland. The hydration liquid they had brought with them wouldn't last very long if they were to continue in this heat. "How far do you think we've traveled from home?" Hector inquired.

"Maybe fifty miles or so. We still have plenty of power in the ATV, it's just this damn heat!" Elijah offered. Stopping the ATV in the middle of what used to be a state road, both men scanned the horizon in hopes of seeing something, anything, that would serve to provide them with shelter. Then Hector shouted out, "There, just to the southwest," Hector pointed excitedly.

Squinting to block as much of the haze from the heat as he could, Elijah could see what appeared to be a farmhouse and a barn in the distance. Exiting the state road, the men made a beeline for the structures. Pulling up to the farmhouse, they exited the ATV and carefully climbed the porch stairs. Hector peeked inside the dirty glass windows of the home and called out to Elijah, "It looks like its abandoned."

Pushing the door open that led to the interior of the house, Elijah carefully went in first. He called out to any occupant that might inhabit this house but received no answer. Then, a shotgun blast rang out with the buckshot barely missing Elijah. Hector's military training kicked in and he sighted the source of the blast behind a couch on the other side of the living room.

With the fluid speed of motion of a predator animal, Hector arrived at the couch and hurdled it to tackle the shooter. Wrestling the shotgun from their hand, Hector prepared to strike a blow to disable the assailant. Before bringing his fist crashing into flesh, he retracted it. Laying on the ground, sobbing in fear was a girl, no older than twelve and perhaps even younger.

Elijah had arrived on the scene to find the young girl frightened and screaming. Picking up the girl, who was squirming vigorously to escape, he held her tight in his grasp and pleaded, "Nobody is going to hurt you, girl. Settle down and quit struggling!" It took every ounce of energy he could summon to finally get the girl to relax. Loosening his grip just enough to allow her to sit down on the couch that once served as the barrier between her and these intruders, she stuttered as she asked, "What are you going to do with me? What do you want?"

"First, what is your name?" Elijah responded hoping that having some familiarity between them might calm her.

Sensing that he might not be the boogeyman, she answered softly, "I'm Venus. Venus Dayholt."

Feeling that some sort of detente had been established, Elijah introduced himself and Hector to the young girl. He proceeded to explain to Venus their reason for being there. "You see, Hector and I are from the spheres. Well, at least near them. We are travelling to get food for our people. An evil man that runs the spheres is out to get us. Does that make sense, Venus?"

She shook her head in affirmation. "We needed shelter from the sun. We still have a long way to go but we couldn't stand the heat any longer," Hector added to the conversation.

Venus acknowledged what Hector had just told her but somehow felt more comfortable with Elijah. Seeking to be closer to him, she moved ever so slightly towards him. "You aren't the Bluebloods. I can tell. Your eyes are...normal."

"You know about the Bluebloods, Venus?" Elijah asked with total curiosity.

"A little. My mom and dad told me about them. They told me that we would never become one of them."

Elijah smiled a broad smile and replied, "Us either, Venus. Us either."

The men listened to the story of how Venus' parents had left the farm in search of water. Their farm well had run dry, but they refused to leave the farm. One day they left her at home. They handed her the shotgun and told her to shoot anybody that tried to come into the house. After that day, her parents never came home.

"Good girl, Venus. You minded your parents even if you could've killed us!" Hector laughed.

"What about food, Venus? With no food or water, how have you survived out here?" Elijah inquired.

With all the innocence of the ages, Venus answered him. "Oh, I know where there is food and water. I go there once a week."

Hector had been sitting and listening to Venus tell her history to Elijah and he jumped to his feet when she proclaimed she knew where there was food and water. "You know where to find these things?" Hector pleaded with their newfound friend to reveal the location of her discovery.

"Yes, I can take you there in the morning. If you want." Venus confided in her companions.

Moving ever closer to Elijah, Venus wasn't sure if she liked Hector's aggressive nature. Elijah sensed she was more comfortable with him and embraced the display of trust that she had in him.

"How old are you, Venus?" Elijah inquired.

"I was eight years old when my parents left me here." She answered.

"And how long have you been alone here?"

Venus wrinkled her nose as she pondered the question she had just been asked. "I think it has been two years."

Elijah glanced at Hector at the answer he had just been provided. His heart hurt for this poor child, but his respect for her resiliency was boundless. "How many people have you seen since your parents left?"

Venus answered, "You two are the first I've seen."

When Lark and he had been making their journey to the spheres they had encountered many that were on the verge of losing their humanity. As food and water became excessively scarce, humans became less human. It was amazing to Elijah that this child had survived. If some of those marauders had found her, the outcome would have been much different than this.

"Would you like to eat, Elijah?" Venus asked as a child that didn't understand the current situation these men had come from. Venus extracted an old propane camping stove from a cabinet in the farmhouse kitchen. Elijah hadn't seen a stove like this since he was a boy. Lighting the stove, she opened three cans of refried beans and placed them on top of the grill.

In what might seem like a trivial thing to the inhabitants of the spheres, eating hot food was a luxury that neither he, nor Hector, had experienced in a long, long time. Elijah savored every bite. He was grateful to Venus that she had become comfortable enough to share her wealth with them.

"Do you like music, Elijah?" Venus inquired as she put away the stove.

He couldn't recall the last time he had listened to music. He had always enjoyed music, but it was a luxury not afforded to the inhabitants of the underground city. Elijah answered, "Yes, I enjoy music very much, but it's been a long time."

Venus went to a cabinet that had a television sitting on top of it. Without electricity, Elijah understood the TV had not been used for several years. The dust covering it told that tale. Underneath, in a sliding door, Venus extracted an ancient device. Elijah remembered it as a CD player. Turning on the player, she pressed the 'play' button, filling the room with sound. Music and lyrics sang out in harmonious delight:

In the heart of the night
In the cool southern rain
There's a full moon in sight

Shining down on the Pontchartrain

Elijah tilted his head backwards with pure delight. He remembered the song, although he could not place where or when. Just when he thought the pleasure he was receiving from the music couldn't get any better, Venus began to sing in time and rhythm to the song:

And the river she rises
Just like she used to do
She's so full of surprises
Oh momma, she reminds me of you

He marveled at her voice. Even though it was young, she sang with perfect pitch and tune. They continued to listen to the music on the CD with Venus joining the songs that she liked the most. After about an hour, Venus brought her legs to a reclining position on the couch that she and Elijah were sitting upon.

With a healthy yawn, she placed her head on Elijah's shoulder and within a few minutes was fast asleep. Elijah did not dare move. He gazed down at the young girl with tattered blonde hair resting upon his shoulder. He believed she was probably tall for her age. Very thin, but that was to be expected.

After he was certain that Venus was deep into her slumber, Elijah slipped carefully from her grasp. Laying her head down on a pillow that had seen better days, he stood over her with the realization that this was probably the first time in a couple of years that this child had felt safe. The relationship this trio of human beings had forged in a very short time was nothing more than astounding.

Moving across the room, Elijah acknowledged Hector was deep into sleep himself. Carefully opening the front door, Elijah stepped out onto the porch. With no ambient light to diminish the glow from the stars or the moon, Elijah located what he thought must be the planet, Venus. He wondered if that is how her parents had come to name her. They stared out into the night sky before this world had gone to Hell.

He thought about Lark. He missed her desperately. There had been several times lately where Elijah questioned if he could be the father his child deserved. If nothing positive came from this journey that he and Hector had started, he knew one thing for sure, and that was, this innocent girl needed him. Elijah knew that he could not leave her here. She needed a father and he had been chosen. Returning to the living room and his sleeping companions, Elijah picked a spot at the feet of Venus and with the song she had been singing echoing in his head, he slept.

The morning came all too quickly. The unexpected trio stepped out of the ATV. Hector had convinced Venus to let him be the one to carry the shotgun. She pointed at a small building that sat adjacent to a church. "That's where the food supplies are," Venus explained. The decaying building had a sign attached to the front of it that was barely readable due to weatherization. It read:

St. James Food Pantry

Opening the front door that was barely still attached to its hinges, the group proceeded inside. Lined on shelves that surrounded the room, Elijah noticed several different types of canned goods. Picking up one of the cans that displayed beets as its contents, Elijah looked to see what the expiration date read. It was clear that most of the canned goods had expired their date for use, but Elijah decided beggars can't be choosers.

Hector examined a can of refried beans just like they had consumed for dinner the night before. In jest he joked,

"These are probably the same beans we ate last night. Hey, we're still alive."

Elijah knew they would need to collect everything they saw here in the pantry. He just didn't know by what means they could do this. Elijah had also failed to consider that these were Venus's food supplies. He hadn't considered if she would even agree to join them in this trek. Here they were, planning on pilfering everything this girl would need to survive. He turned to Venus, asking, "You said there was water here too. Where would I find the water?"

Venus pointed at a pallet sitting in the corner of the pantry. Sitting upon the pallet were several cases of a diet cola product. Elijah let out a laugh that probably scared both Venus and Hector. He apologized to both his companions and took one of the cans and opened it. Taking a large gulp of the liquid, he was surprised to taste something sweet, but most importantly, wet.

The exploring companions loaded up a few of the canned items and a case of cola into the back of the ATV before heading back to the farmhouse. Hector, with a concerned expression, sought Elijah's attention. "This is a good start in the food supplies we're seeking. It's enough for a lone child to survive on, but we'll need much, much more than this. Plus, we have no means to transport it. We need to move on to the armory location. If my memory serves me, not only will we find some firepower to battle these bronze demons, but we hopefully will discover additional food supplies."

Elijah stopped the ATV to address Venus. "I want you to come with us, Venus. I don't want you to stay here any longer. I don't want you to be alone."

Hector was speechless at the offer that Elijah had just extended to Venus. He certainly hadn't seen it coming. Venus reached over to embrace Elijah. "Yes, I will go with you and this scary man in the backseat!" Elijah let out another laugh that could have woken the dead. Hector simply stared out at the wilderness, holding the shotgun like a long-lost friend.

Bringing the ATV to a stop in front of the farmhouse, each of them grabbed some of the supplies they had retrieved from the pantry. Walking towards the steps that would lead to the porch and front door, Elijah looked out upon what used to be the Dayholt Farm. He casually asked Venus, "Were your parents always farmers?"

With total oblivion to his question, Venus answered, "Oh, not at all. Daddy wanted to be a farmer, but he had to do another job to provide for us."

Hector continued the conversation out of curiosity, "What job did he do, I mean, to provide for you?"

Venus pointed at the large barn on the property replying with a nonchalant attitude, "He owned a semi and a trailer. It's a Kenworth. Both are in there. He was a truck driver."

Turning towards the barn and then to each other, Hector and Elijah stood speechless. At that moment, Elijah had to consider that if there was a God who looked down upon this planet, perhaps, just perhaps, He had smiled upon them.

CHAPTER 31:
HARVEST

TREMONT STOOD AT ATTENTION as Hendricks entered the room. He always marveled at the handiwork of Silver James every time he encountered this being. The specimen before him was intimidating and Hendricks was thankful that it was totally loyal and allegiant to him, and him alone.

"How may I serve you, Dr. Vesper?" Tremont inquired as if he were a loyal General seeking his orders.

"New orders, Tremont. New orders," Hendricks answered before continuing to provide the commander of his military force exactly what he desired to be done. "I want you to take a small force, maybe fifteen of your soldiers, and go to the underground city. I need you to go door-to-door and gather all the inhabitants of their city and march them to me, outside of Sphere2. Leave nobody behind, including Elijah and Lark Price."

"What are my orders if they resist our presence?" Tremont asked.

Hendricks, without pause, answered, "If they resist, shoot them. I cannot tolerate their ignorance any longer. Their refusal to accept their future and take the injection will only prolong their suffering. I will have an injection site ready once you bring those that have come to their senses to me."

Tremont acknowledged his new orders and went to gather his elite soldiers to complete the mission assigned by their leader.

Having gathered everything they could transport to the cavern that would be their new home, the two hundred former inhabitants of the underground city made their exodus from the stark quarters that had been provided for them by the man that now despised them. Lark, Andrea, and Lena were the last to begin the walk that was probably ten miles west.

"You going to shut the door and lock it?" Lena jested.

"No, if somebody wants what's left in there, they can have it!" Lark returned the humor.

Klous had long ago reluctantly left the women. He understood that his talents and skills in helping set up the temporary accommodation of the cavern's inhabitants was needed. Still, he had much angst about leaving them. Lark and Lena carried the remnant of what had been harvested from the hydroponic gardens. Most of what they carried would be used for seed to begin anew.

Sensing that they were all in harm's way, Lark had insisted that the inhabitants leave their homes very fast. Her intuition spoke to her like the Hebrews when they were set free from Egypt. She had this feeling that the Pharoah Vesper would soon be on their heels, and it wasn't to help them. When the women arrived at the entrance to the cavern, Lark was astonished by the work that had already been accomplished.

Even if Hendricks' bronze goons would happen to come this far, the entrance to the cavern was camouflaged and undiscernible. Her astonishment at just how resilient these people were was heightened by what they, and Klous, had accomplished in a very short time. The cavern itself was deep and vast. She had no idea just how far it extended.

Makeshift camping sites had begun to be formed along the banks of the underground lake. With lights beginning to illuminate not only the size of the lake, but also a cavern that provided more room than they had been accustomed to or their wildest imaginations could perceive.

Several of her fellow inhabitants came up to her once word got out that Lark had arrived. She received many warm hugs of thanks for leading them to this sanctuary. One of the ladies brought Lark, Lena, and Andrea a container of water from the lake. "Taste it, Lark. It is fresh, cold, and wonderful," the woman announced with glee abounding from her.

All these accolades were nice. Lark found their gratefulness and happiness a pleasant change from the fear and anguish they showed only a short time ago. Lark's thoughts quickly changed to concern for Elijah and Hector.

She wondered what they were experiencing. What dangers or discoveries had they encountered. Deep down, she hoped they would fail. Fail at finding weapons and at last turning tail to return here. Conflict with the madman Hendricks Vesper could be avoided. Here in this cavern, their new home, they had more than enough water to last several generations and she could show them how to grow and harvest food.

Lark anticipated that of the four hundred inhabitants who had lived in the underground city, two hundred had the energy and belief that humans could survive without injecting something they knew nothing about into their bodies. The others had gone to the spheres. The two hundred that were here with her now could survive with rations to the food supply, just long enough for the gardens to be harvested with abundance. All of this was within reach.

Hector climbed into the cab of the Kenworth diesel powered truck that had been resting and waiting for somebody to revive it. "She is a beauty!" he excitedly announced like a kid opening his birthday presents.

"Hector, what about the fuel? Won't diesel fuel go bad?" Elijah called out fully anticipating that their discovery of this transportation would be fruitless.

Hector leaned out the open window of the truck's cab and loudly answered, "Yes, my friend, diesel fuel will go bad in about six to twelve months."

"Then this idea will never work. We can't use this truck or the trailer," a disappointed Elijah proclaimed.

"Ah, this would be true, very true, if..." Hector responded.

"If what?" Elijah curiously asked.

"If this girl's daddy hadn't been a genius. The gas tank in this truck is bone dry. I suspect her daddy drained it." Hector laughingly explained.

"We are back to my original comment then," Elijah responded.

Hector pointed across the barn. Sitting in the corner of the barn was a large tank with a pumping apparatus attached to it. "See that tank, mi amigo, I'll bet it is full of diesel fuel. Sitting right next to that tank is a chemical tank, inside that tank is a chemical that rejuvenates diesel fuel and restores it like new!"

Hurrying to the tanks that Hector had pointed at, Elijah peered at the gauges that indicated just how full these tanks were. Elijah bent his torso backwards and pumped his fists toward the roof of the barn. Immediately, Hector's intuition was correct, these tanks were full.

The fact that Hector called her father a genius elevated his standing in the group immensely with Venus. It took several hours, and a jump start from the ATV before they pulled up in front of the pantry and loaded the entire pantry into the trailer. They each popped a can of diet cola and toasted the accomplishment.

Hector was driving the rig. Having much more experience with this type of machine, he was the obvious choice to be the captain. As they traveled south and the home of Venus disappeared from view, Elijah questioned Hector, "How long do you estimate before we find the armory?"

Hector shrugged his shoulders upon hearing Elijah's question. "Maybe two hours, more or less."

Like a seasoned veteran, Hector backed the trailer up to a loading dock of the National Guard Armory. The trio exited the semi-truck with Hector carrying a large cable cutting device he had discovered in the Dayholt's barn. A large padlock kept the door to the dock from being breached. With muscles showing, Hector snapped the lock with what seemed like very little effort.

Pulling the door up, it rolled on its tracks to extend into the ceiling. It reminded Elijah of the large doors at the extrusion facility. Having procured several flashlights during their stop at Venus's home, they turned them on and shone their lights into the Armory. Hector let out a powerful yell. It was not a yell of fright or anger; it was a yell of triumph.

With the brilliant sun beginning to disappear behind the Rocky Mountains, both men were physically spent. The trailer was completely full of weapons and ammunition. Elijah and Hector both agreed that the majority of weapons and ammo should be handheld missile launchers, deciding that the highest probability of damage they could do to the bronze soldiers would be to blow them up, or at least, take off their limbs.

Although the food they found consisted mostly of 'meals-ready-to-eat', also known as MREs, they found several cases of water. They both considered it a win to find what they had. Venus helped as much as she could, but it became clear that her stamina was lacking compared to her adult male companions.

"I say we get some sleep tonight and head back to the underground city early tomorrow morning," Elijah proclaimed.

Hector pointed at Venus who had already consumed her MRE and had crawled up into the sleeping cab of the semi and fallen asleep. "I guess she's confirmed your idea, my friend," Hector chuckled.

As the stars appeared and the moon shone brightly in the night sky, they all found as much comfort in the semi cab as was possible. The last words from Elijah's mouth that his exhausted body and mind could manage was, "I will need Lark's lake when we get back because I stink." With that statement, he began to snore.

CHAPTER 32:
REVENGE

TREMONT MOTIONED AT A SOLDIER positioned on his left to pull open the door of the underground dwelling. Once the door was open, he signaled for several of the bronze soldiers to quickly descend the steps. With their weapons drawn, they invaded the residence below. He stood at the top of the stairs waiting to decipher how much commotion and resistance was occurring below.

When he determined he had waited long enough, he sent a signal to the soldiers to report their status. The voice of one of his soldiers announced, "No inhabitants present, sir." Tremont found the absence of any humans below, curious. Vesper had commanded these raids to commence during daylight hours in anticipation that most of the inhabitants of the underground city would be in their dwellings.

"Return to the surface!" Tremont commanded. Once the bronze soldiers had returned to gather around him, they moved to the next underground dwelling only to discover that it had also been abandoned. Unit after unit revealed that the underground city had been abandoned. Tremont immediately called out on his radio to inform Hendricks Vesper of the situation. Vesper ordered his Commander, along with the force of soldiers, to stay put at the underground city. He expected them to stand vigil. Even though no inhabitants had been discovered, he decided to dispatch a crew to build a barricade around the city. Setting his radio on his desk, Hendricks walked over to the large window that encased his Palace office and looking out upon the green landscape of Sphere2, thought to himself, "Interesting, I wonder where Price and his cohorts could have ventured off to? Certainly, he wouldn't be foolish enough to lead them into the wasteland, would he?"

Certain that the radio conversation between Tremont and he wouldn't have been heard by any other ears, Hendricks exited his office to attend to Antonetta who was desiring to gain his attention. Silver James turned off the radio and pondered what he had just heard. He sensed that this exercise that the A.I. force had engaged in had sinister motives.

"What about the ATV, Elijah? Are we just going to leave it at the barn?" Hector inquired, hoping that his leader had another plan. He understood just how important that ATV could be.

"I hope to retrieve it someday. For right now, we need to get these weapons and supplies back to the underground city as quick as we can," Elijah responded with clear regret about having to leave the ATV.

"Well, I hope nobody ventures upon it until we can come back for it," Hector replied.

Venus looked over at Hector and then turned her head towards Elijah. With a smugness well advanced for her age, she casually injected herself into the conversation. "It will be very hard for anybody to do anything with that ATV. After you guys got daddy's rig running, I took the batteries out of the ATV. They're in the trailer." Both men laughed in delight at just how cunning their newfound companion could be.

Fanning his soldiers out to form a perimeter around the underground city, Tremont waited patiently for the crew that was coming to install the barricades. With keen eyesight and technology that allowed him to see great distances, his head cocked to scan an area south of where he stood at attention. Canting his body slightly to face the south more directly, he increased the periscopic intensity of his vision. Tremont could see that, about ten miles out on the horizon, something was casting dirt and dust into the air.

His senses directed him to be on high alert. Commanding three of his soldiers to leave their posts to follow him, they began a march towards the source of the dust to investigate.

"It sure will be nice to see everyone," Hector acknowledged as the semi-truck and trailer moved ever closer to home.

"Yes, it sure will," Elijah agreed.

"Do you think she'll like me?" Venus innocently inquired of Elijah.

With his arm draped over her shoulder and pulling her closer to him, Elijah looked intently at Venus and replied, "She will not only like you, she'll love you!" Suddenly, Hector slammed the airbrakes on the truck all the way to the floor practically sending his passengers through the window.

"What the hell?" Elijah yelled.

Hector pointed about half a mile to the north of where the truck had come to an abrupt stop. "Bronze demons! Twelve o'clock!" The soldiers approached the vehicle with a quickness that Elijah had never seen before. Knowing that it was too late to react, Elijah held Venus close to him in the cab of the truck. He was shocked that Hector bailed out of the cab and began running directly towards the rear of the trailer.

"Where does he think he's going!" Venus screamed. Elijah saw a flash of light emitted from a weapon that one of the soldiers held erect and pointed towards the driver's side of the truck. Elijah feared for his friend, sensing that whatever ammunition that creature had fired might have hit its mark.

Three of the soldiers stopped ten yards away from the front of the truck. With weapons drawn, they waited for their commander to walk past them and address the occupants inside the truck. Elijah thought he heard a noise coming from behind the trailer but couldn't decipher its origin. He considered it might be Hector trying to hang on before succumbing to his wounds.

"Humans, exit the vehicle! By the orders of Hendricks Vesper, leader of the Sphere cities, you are to come with me to receive the injection!" Tremont forcefully ordered. Elijah slipped out of the cab and extended his hand to Venus to assist her to the ground. She would not let go of Elijah's hand and was clearly terrified by these bronze creatures.

Elijah had to force Venus to release his hand and grabbing her by her arm proclaimed, "Stay here, Venus!" He slowly advanced towards Tremont. Once he had arrived to face him, Elijah was amazed at just how large this thing was. He wasn't sure where he miraculously found the courage he did at this moment, but he spontaneously spat on Tremont with his spit landing on the chest plate of the bronze commander.

Facing the realization that Venus would soon become a Blueblood, and his child would grow up without a father, Elijah found himself elevated into the air with a bronze hand choking him by the neck. The moment should have brought a sense of terror to Elijah but all he could think of at that moment was, "I guess he doesn't like to be spit on!"

While struggling to remain conscious, Elijah heard the one voice he did not want to hear cry out. "Put my dad down. Put him down or I will kill you," The voice of Venus rang out, directed towards Tremont.

During the commotion of the interaction between Tremont and Elijah, the force that had joined him to intercept the humans was distracted, not noticing that the small female human had climbed back into the cab and retrieved a shotgun that was now pointed directly at Tremont.

With his protective senses now activated, he raised his weapon with his right arm while still holding Elijah Price extended in the air with his left. Elijah wanted to die, but to die at the hands of Vesper's goons was something he couldn't bear to have this girl watch. This girl who had been through so much. Just then, when Elijah was sure he saw the flash of Tremont's weapon with death certain to find its mark, Elijah fell to the ground.

Stunned and gasping for air, Elijah stumbled to his feet. Having gained enough of his senses with the revival of oxygen to his brain, he saw Hector throw down the handheld rocket launcher and bring an automatic assault weapon to the ready. With several repetitive blasts from the weapon, he effectively destroyed the torsos and limbs of the remaining bronze soldiers that had confronted them.

With destroyed circuit boards and wires protruding from broken and dismembered artificial body parts, Elijah watched as Venus approached one of the soldiers that was wiggling on the ground. With two quick shotgun blasts, the bronze soldier learned today what death was like.

Hurrying over to where Venus stood holding the shotgun, Elijah held her tight. "I was afraid you would die," he cried with all the relief of the ages being released from him.

"I was afraid for you too!" Venus echoed his relief.

Joining his friends, Hector stood before them. Elijah and Venus nearly knocked him over with hugs of gratitude.

"Guess we made the right choice about which weapons to bring with us, huh, my friends," Hector laughed.

It would be a while before the trio would release each other from their mutual embrace. A short distance from where they stood together, Tremont did his best to evaluate his current status. Self-diagnosis revealed that a good portion of his right torso and his entire right leg were not responding due to mangled metal, circuits, and blue liquid excreting from his wounds. He sent out a distress signal requesting recovery.

"I am deeply worried that if these things were here to intercept us, it seems like they came from the direction of our home," Elijah reluctantly professed.

"Yah, we need to go, now! Where there's smoke there's fire. There's liable to be more of them where we're heading," Hector agreed.

Climbing back into the cab of the truck, Hector started the engine. As the truck moved forward, it was apparent to the three that a tire ran over one of the soldiers' bodies. Behind the cab, in the sleeping quarters, sat five rocket launchers, two AK 47's and enough ammo to wage a war.

Elijah spoke to a still trembling Venus who was resting her head on his shoulder, "When I was being molested by that big hunk of bronze junk back there, you yelled at it to put your dad down. Did you mean to say that, or…"

Venus wrapped an arm around Elijah's torso. This action meant she didn't need to answer his question.

CHAPTER 33:
BARRICADE

BEN TOLMIE LEANED OVER the disfigured remnant of the Commander of Vesper's Army. Laying on an examination table, Tremont had been severely damaged, and Ben was doubtful he had the skills to restore him. Hendricks paced frantically around the lab where the Commander of his A.I. force lay prone, mangled and defeated.

"This is Price's doing. How dare he do this to my property!" Hendricks screamed as if Ben could not already tell how aggravated he was. "Can you fix him? Can he be repaired and reactivated? I need him to confirm to me who is responsible for this abomination."

Ben looked up from the work he was frantically trying to do and responded to Vesper's rant and inquisition. "I don't have the knowledge or the skill, Hendricks. This amount of damage is beyond my expertise. This will require Jon James. If you want this A.I. restored, he's the only one who can possibly do it."

Still frantically pacing, Hendricks finally came to a stop and with no hesitation replied, "I'll have him come here immediately. You and he are to work non-stop to restore my commander."

Ben acknowledged his command and spoke, "I wonder what could have done this kind of damage, Hendricks?"

Hendricks turned away from Tolmie and replied, "Just fix him and we will find out!" With that statement, Ben recognized that this was the man he had worked with for several years, and really didn't like very much.

"I don't think we should drive this rig into the heart of the city. We had better park it behind this dirt hill and then we can hike up the hill and see what's up," Elijah said. Hector agreed with the plan and carefully positioned the semitruck and trailer behind a large pile of excavated dirt. Each of the men grabbed a rocket launcher and automatic rifle as they exited the truck cab. Venus attempted to follow but Elijah abruptly stopped her. "I need you to stay in the cab, Venus. Just stay here until we can investigate what the status of the city is."

Venus wasn't happy about being left behind but reluctantly agreed with Elijah's wishes. The two men, with weapons strapped to their torsos, slowly navigated a path towards the underground city. Stopping at a tall apparatus that used to serve as a fracking rig, the men slowly navigated the ladder upward to gain a better and less noticeable position to survey any activity that might be underway.

Reaching a small platform that was at least two hundred feet above the ground, laying prone on a metal mesh surface that was barely large enough to accommodate them, Hector pulled out a set of binoculars that he had procured during their recent visit to the Armory. After looking, Hector handed them to Elijah so that he could see what Hector had seen. Elijah sighed at the activity in the city.

"Maybe ten soldiers. Could be more," Elijah proclaimed.

"Probably more," Hector affirmed.

Continuing to peer through the binoculars, Elijah was concerned and curious why the Blueblood workers from the spheres had begun laying down barricades.

"What's the reason for imprisoning our people? Vesper has already cut off our food and water supply. What's his purpose behind this? Wait until we all stumble up to the surface, half dead, so he can inject us all when we are near death?" Elijah pondered the mystery he was watching.

Taking the binoculars from Elijah, Hector took another look at the scene before them. "I don't think this is a barricade to keep us in," Hector declared.

Looking at his companion as he peered through the field glasses, Elijah responded. "If it isn't to keep us in until we submit, then why the barricade?"

"It's to keep us out. There ain't any of our people down there. Vesper's soldiers are down there to stand guard." Hector declared.

"Guarding what?" Elijah seemed confused.

"Vesper doesn't know where we went, but we ain't there. He knows we can't survive out in the open. He's counting on that fact. Our people will have to come crawling back to the underground city to stay alive," Hector declared with a tinge of admiration for the tactic.

"Do you think Vesper has discovered his things we annihilated?" Elijah quizzed, fully expecting what Hector's answer would be.

"You can bet on it. Those soldiers standing vigil at the barricades are there because of it. Vesper has ordered them to stay there," Hector revealed what his intuition was saying to him.

"So having our people surrender is that important to him?" Elijah quizzed.

Laughing softly to not create the possibility of being detected by the troops below and in the distance, Hector tried to spit, but his mouth was too dry. "Vesper couldn't care less about our people surrendering. Those soldiers are there because Vesper is betting that you will be with them."

Inching their bodies backwards to descend the ladder of the fracking rig, the men returned to where Venus was sitting in the cab of the truck, holding a rocket launcher that would have propelled her farther than the rocket, if she had reason to use it. Elated to see Hector and Elijah approaching the truck, she placed the rocket launcher on the seat that she had been sitting upon and ran up to hug Elijah.

"It's alright, baby. Everything's gonna be fine," Elijah comforted her.

"Where do you think our people went? They certainly couldn't have gone too far," Hector inquired of his leader.

Still holding onto Venus, he shook his head in a manner that indicated he didn't have an answer. "I have no idea, Hec…" Stopping in mid-sentence, a smile came to Elijah's face.

Even more confused by this precarious expression on Elijah's face, Hector raised both arms in a posture that meant, "What?"

"We need to ditch this rig somewhere where it can't be easily detected. I think I know where our people are. I'm betting on it because, if I know my Lark, she saved the entire bunch of us!" Elijah proclaimed as he encouraged his companions to follow his lead.

Sentries at the cavern entrance signaled to the people closest to them to let Lark and Klous know that there were three figures approaching. Upon hearing the news, Lark sprang from the garden she was planting and bolted for the entrance. Unafraid that intruders had stumbled upon their sanctuary, her intuition provided overwhelming clarity in the belief that her husband had come home to her.

Lark's senses hadn't failed her. Entering the cavern like he had been there a hundred times before, Elijah, leading Venus and Hector, stopped in front of Lark and the inhabitants of the cavern city that had gathered, rejoicing on the return of the men who had left to try and save them. Not only save to them, but to give them a fighting chance.

Flinging her entire body to embrace Elijah, he delighted in feeling her lips upon his. A young, blonde girl, looking like she had been hurled by a hurricane, stood shyly near Lark and Elijah. Realizing that she had ignored Hector and the young girl, Lark released her embrace of her husband and gently gave Hector a hug. "Thank you, Hector. Thank you for bringing my husband back to me."

Elijah walked over to Venus and placed an arm around her shoulders. "Lark, I'd like you to meet Venus. Venus Dayholt" The look in Elijah's eyes indicated that there was so much more to tell his wife, not only about Venus, but about the journey they had started several days ago.

Lark, sensing that rest, nourishment, and fluids were the most important things for this magnificent trio, placed one arm around Elijah's waist and the other around Venus's shoulders to direct them towards the camp that would become their home.

"It's pleasantly cool in here," Elijah remarked.

"The temperature never fluctuates. It is cool but not cold." Lark answered.

Handing Elijah and Venus each a container of water, both drank like they had never tasted anything so good. "Go slow, this is genuine fresh water and there is plenty more of that. Much more than you can fathom."

Venus smiled with water dripping down her tattered clothes. "Thank you. Can I have somewhere to sleep? I'm very tired," Venus requisitioned.

"Of course you can have somewhere to sleep, darling. But first, all that wonderful water you just drank, it can also be used for bathing and you, and this wonderful man, need to clean yourselves because you smell!"

CHAPTER 34:
ALTERNATE PLAN

"DAMMIT!" HENDRICKS YELLED as he threw some papers haphazardly across the room in anger. Silver James stared blankly at his leader, not knowing how to respond to his tantrum.

"You don't want me to lie to you, Hendricks. I'm simply trying to tell you the truth. Tremont can eventually be restored. It will just take a long time. Even working around the clock, Ben and I can only go so fast with these creatures. It's almost like starting from scratch," Silver reluctantly said.

Seeing that Vesper had finally started to gain his composure, he waited for him to respond. "How long, Silver? What are we looking at here, time wise?"

"It's hard for me to estimate. Since I need to rebuild his torso and rewire his synapsis, it might take a couple of weeks. Maybe longer." Silver answered.

Hendricks pondered the timetable he had just been given. "Then make it two weeks. I need it reactivated in no more than two weeks," Hendrick's proclaimed the ultimatum.

Silver didn't acknowledge the ultimatum but posed another question. "And what about the people or person that did this? If they weren't Blueblood's, how did they get the firepower to accomplish this damage? If they were from Sphere City, they should be easy to find."

"Just leave that to me. The discovery of the culprit in this matter may not necessarily require Tremont. I have another plan. I might have a way to flush these cockroaches and their King Bug out into the open," Hendricks answered Silver's question in a sinister manner.

Turning to leave the laboratory and Silver James to the daunting task of restoring Tremont, Hendricks pushed open the door and walked out.

Elijah sat on the edge of a cot that would provide somewhere for him to get some much-needed rest. He marveled as he watched Lark gently brush the clean and wet tangled hair of Venus. It delighted him to watch them engaged in conversation that usually yielded laughter. Watching Lark's interaction with this girl that he had rescued from the wasteland warmed his heart.

When Lark was content that she had removed most of the tangles from Venus's hair, she directed the young girl to a cot close to where she and Elijah slept. Pulling a blanket up and around her shoulders, Lark leaned in to give Venus a kiss on the cheek. Rolling to her side, Venus quickly fell asleep.

Lark walked over to where Elijah was reclining and slid inside his embrace. She had longed to feel her husband beside her, and she took great pleasure that he had returned to her safely. "What were you girls talking about? You weren't agreeing about how weird I am, were you?" Elijah joked.

"Of course, we were, silly," Lark fed right into Elijah's humor with her reply. "Poor thing, she filled me in on her history. I'm grateful that you and Hector found her and brought her back here. She needs us. She needs this community."

Pleased with Lark's acceptance of this girl, he was even more in awe of her resiliency and insight to bring the remnant of the underground city to the cavern. "What you've done here is nothing more than remarkable. These people have come a long way in such a very short time," Elijah said with a glow of admiration emitting from his words.

"I'm worried about power. The generator has been sufficient to get the gardens started, and the lanterns we brought with us from the underground city help to light the camp sites, but even though those batteries are rechargeable, they won't last forever." Lark confided in her husband.

"Who's helped you with what you've done so far? I hope you haven't done all of this yourself. After all, you are carrying something very precious to me. Is all well with the baby?" Elijah inquired.

"Lena is making sure I don't over task myself," Lark replied. "To answer your question, it's been Klous. He has been instrumental in helping get this all set up. The others…it just seems like everybody wants to pitch in and build our new home. This cavern, it represents freedom and hope to them."

"Good ol' Klous. I love that man!" Elijah offered.

"Well, apparently so does Lena. I glimpsed them kissing yesterday. Who'da thunk?" Lark said.

Elijah smiled at the thought that this community had turned from despair, to hope, and even love.

Lark turned the conversation to a serious note, "I saw the weapons you and Hector brought with you. I hope that's all you were able to find out there. I just don't believe we have to fight Vesper any longer. We can live here undetected, and he will think we are gone and probably dead."

Before Elijah could answer her and reveal the truth of what they had found, and brought back with them, she heard her husband snoring.

Hendricks touched the speak button on his radio which was connected directly to Tremont's second in command, inside Sphere2.

"I want small recognizance forces to begin fanning out from the underground city. Go out in all directions from the barriers and report directly back to me if you discover any of the traitors lurking about. I especially want to be alerted if you capture Elijah Price. I don't want him harmed, just brought back to me. Do you comprehend?"

"Yes, sir. I copy your command," the soldier confirmed.

CHAPTER 35: RECOGNIZANCE

A LARGE GROUP OF THE CAVERN PEOPLE gathered around Elijah. Lark had to show a great deal of patience in waiting to hear about the mission that he and Hector had undertaken. Elijah did his best to explain to her that he needed to share what they had found with everybody. It was then that she realized that he was more than her husband. He was their leader.

Holding Venus close by his side, Elijah addressed the crowd. He told them about how they were lucky to find Venus who led them to the food pantry and the semi-truck and trailer. About their drive to the Armory and the retrieval of the supplies and weapons. He also told them about the skirmish they had with the bronze soldiers and that if it hadn't been for the military training and quick wit of Hector, they would be dead.

Lark felt some degree of relief when Elijah confided with them that they must all prepare themselves to defend their new home and freedom, but maybe they could seclude themselves in this sanctuary and live and let live. Some cavern residents called out for revenge for the fallen members of the underground city, but Andrea squelched that speech just as soon as it was uttered.

"Nobody hates Hendricks Vesper more than I do. He has taken away the love of my life, Tobias Krill, and left me, and this child growing inside me, without a husband

and father. Elijah is right, we need to move on and build a community here, of peace."

Elijah appreciated her moving words as they seemed to calm everyone down and begin to focus on their future. He called for a team to help empty the trailer and transport the contents back to the cavern. Plans were drawn up to accomplish this and Elijah appointed Hector as the head of security and training on how to use the weapons. With those plans set into motion, the meeting was adjourned.

Lark and Venus joined Elijah as they returned to the campsite. Each with a hand holding one of Elijah's. Later that day, Klous and Lena joined Elijah, Lark and Venus at their camp.

"Ve are going to need sun panels eventually," Klous admitted.

"I agree, Klous. At least to charge the batteries. We need more illuminating light here in the cavern."

"Vell, the only panels I know of are back at our former home," Klous revealed.

Braden Samuleson cautiously entered the room where Hendricks was standing. Motioning for him to enter, Hendricks asked Braden to sit down. This meeting was something he did with all newcomers to Sphere City. Like a long-lost brother, Hendricks appeared excited to have Braden visit and sit with him. "So, tell me, Braden, how are you and your wife doing? Since coming to Sphere City, are you pleased with your decision to join us?"

Tentatively Braden answered, "Of course, Dr. Vesper. Life here is much better for us."

"And your wife, does she feel the same way?"

"Yes, definitely. Natalie was the reason we decided to leave the underground people and join the Bluebloods. She felt it was the best decision we could make," Braden confided to an attentive listening Hendricks.

"Smart girl. Well, we are happy to have you. How is everything going at the extrusion facility?"

"We have our struggles. Since Elijah Price abandoned the project and us, failures in the panels have been frequent," Braden replied.

"Ah yes, Price. He has been a disappointment to us all, hasn't he? Speaking of Price, you were there that night he decided to go rogue. Isn't that correct?"

Unable to resist the inquiry, Braden answered, even though it made him feel uncomfortable, after all, Elijah had been a good friend and mentor of his. "Yes, Dr. Vesper, I was there. The last I saw of him, he and another resident of the underground city were going to travel south in search of weapons."

Hendricks smiled a broad smile that made Braden feel even more uncomfortable than he already was. "Weapons, huh? Obviously, a fruitless trek, wasn't it, Braden?"

"Obviously, Dr. Vesper," Braden replied as though he had just snitched on a cellmate in jail.

Hendricks thanked Braden for his time and finished the meeting. Braden gladly left the room feeling sick to his stomach. The pain he felt was a twinge of betrayal.

Twilight revealed itself as figures emerged from the cavern. Moving cautiously towards their former home, Hector, Klous, and a small group of men crept slowly towards a vantage point to gain a better view of the location of the solar panels. Having settled in on a hill just overlooking the underground city, Hector slipped on the night vision goggles he had procured from the armory.

He spied the bronze soldiers still standing vigil with some of them patrolling the perimeter of the barricades. His reason for joining this recognizance group was to gain some insight into what the plan might be if military action was required. Scanning the area, Hector was satisfied that he had seen what he needed. Removing the goggles, he handed them to Klous who put them on and began looking for the objects of this operation.

Klous was pleased to see something he had not expected. "Vell, it seems as though Vesper didn't expect our return after all. The sun panels have been dismantled and are stacked neatly where they once vere. Dis vill make it much easier for us."

Having gathered all the information they required to convey to Elijah, the men retreated and returned to the cavern to report on their findings. The men discussed what they had witnessed with Elijah and began formulating a plan to retrieve the panels. Hector felt the best action from his people would be to create a diversion, drawing as many of Vesper's soldiers away from the underground city as they could.

When they came to investigate the diversion, they would find nothing but several detonated explosives. "Hopefully this will allow our people time to get in and get the panels without having to face many of Vesper's pukes," Hector commented with a matter-of-fact attitude.

Elijah always enjoyed Hector's descriptions of the bronze A.I. solders. Once the plan was set in place, it was decided that they would commence with the operation in two nights, deciding that darkness was their best ally. It was also decided that using the semi-truck and trailer would be the best way to transport the panels. They knew the size and loud noise it made could be risky, but they had to get in and out as quickly as possible.

Hector had found a dilapidated barn that was close to collapsing that was near the caverns to hide the truck and trailer. The barn provided a reasonable cover for the vehicle to avoid detection should soldiers come close to its location.

"Okay, we're all set. Does anybody have any questions or anything else to add?" Elijah offered, closing the meeting. One of the men that had been on the recognizance mission spoke up.

"Did anybody else see the structure that the Bluebloods have built inside the central compound of the underground city?" he asked.

After a moment of silence, Klous answered. "Yah, I seen it. I didn't want to say anything because it looked like something I didn't vant to recall."

"What is it you think you saw?" Elijah encouraged his friend to explain.

"Ven I vas a boy, my daddy vas a prison guard. My daddy would tell us about ven a prisoner vas in there because he killed somebody, sometimes they vould hang him vith a rope around his neck. It reminded me of vat my daddy would describe as *gallows*."

The men who were gathered at the meeting all grew extremely quiet.

Antonetta, seeking to gain Hendricks attention was finally successful. "Sorry to interrupt your thoughts, Hen, I just want to make sure you're okay. Lately, you've seemed…so distant."

Hendricks smiled at her and replied, "Sorry, Netta, I've just been preoccupied lately. Maybe even a little troubled."

"Anything I can do? I was thinking you were having second thoughts about becoming a father," Antonetta joked.

"Not at all, my dear. How are you feeling? I wasn't going to say anything to you, but I think you're starting to show," Hendricks confessed.

"Ah, that's the Hendricks I know. Yes, I'm beginning to get the baby bump!" she excitedly exclaimed. "What's troubling you, then?"

"The rebels. I fear they're plotting against us. Plotting against *me*! Sphere3 isn't proceeding as I expected. Price had the touch when it came to the panels. Now he's turned against me."

Antonetta moved closer to Hendricks and sat beside him. Taking his hand in hers, she spoke, "How can they be a threat to you? They and Price have chosen to live in squalor with no future. Why not just let them be? They'll all die sooner or later. Their decisions aren't your problem. Your focus should be on continuing to build this Utopia for your people, your child."

Hendricks, letting go of Antonetta's hand, slammed his fist on the table in front of where they were sitting. It was clear to her that she had touched a sensitive spot with him. After calming down, he thought intently about what she had said. He couldn't reveal to her the anger built up inside of him. His entire life he had known the answers. Those that refused to listen were *traitors* to him. He couldn't, and wouldn't, tolerate those who didn't believe in him any longer.

After Antonetta had gone to bed, Pi stood quietly in the presence of Hendricks. Acknowledging that his synthetic creature was standing there, Hendricks addressed him, "You seem deep in thought, Pi."

"Just learning, Hendricks," Pi responded.

"Learning what, Pi?"

Pi's facial features indicated he was processing how to answer the question he had just received. "These rebels, as you call them, I have researched that word. The definition is short for the word rebellion. Do you feel threatened that there will be a rebellion against you?" Pi asked.

Hendricks chuckled at the innocence of this creature. "There are ways to squash a rebellion, Pi."

"Then I will help you, *squash* it," Pi affirmed.

CHAPTER 36:
THE WAR

WITH THE PLAN TO RETRIEVE THE SOLAR PANELS in place, Elijah and Klous led a small group of men that were heavily armed. Hector, who had spent the better part of two days giving these men a crash course on how to fire a hand-held rocket launcher along with various other weapons, moved to get the semi ready for the signal to proceed to the underground city.

Nighttime had arrived and Elijah and Hector had determined that that would give them the best advantage to begin their mission. Reaching the vista above the underground city, Elijah placed his men in position. Hector had programmed two radios on a frequency that only he and Elijah had so that they could communicate with each other.

Hector sat in the cab, impatiently awaiting the call to ignite the explosives that would create the diversion to attract Vesper's soldiers away from the city. His hand trembled slightly as he held the switches that would trigger all hell breaking loose. His hand didn't tremble with fear, it trembled with the thought of failure.

Explosives weren't his expertise in his former military life.

The moon was in its crescent phase, emitting the least amount of reflection from the sun. Elijah considered this a good thing because it was extremely dark. Putting on a pair of night vision goggles, Elijah surveyed the area below.

Suddenly, he was alerted and confused by what appeared to be an excessive amount of activity down below. He witnessed not only Vesper's military patrolling the barricades, but he also saw what appeared to be a series of floodlights surrounding the platform that Klous had so fearfully referred to as 'the gallows'.

What he saw next explained that Klous might have been correct with his analogy. There were two ropes displaying nooses tied on the ends of both. The nooses dangling from the ends of the ropes appeared ready to accept a human sacrifice.

Elijah called out on the radio to alert Hector that there was a problem and to hold.

"What's the problem?" Hector inquired.

Just when Elijah was going to explain what he was seeing, the floodlights came on, illuminating the area as if it were daylight. Elijah was flabbergasted to see Bluebloods in the city surrounding the gallows. Then one of them climbed the stairs and stepped up to a microphone that had been placed to the side.

Leaning into the microphone that was connected to several amplifiers to ensure that anybody within a couple of miles could hear, he spoke. "Per the decree of Hendricks Vesper, these two traitors before you have been sentenced to die by hanging from the neck. Our benevolent leader is saddened by this. He desires no more humans to perish. He desires that all who will surrender and come live in harmony with us, will live a peaceful and serene life. Our leader will gladly accept the surrender of Elijah Price as payment for your short rebellion. Should Elijah Price present himself to us, he will allow the remainder of those who resist him to coexist with those of us from the spheres."

Mortified by what he was hearing and fully knowing it was a lie, Elijah was paralyzed on what action he should take next. Then, it became even more real as the man at the microphone motioned for a couple of the bronze soldiers to escort two people up the stairs to the platform. Once the two people being escorted reached the platform along with the soldiers guiding them, the light shone on their faces.

Elijah was terrified at the sight. Standing next to the soldiers with their hands tied behind their back were Braden Samuleson and his wife, Natalie. Elijah felt sick to his stomach. "What the hell, this has to be a bluff by Vesper to get me to surrender," Elijah spoke in hopes that even he could believe it to be true.

A few minutes passed and the soldiers were commanded to place the ropes over the Samuelson's heads and tighten them around their necks. Calling out one additional time to the audience he knew existed in the nearby wilderness, the Blueblood on the podium added to his soliloquy, "Our benevolent savior, Hendricks Vesper, has also decreed that for each month that Elijah Price remains protected by the rebels, he will execute two more. Make it known that he is a man of his word."

With the finish of these words of horror just uttered by the Blueblood, he raised his right hand to instruct the one who controlled the trap doors beneath the Samuleson's feet to open them. Elijah watched as his best friend's bodies plunged through the opened doors, their sudden plummet stopped by a rope that had been pulled taught, hopefully killing them instantly.

Still in a state of horror, Elijah hadn't realized that he had left his radio mike keyed. Hector had heard the entire speech and knew precisely what was happening without having to see it. With Elijah unable to rationalize what was happening, Hector took matters into his own hands. Pushing the switch forward without hesitation, far off in the distance, all hell broke loose.

With the sight of Hector's explosives igniting, and many of the bronze soldiers beginning to move towards them like mosquitoes drawn to a bright light, Elijah snapped out of his trance. With a yell of defiance, the cavern cities leader, once again, took control, "FIRE!"

With streams of bright light followed by the explosions of missiles hitting their marks, Elijah's force proceeded down from the vista like ants scattered from their home. The Bluebloods that had come to watch the spectacle screamed in terror. They were unarmed and had no means to defend themselves. Many of the fired missiles found their targets. Elijah rejoiced to see several of Vesper's soldiers squirming from missing limbs or even better, obliterated into a pile of metal and wires.

He came upon a Blueblood that was wounded and begged for her life. For a moment, he felt sympathy for the woman. Then, just slightly over one hundred feet away from his current position, amongst the smoke and screams, he saw his friend's lifeless body hanging from a rope. Elijah realized he could help this woman. She could have a better future. Reaching for the .38 Colt revolver on his hip, he drew it and put a bullet in her head.

Hector pushed the semi-trailer as fast as it could go on the makeshift road leading to the underground city. As the truck whined with the process of using its air brakes to slow it down, he fired shots from his automatic rifle the best he could manage. Driving through a barrier that had been placed around the solar panels, he abruptly stopped the trailer near the panels. Exiting out of the back of the trailer, his retrieving team went into action. Within minutes they had loaded the panels into the trailer. Several of the bronze soldiers who had stayed behind moved quickly to confront Hector's team. A fierce firefight ensued with the cavern force defending their treasure with a spirit that made Hector proud.

Hector ran to the cab of the truck. Climbing into the cab, he placed it in gear. As he drove off, he could hear the blast of handheld missiles as they attempted to fend off the foes that sought to stop them from taking the panels. After pulling the truck into the barn that served as its hiding place, he jumped out of the cab and ran to the back of the trailer.

Hector estimated that he had lost seven of his men and women. He grieved for them. They had fought gallantly. Their sacrifice would not be in vain because resting in the back of the trailer, unbroken, were seventeen solar panels. The goal of their mission was to get ten.

Far off in the distance he could hear explosives beginning to succumb to the quiet of the night. The remainder of his people, exhausted and with several wounded, accompanied him slowly back to the cavern. Their friends gathered around them to assist with caring for the wounded.

Lark approached Hector with fear on her face. "Any word yet from Elijah?"

Still recovering from the events of the night, Hector realized he hadn't had time to contact Elijah. "I'm not sure about Elijah's force. I haven't heard from him. Wait, I have the radio!"

Lark impatiently grabbed the radio from Hector's hand. "Elijah, this is Lark, do you copy?" Seconds went by with no answer. "Elijah! Answer me! Do you copy?"

Still with no answer, Venus approached Lark with a plea to let her try the radio. Reluctantly, Lark handed it over to her. "Daddy, this is Venus. Yes, I said, Daddy. We need you to answer us right away. Mommy is terrified and so am I!"

Moments later a voice came over the radio, "How're my girls? Daddy, boy does that sound nice. Daddy returning to base momentarily, over," Elijah spoke as though they were long-lost friends being reunited.

With tears streaming from their eyes, mother and daughter embraced, never wanting to let go of each other.

CHAPTER 37:
IN THE STARS

18 months later

LYING FLAT ON HIS BACK, Elijah held his son, Zenith, next to him as he pointed towards the stars that formed the Big Dipper. Zenith mimicked his father as he pointed around the starlit sky saying, "Whazzat... whazzat?" Elijah enjoyed these moments. They distracted him from the trials and turmoil of everyday existence.

Climbing up to the where her son and husband lay stargazing, Lark approached them, laying down beside them. "I thought I would find you two up here," Lark commented like just catching somebody with their hand in the cookie jar.

"He loves to look at the stars. Like father, like son," Elijah chuckled in response.

"I'm glad you're taking some time. Time to relax. Time to be a father," Lark replied in honesty.

"Speaking of being a father, where's Venus?"

Lark smiled at her husband and revealed, "She's with Lena and Klous. He's installing a new latrine system. Not sure why she's interested in that, but to each their own."

They both laughed at what Lark had just revealed and continued to enjoy the peace and quiet of the night and starlit sky.

As Zenith moved in to receive the embrace of his mother, Lark, despite wanting to delay the inquiry, had to ask her husband a sensitive question. "You don't believe any of our people blame you for the executions, do you?"

"Sometimes I can't help but believe they do. Every time Hendricks executes those people, even though they finally accepted his false view of the future, I can't help but believe it is my fault."

"Those people bought into Vesper's treachery. They made a decision. That decision led to their death. Our people know it makes no difference to him if you turn Blueblood or not. Elijah, you are simply a pawn in his desire for power," Lark strongly said.

"Those people who have died with their Blueblood on his hands had no choice. The injection was engineered with a substance to control them, control their thoughts. That's why they don't resist him, they can't," Elijah preached.

"All the more reason why we need to continue to resist. Our people will follow you anywhere. They would rather die as free people than as a controlled people." Lark's words rang true.

Elijah glanced at his son who was thoroughly enjoying this time together with his parents. He marveled at the deep purple color of his eyes. He attributed the unusual eye pigments of the children being born to the Cavern people as the effect of underground living. It was just amazing to him, the different colors. Some of the children had dark green, some turquoise, and some even had orange. The one eye color that was not appearing in the Cavern children was blue, and Elijah was grateful for that fact.

Antonetta watched with pleasure as her son, Cyrus, named after a word that meant sun, played with Pi. The child laughed as Pi teased him with a toy, attempting to play hide-and-seek with it. She delighted in how Pi had learned to be a companion. a fun one at that, and Cyrus adored him.

"Pi, I think it's time for Cyrus to eat his lunch and take a nap," Antonetta requisitioned of her synthetic servant.

"Very good, Antonetta. I will go and prepare his nourishment."

Antonetta got down on her knees and picked up the toy that Pi had so affectionately used to tease Cyrus. He smiled and giggled at her. She found his deep ocean blue eyes truly beautiful. Hendricks had been so relieved when he was born with the Blueblood trait. All children born to the Sphere people displayed the same characteristic of eye color. Deep down, her greatest pleasure was that neither Cyrus nor his kind would have to take the injection. They were born to parents that had become Bluebloods and, by natural DNA, these children were true Bluebloods.

The leadership council of the Cavern gathered to discuss the war that was raging with Vesper and the Sphere people. Hector reported to the clan that they had suffered some casualties, but his force continued to engage the Bluebloods and their bronze A.I. force whenever there was an execution, or to divert them away from this cavern.

"Do they still call for my surrender, Hector?" Elijah asked.

"Of course they do, boss, but that ain't gonna happen on my watch!" Hector proclaimed with total agreement from all who were present at the gathering.

Lark stepped forward as a respected leader of the community. If it hadn't been for her, starvation would have been imminent. Now the gardens of the cavern were flourishing, and the Cavern people had all the comforts for their future. A future without being Vesper's slaves or sacrifices."I still can't help but feel for those people. The ones that are being used as bait for Vesper to use to get revenge on my husband!"

Elijah stepped up on the heels of Larks' testimony regarding just how wicked Vesper had become. "For the sake of our children, our blessed children of the Cavern, and yes, even the children of the Spheres…"

Mumbling amongst the clan interrupted Elijah's statement, so Lark proceeded to address the discomfort they were feeling about the children of the Spheres. "People, these are children! Innocent children. They need to be protected, just like our own."

The group calmed down at her words. Elijah then continued to speak. His words surprised Lark but didn't surprise all of those that were in attendance. "I see that the only way to provide for all of our futures, both Blueblood children and our own, and to stop the senseless sacrifices of a sick and demented man, is…"

Lark barked at her husband, fearful of what he was about to say. "No, Elijah!"

Failing to heed the fears of his beloved wife, he revealed the inevitable truth that they had all been waiting for. "We need to kill Hendricks Vesper!"

CHAPTER 38:
EXPOSURE

HE HAD ALWAYS BELIEVED he had all the answers, but Hendricks sat in the thirteenth-floor Boardroom that overlooked his empire and addressed Ben Tolmie and Silver James. "I'm at a loss. Why would these traitors continue to protect this fiend, Elijah Price? These last months I have intensified my reasons for them to surrender him to me. Still, they wage war on my people and my creations!"

Ben answered Hendricks statement and question, "Perhaps they aren't suffering as much as you believe they are, Dolion?"

Hendricks pondered his partner's rebuttal for a moment but then his face grew flush and discerning. "How long have you known, my friend?"

"Long enough, Hendricks. Long enough to know that none of us can reject you. None of us can deny you. We lost that ability when the needle went into our arms," Tolmie responded with a reality like a flash of lightning preceding the imminent clap of thunder.

Silver James sat astonished and at the same time confused by the exchange between Hendricks and Ben.

"Perhaps I should fill you in on our little secret, Mr. James. You see, Dolion Cozbi, the great environmental scientist and creator of sphere technology, whose suicide tossed his lifeless body out into the ocean never to be seen again, well, apparently, the stories of his demise were…you know, greatly exaggerated." Hendricks explained with an attitude that seemed more like telling a fictional story.

It suddenly seemed to make sense to Silver. He was sitting in the presence of a man that had been resurrected as somebody else. A man that had resurrected himself.

"I was wrong about my sphere technology. Of course, only to a certain extent. What we are doing here is the short-term answer. The answer on a much smaller scale. The truth was what I discovered later, after the world thought me dead. That truth was to alter human DNA. Nobody would have accepted that truth then, just like they refused my sphere technology. I vowed to return when the situation was more, shall we say, desperate, and I was more powerful. Dolion Cozbi is truly dead. In my mind, he did die. I am Hendricks Vesper, the savior of humanity."

Ben stood up from his seat and spoke, "So, killing humanity is also part of your plan?"

Hendricks laughed at Ben's statement. "No, Ben. I need Price. Even my superior brain can't overcome the failures of the Sphere3 panels. Price was more than an extrusion expert. He came to understand my creation. He knows how they work. How they think. I need him to come back to me. I need him to be submissive to me!"

"Then we will help you find him, Hendricks. I don't have the ability to deny your commands. Somewhere, inside me, I still have a conscience. I just don't know where it is." Ben replied.

Silver stayed seated. Hendricks looked at him waiting for a response…any response. He shifted uncomfortably in his chair and replied, "Tremont has been reactivated. He's better than before. Stronger and more powerful, and resistant to any of the weapons being used against your A.I. force. I guess that is my response, Dr. Vesper."

"Excellent work, my friend. Tremont is how I will restore peace. You have been very allegiant to me, Silver,"

Hendricks spoke while approaching Silver to provide him with an embrace that seemed forced and artificial.

Silver reciprocated the show of appreciation, but his conscience had been found and the blueblood serum that altered his DNA had not controlled his mind quite as much as the other recipients.

CHAPTER 39: JOURNEY TO ASSASSINATION

HECTOR SAT ALONE WITH ELIJAH discussing a way that they could possibly assassinate Hendricks Vesper. Several options were presented by Hector, but even he agreed they were almost impossible to carry out. "Obviously, if there was a way to lure him out into the open, away from the protection of the sphere, we would have a chance."

"Hendricks wouldn't be so foolish. Even if I were used as bait, I don't believe he would risk coming out of the sphere," Elijah resigned himself to the truth.

As the two men sat pondering the many hypothetical possibilities, Elijah had an idea pop into his head. "What if we don't lure him outside? What if we get to him inside the sphere? Inside his Palace?" Elijah proposed.

Hector smirked and responded to Elijah's proposal, "Sure, Elijah, we'll just roll up to the front door and knock on the sphere and ask one of those bronze turds if Hendricks can come out and play!"

"I'm not saying getting into the sphere at an entrance, I'm saying we get into the sphere where nobody expects," Elijah revealed.

"And just where is that?" Hector questioned.

Elijah smiled like a Papa that knew exactly what his children were up to. "Beneath the spheres. When I built

Sphere2, we reduced the temperature of the bottom middle panel, at its center, so we could insert a pipe through it. That pipe was for the water supply to the spheres. Those panels were structurally sound but had a circular gap around the water pipe just wide enough to allow a human to fit through them and up into the sphere."

Hector waited a few moments for Elijah's revelation to fully sink in. "Even if we can find where those pipes enter the spheres, what guarantee do we have that they aren't covered with tons of dirt and God knows what else?"

"I've seen them. They have huge valves and pipes jutting off in all directions, but if you were to look down on the pipe that enters the sphere, you would see the gap," Elijah answered.

"Just how are we supposed to find the source of the pipeline? It could be anywhere. It's probably buried so even if we could follow it, we would have no way to do so." Hector pleaded.

"Oh, my Commander of little faith," Elijah joked. "The concrete tubes we lived in at the underground city, they're the same as the ones that carry the pipeline that feeds the spheres. It will be a tight squeeze, but it will be large enough."

Hector was becoming quite intrigued by Elijah's plan but had to ask another question. "How do we find a concrete tube that might carry the water pipeline that leads to Sphere2?"

"When Vesper had our water turned off, I know that the pipeline that fed the underground city was an offshoot from the sphere's water supply. My best guess is that whatever water source Spheretech tapped into, also fed us water. I'll bet they discovered an endless underground stream or well, and that is why they decided to build the spheres where they did."

"Little did they know that water source had a very large, big brother that sat inside a very large underground cavern," Hector admitted.

"Exactly," Elijah agreed.

The plan was set to break into the underground city, get into the concrete tube that held the water pipeline, and follow it to what they hoped would be the entrance to Sphere2. Breaking through the concrete wall, a small force would ascend through the gap in the base of the sphere and navigate their way to the Palace of Hendricks Vesper.

Once inside the Palace, they would locate Vesper and complete their mission. Both men agreed on the possibility that they might not be able to escape and return to their home. And both agreed that was a risk they needed to accept. Elijah had never lied to Lark. He loved her too much to ever do that to her. He was saddened to realize that for the sake of his family, Lark, Venus and Zenith, and their futures, he would have to lie about this plan.

Hendricks walked a circle around Tremont. He was in awe of the work Silver James had done to restore his synthetic commander. "Tremont, are you pleased to have been repaired and returned to service for me?" Hendricks asked.

"Of course, Dr. Vesper. I am prepared to resume my command and fulfill your orders to capture Elijah Price," Tremont stoically responded.

"Very good, Tremont. But, for right now, I am ordering you to stay close to the Palace. I perceive there is treachery afoot and it pleases me to have you close by to protect my family."

"I'm here to serve you," Tremont acknowledged as he turned to attend his post outside the Palace.

Pi entered the room with Cyrus. The young toddler was excited to see his father and bounded over to him to be hoisted into his arms. "Hendricks, I overheard you say to

Tremont that you sensed treachery afoot. That treachery you are sensing, is it the rebellion?"

"Perhaps, Pi. But don't concern yourself with that. Just continue to take care of my boy here," Hendricks replied.

Scanning the horizon and the underground city off in the distance, Hector and Elijah considered how they would be able to invade the underground city and progress to the water supply tube without detection. They were pleased to see that the barricades were only manned by three bronze soldiers. Apparently, Vesper had grown tired and bored with using additional resources to guard the city and had begun reducing them.

"I guess Vesper's given up on us and believes we're all dead, huh, Elijah?" Hector commented.

"Apparently so," Elijah responded. "We're going to have to devise a plan to get those soldiers away from the city," Elijah said.

"Leave that to yours truly. I'm an expert at diversions," Hector said, tongue in cheek.

Elijah gently stroked the hair that fell across Lark's forehead. She enjoyed these moments of tenderness from him, mostly because they had been so infrequent lately. She fully understood the pressure and strain that leadership had placed upon him. Turning towards him, she rolled to reciprocate the affection he was displaying. She loved this man, more than life itself.

After the couple had completed their union together, Elijah lay next to Lark and nonchalantly said, "Tomorrow night, Hector and I need to go to the underground city and fetch some cable that Klous needs for the solar panels." This was lie number one told to his beloved, and it pained him to tell it.

"Why can't Klous and his crew go get it themselves?" she asked with curiosity.

"There might be some soldier activity there. Even though Vesper no longer uses the gallows to persuade my surrender, Hector seems to believe the soldiers patrol it regularly," Elijah answered, knowing that this was lie number two.

"Just be careful, my love," Lark replied.

"I always am," he answered, completing the trifecta of lies.

With dark hoods over their heads, Hector, Elijah, and two other men waited for the pyrotechnics show to begin that would draw the three bronze soldiers away from the underground city. During this idle time, Elijah's thoughts wouldn't depart from remembering last night and his conversation with Lark. "You know we can do this without you, Elijah. The risk we're undertaking is great," Hector honestly revealed.

Elijah replied without even a second thought. "Even if you can get inside the sphere, I'm the only one who knows how to get to the Palace. I've been there and know the layout."

The diversion began and the soldiers responded just as Elijah and company thought they would. Moving quickly to where the men believed the entrance to the water supply tunnel existed, they found that the door that allowed their descent was not locked.

Once down the stairs, they found themselves in a concrete lined room. Just as they imagined, right before them were several spindles connected to a large concrete cylinder. Taking the sledgehammer that he had packed with him, Hector began swinging at the cylinder. Within a few minutes the concrete had succumbed to his efforts. Inside the cylinder was a large pipe that extended forward and, if all went right, would lead the men directly to the entrance of Sphere1.

With barely enough room to navigate on all fours, the men proceeded, following the pipe. After approximately an hour, the men, with sweat dripping profusely from their brows, reached a section of the pipe that forked to the right. Following the right fork for about thirty minutes, they believed they had discovered paydirt. The pipe, with a ninety-degree angle turn, went directly upward.

Chipping away at the concrete cylinder that confined them, they eventually broke through. Crawling out of the tube, the men found they could stand upright. Elijah was grateful for this. Inching up with their legs on the tube and their backs against dirt, the men reached the promised land. Just above them was the gap between the sphere panel and the water pipe.

Elijah eased up through the gap first and signaled to Hector to hand him the supplies and weapons. Soon, all four men were inside Sphere1, knowing it was too late to turn back.

"The connecting sphere that leads to Sphere2 is that way," Elijah pointed as though he were a tour guide. With that instruction, the four men set off to complete the assassination.

CHAPTER 40:
TRAGEDY

HENDRICKS SAT QUIETLY READING the journal of his former self. He perused the notes about the compounds that made up the organic material that formed the sphere panels. He thought to himself, "I have to be missing something."

Pi entered the room. "I have put Cyrus to bed. He is sleeping."

"Thank you, Pi. Where's Antonetta?"

"Miss Antonetta is practicing personal hygiene," Pi responded.

Laughing, Hendricks nodded his head and said, "It's called a shower, Pi."

"Can I get you anything, Hendricks?" Pi inquired.

"No, just stay in here with me. I feel uneasy tonight and your company is comforting," Hendricks admitted.

Outside of Hendrick's Palace, four men crouched near a wall that led to a terrace that was attached to a living area. Throwing ropes up and over a banister onto the edge of the terrace, the four men scaled the wall to arrive on the terrace. Elijah remembered that the living area where Hendricks frequented was open with no doors or windows. The weather inside the spheres provided no reason to close it off, plus it allowed Hendricks easy access to look out over his empire.

Moving stealthily, the four men proceeded to the entrance of the living area and were elated to find

Hendricks occupying a chair, reading. The men readied their weapons in preparation to shoot Vesper, retreat, and escape the spheres to return to safety.

With one finger erect and spun in a circular motion, Hector signaled the men to commence with their mission. Suddenly, sirens blasted, floodlights came on, and the men were exposed and compromised. Coming out from behind a wall in the living area, Tremont, who was accompanied by four of the soldiers under his command, shouted at the intruders to drop their weapons.

Knowing that they had been bested, all the men, including Elijah, dropped their weapons, tossing them away from their bodies as instructed. Stepping up to confront the men, Hendricks, in an arrogant fashion, proclaimed, "Good evening, Elijah. So nice of you to visit me again." Elijah removed his mask, saying nothing.

"Did you believe I could be so naïve that I would not prepare for this very moment? Although, I must admit, your plan was ingenious. Your knowledge of my sphere organics certainly served you well," Hendricks commented in the manner of a parent catching their child misbehaving.

Antonetta emerged from the bathroom to find the confrontation that was currently taking place. "Hendricks, what…what's going on here?" she cried out.

"No worries, my dear. Mr. Price and his friends here were simply attempting to make you a widow."

Antonetta gasped. Elijah realized that no matter what happened, the events of tonight would change his life forever. He could be forced to take the injection, hung as a traitor, or he could complete the mission, whether he lived or died. With Hendricks standing approximately five feet directly in front of him, Elijah, in one swift move, withdrew a .38 caliber pistol that he had tucked inside the back of his pants.

So as not to be vanquished in his attempt, Elijah took no time to aim, but, before he could pull the trigger and send the bullet projecting towards Vesper, he heard at least two projectiles that had been fired from behind him speeding past his left ear. Antonetta, who had been focused on Elijah, had sped to move in front of Hendricks to protect him from Elijah's bullets. Both rounds that were fired from an unseen weapon struck her in the back.

Antonetta collapsed to the floor landing in front of Hendricks. Confused, Elijah pivoted around. Standing behind him, with his weapon extended in Vesper's direction, was the A.I. Commander, Tremont. In rapid succession, he cut down the soldiers who had accompanied him to thwart the attempt on Hendrick's life.

Crouching in disbelief of what had just happened, the intruders received an urgent command from Tremont. "If you want to live, you must follow me. NOW!" Not being in a position to argue, they stood to follow Tremont to wherever he led them.

Pi stood in the background. He fully processed what he had just witnessed. Not having aggression as part of his programming, he noticed that one of the intruder's weapons had been tossed near to where he was standing. He picked it up and examined it. What Pi's learning had taught him is that the treachery, of which Hendrick's had spoken, had come true tonight.

As the men started their retreat following the biggest traitor of all, Pi fired the weapon in the direction of the men. One bullet hit its mark and Elijah Price dropped to his knees and then to the floor.

Tremont turned to return fire towards Pi. Deep down in his circuits, he admired Pi's moxie. Barely missing Pi, Tremont scooped up a wounded Elijah like he was a rag doll. He then turned to lead the would-be assassins out of the Palace and into a vehicle waiting just outside.

As gently as he could, Tremont laid the body of Elijah in the back of the vehicle and, after Hector and the two other men had jumped in, Tremont instructed the driver to "GO"! Punching the pedal that enabled the vehicle to move forward, Silver James stared directly in front of him, knowing that multiple tragedies had just occurred, and it would change everything.

Hendricks lay beside Antonetta's body. His grief blocked the fact that blue colored blood was flowing rapidly from her body. Looking up from the body of the only human he had ever truly loved, he saw Pi with his toddler child, tightly holding onto the bronze leg of his servant.

CHAPTER 41: DEVASTATION

As TREMONT APPROACHED THE ENTRANCE to the cavern, he carried the limp, lifeless body of Elijah Price in his arms. Hector and the men that accompanied him on this tragic mission frantically stopped as several men coming from inside the cavern were rapidly approaching them carrying handheld missile launchers. The weapons were angrily pointed directly at Tremont.

"Stop! Lower your weapons! He is not our foe!" Hector screamed at the top of his lungs, hoping to diffuse an already chaotic situation.

Lark appeared at the entrance with terror etched on her face. Her terror was warranted upon discovering that the body the bronze giant held in his arms was Elijah. She yelled at Tremont to put her husband down. He complied immediately. Screaming hysterically, she fell upon the body of her husband.

With tears streaming down her face, she looked up at Hector. "Why did you bring that thing here? That thing killed my husband!" Lark screamed with hysteria at Hector while a shaking finger pointed directly at Tremont. Hector moved quickly over to embrace Lark to try and comfort her grief. "I'm so sorry, Lark. I didn't mean for this to happen. It was a trap! That bronze thing was part of a different plot to assassinate Vesper. Had we...had Elijah known, we would have let him do it! We would have never been there," Hector cried out to try and ease her pain.

Nothing helped to ease her pain. Her husband was dead. "And what about Vesper? My husband is dead, and I'll bet he's just fine!" Lark cried out. Venus had joined her mother at Elijah's body and had broken down in tears. Lena, who held Zenith in her arms, came to kneel by the body of their leader. Tears were flowing profusely from her face.

Lena gathered what small amount of composure she could summon and addressed the group of cavern dwellers that had gathered since the commotion started. "I don't care why that abomination was at Vesper's! I don't care what it did or didn't do! That thing is not welcome here!"

Tremont could only stand idle and listen to the hatred directed at him that was not only spilling from Lena's words, but also from the faces of Venus and Lark. That same hatred was also etched on the faces of the Cavern people. He processed their reaction with a sense of understanding. That was the best he could do.

From behind Hector, a figure emerged. Lark recognized the silver covering on his tooth. "Lark, had I known your husband had planned to assassinate Vesper, I would have stopped him, trust me. I have no love for Hendricks Vesper and what he has become. I know one thing for sure, my creation here, and myself, are no longer welcome in his empire either. Like your husband, who I greatly respected, we will be hunted for our treason."

Lark battled through the tears streaming from her eyes and the snot dripping from her nose. "Did he kill my husband? Was it Vesper that killed my husband?" Lark pleaded with Silver to answer her question.

"I understand it was his A.I. servant, Pi," Silver answered.

"Another one of your creations then. Another one of your abominations!" Lark bellowed.

"Yes, I created Pi. I did not create him to be a killer."

"Maybe not, Mr. James, but then tell me why I shouldn't have this freak standing here destroyed? This freak you created! And tell me, why I should allow you to live?"

Silver lowered his eyes in submission to her, then he raised his blue eyes up to meet her eyes that were red and swollen. "Because, someday, you will need him. Someday, all of us will need him. One day, Tremont will be able to make his own decisions, but until that day, he listens to and obeys only me."

PART 3:
THE SECOND-GENERATION WAR

There's a room where light won't find you

Holding hands while the walls come tumbling down

When they do I'll be right behind you

So glad we've almost made it

So sad they had to fade it

Everybody wants to rule the world

Lyrics: Everybody Wants To Rule The World

CHAPTER 42:
THE CHILDREN

18 Years later

LARK CALLED OUT TO VENUS to gain her attention, "Do you know where your brother is? It's almost dinner time."

"Where do you think he's at, mom? Once it starts to get dark, he's always in the same place. I'll go and get him," Venus reluctantly offered.

Just outside the cavern entrance, Venus climbed to a bluff that sat atop the secluded opening of the cavern. Lying there, flat on his back was her brother, Zenith. "Gee, just how did I know you would be up here, dear brother," Venus jokingly exclaimed.

Patting the ground, he motioned for his sister to come join him. Pointing into the western sky he asked her, "See that bright star right there? Well, that's no star, that's a planet. That planet was named after you since you're so old, you were here before it was formed," Zenith barked with glee at teasing his sister.

"You're a dork, brother, and mom wants us for dinner, right now."

Letting out a sigh, Zenith pushed his sister in playful retaliation as they got up from stargazing to descend to the cavern entrance. As they entered the opening, Zenith waved at the two guards that were on duty this evening. Off in the distance, he could see several airborne drones.

Drones that searched for whatever remnant might still exist that was in rebellion against Hendricks Vesper.

"Dinner was great, mom," Zenith commented as he washed and dried his plate. Lark came over to where he was doing the dishes and leaned into him with appreciation. Stopping what he was doing, he hugged his mother, sensing that she needed it right then. Placing her older and calloused hand on her son's cheek, she gazed for a moment into the purple hue of his eyes. He had grown tall and strong, just like his father.

Lark brushed his shaggy black hair in a playful manner indicating that he needed a haircut. "I know, I know, I promise I'll let Lena cut it soon. I have plans with Dyce tonight. Silver's going to let me, Dyce, and Chip, play a game with his talking head," Zenith pleaded for his mom to approve.

"Well, I don't particularly care for that talking head. I think it's...you know, freakie," Lark expressed with total honesty.

"I know, but he is way more fun than Tremont. All that big lug wants to do is wrestle with Blaze. Then Blaze winds up getting frustrated and then Silver makes us all go home. I feel kinda bad, but that's why we didn't invite Blaze tonight."

"Well, I think Blaze is the lucky one. I'm not so sure his mother would be too happy if she knew he was wrestling with Tremont," Lark acknowledged.

Having sought and received Lark's approval to go to Silver's camp, Zenith kissed her on the cheek and departed to meet up with his friends. "Does Zenith know that it was Tremont's former self that probably killed Blaze's dad?" Venus asked.

"No, and I don't want him to find out, so don't you go and tell him, young lady! He will go off with visions of grandeur just like his father," Lark expressed with a small tear forming in her eye. Venus could sense that even after all these years, she still longed for Elijah.

"Do you want me to sing for you, mom?" Venus tenderly inquired.

"I always want you to sing for me, baby," Lark smiled and answered. With that response, the camp was filled with songs befitting when the robins and sparrows used to fly on the earth.

"Crap, lost again!" Dyce slammed down the game controller.

Primus laughed and responded, "I thought you were getting better at this game?" This evoked a chuckle from the usually stoic Tremont. Silver watched on with amusement. He enjoyed it when these young men came over to challenge Primus. The only thing that enjoyed their company more than him was Primus.

Sensing that it was highly unlikely that he would return after the fateful night that the assassination of Hendricks Vesper turned into the assassination of Antonetta Valde, Silver had taken Primus and his computer equipment to a secure location outside the spheres. He couldn't and wouldn't leave his prized possession behind.

The computer equipment had also become invaluable for hacking and the tracking of Vesper's movements. Zenith's friend, Cedric Lee, had grown to show a proclivity for intruding into Blueblood business. He also was the only person that could beat Primus at his game. Chip, as his friends called him by his nickname, was brilliant. His parents were killed during a skirmish with A.I. forces when he was barely two months old. Klous and Lena adopted him and cherished Cedrick as their own.

Absentmindedly working on a circuit board, Silver was deep in thought. Several times in the last eighteen years, he had laughed at the thought that Vesper believed he owned the market on human repopulation. The people of the cavern were rapidly growing their community without the addition of the blue serum into their lives. He considered that Hendricks might just drop dead from a heart attack if this discovery ever came to light.

Zenith was doing his best to engage Tremont in meaningful conversation, but the bronze soldier was not having any of it and he decided it was an appropriate time to ask Silver about something that had been bothering him all night. "Hey Silver, tonight when I was outside stargazing, I noticed quite a few more drones than normal, any idea why that might be?"

Looking up from the circuit board he was working on, Silver pondered the question. "I've also noticed them when I go out in the daytime. I've been watching the development of housing outside the spheres. With the failures in constructing Sphere3, the Blueblood people have been forced to go outside to live."

Then Silver continued, "Sphere1 and 2 are needed to be used for what Vesper originally designed, which wasn't to house his people. They're running out of room. Just like here, humans are being born, even to the Sphere people. Vespers concerned that he can't protect his people. The drones are his paranoia that we're still out here. That we exist. That we're a threat!"

Zenith thought carefully about what Silver had just explained. "Even after eighteen years? Vesper is still afraid of the ghost of my father, isn't he?"

Hendricks sat alone in the vast living quarters of his Palace. It was darkened, only illuminated by the moonlight that penetrated through the sphere. The hexagonal beams of golden moonlight slanted through his large window.

He *stared*.

It was moments like these when Antonetta would creep into the silent crevices of his mind. The quiet ate at him as his thoughts seeped deep inside. He sat, slacked, in his usual leather seat, where just across the way stood the matching piece, virtually untouched. The seat that his wife, the mother of his child, would often inhabit, staring back at him.

His hand was creased around a small, cold glass, filled with a splash of whisky on ice. In one lingering movement he pressed the glass to his lips, tipping it and allowing the liquor to rewire his brain and smother the thought of Antonetta's haunting blue eyes.

He pushed himself up from his chair, gathering his balance, he stumbled towards Antonetta's seat. With hunched shoulders rising slowly to meet his tall stature, eighteen years of loneliness was carved into his face. A deep curved frown elongated it. With one hand filled with his small glass, he leaned down with the opposite. Smudging his index finger against the grime of the cold leather that adorned the seat where she had sat, he brought his finger to his gaze, with a soft layer of dust nestled on the tip. He rubbed his thumb and forefinger together.

He ticked; his pupils turned black with an utter torrent of rage that coursed throughout his entire body. With a swift stride forward and with all his strength and unbridled anger, he threw the glass which struck the large window, the expensive organic alcohol waterfalled down the window in strong honey-hued beads as the whiskey glass shattered on impact.

Pi emerged instantaneously. "Are you alright, sir?"

"Fine, Pi." Hendricks responded matter-of-factly, rubbing circles into the sides of his temples.

Pi swiftly scanned the area, synthetic eyes beamed over the out-of-place mess. "Shall I call for clean-up?"

Hendricks waved his hand, giving Pi the approval. With an attempt to remove the ache that was slowly spreading in his head, Hendricks returned to his chair and cupped his hand over his eyes.

Small flat robots entered the room to collect the glass and spilled liquid. Pi marveled at the efficiency these machines operated with. He was curious if they had been created by his creator, Silver James. With arms that extended from their torsos, they cleaned the window, then disappeared after removing the broken glass from Hendricks domain.

Pi slowly and cautiously intervened, knowing and recognizing the mental state in which Hendricks was in. "Is there anything I can get for you, sir?" Pi stepped forward and, with a robotic tilt of his head, added, "Analyzing the current state of your alcohol levels and tracing back to when they were as high as this at a prior time of intoxication, you've always asked for more alcohol."

"Get me my son!" Hendricks commanded, slumping back in his chair.

Pi hesitated.

"Pi..." Hendricks reiterated intimidatingly, blue eyes glaring at his servant, and piercing like daggers. "I need to speak with my son!"

Pi's head tilted back to return to a straight position and processed the command. "Sir, your blood alcohol levels currently are at 0.11, maybe it's time for you to rest."

Hendricks sharply cut off his servant, "Obey my command and retrieve my son, *now!*"

"I can't, sir."

"Why not, you disobedient scrap of metal..." he bellowed, showing his drunken state.

"One of my program functions is to remain inside the Palace and serve you. I'm forbidden to leave the Palace. I'm certainly not allowed to venture *outside* the Sphere." Pi confessed, stepping backwards.

Hendricks's jaw fell slightly agape, then clenched. As unremitting, pulsing strikes of anger coursed throughout his body, his eyes flew wide open, revealing an illusion that his blue eyes had turned to flickering flames.

His sapphire eyes were radiant against the darkness inside his father's Sphere. Cyrus Vesper peeked around the edge of a cold grey stone building, hugging the corner to take note of his surroundings.

The obnoxious sounds of his father's drones buzzed in the air above him. Flinging himself to press his back against the wall, he closed his eyes tightly, exhaling uneasily due to his heart rate and breathing being accelerated because of fear. The full moon above the Sphere cast the only light available to help illuminate his way. Despite despising the prison this Sphere had become to him, Cyrus found himself awestruck by the sight of it.

He had no destination. All he knew for sure was that he wanted to escape. Glancing back around the corner, he darted forward. The further he went towards the area that was forbidden to him, the more exhilarated he felt.

A subtle breeze was kind to him as he took in a deep fulfilling breath, letting the fresh air flood his system. The wind blew through his hair, a blonde color that was intensely light-hued like bleached ivory bitten by frost, tangling the strands of it that just barely hovered over his ear.

He reached the border of Sphere2 and hid himself from the A.I. force that was perched there, standing guard. Upon receiving instructions to search for Cyrus Vesper, and the command not to alert the population, the bronze-colored force panned out in compliance with their orders. Cyrus, believing that his father's henchmen had abandoned the portal that would take him outside the Sphere and, for once, let him taste the sweet nectar of freedom, slowly approached the meager hut that contained the key that would deactivate the Sphere portal. He recalled how once he had asked Pi how people entered and exited the spheres. His artificial servant politely answered him, being unaware that Cyrus had ulterior motives. Cyrus laughed at just how naïve Pi could be sometimes, to have believed his question was purely innocent.

Quietly reaching the hut, he crouched down at the entrance which had been left open. "Foolish artificial creatures," he thought. Bursting into the hut to grab one of the rods that would allow him to exit the Sphere, he was startled to realize he wasn't alone. Not all the bronze soldiers had gone in search of the disobedient son of Hendricks Vesper. One lone synthetic soldier had remained and, immediately upon sighting Cyrus, sounded alarms. Quickly, he was surrounded by several of the soldiers.

Without thinking clearly, Cyrus began to run. Having travelled a very short distance from the guard station, Cyrus looked back to see if he had a chance to escape their chase only to crash into one of the soldiers that had stepped in front of him while he retreated. The blue eyes with a red pupil of the A.I. soldier told him that his escape attempt had been thwarted.

Cyrus let out a beaten exhale. He breathed in, shakily turning his head to meet the cold stare of several of his father's force. The bronze hand of the capturing soldier reached out and the palm was swiftly slammed against Cyrus's mouth. A torrent of pain riddled through him, and he instantly tried to writhe away as his scream was silenced. His body was lifted from the floor as cold steel pinched the sides of his cheeks. The hand moved from his mouth allowing his scream to travel as he pushed himself away from his captor. He searched for an escape as he read *HF-00137* engraved in a small font along the forehead of his captor.

"Hendrick's Force-00137! Let me go!! Unhand me!! Your function is to obey Vesper command, and I demand you unhand me! I am Vesper!" Cyrus screamed his command.

HF-00137 then forced Cyrus to the ground pinning his arms down to the cement, with his focus narrowing in on his previously given task. "Function override, you have no authority over Hendrick's Force," it answered.

Metallic fingers revealed a syringe filled with an unknown substance.Cyrus's eyes widened, fear thumping in his chest as he watched helplessly. "What are you doing? What are you doing? Stop! Please! No!"

HF-00137 shoved the syringe into the crease of Cyrus's arm, pushing the liquid into his veins.

His body almost instantly relaxed. "Please, don't do this…" he whimpered, his lips parting slightly as his eyes began to slowly blink. Cyrus continued to try and push himself away, but his arms could barely lift from his sides, even without the A.I.'s constraint.

Lethargically, his head slipped backwards, bumping into concrete with a short thud as his eyes rolled back into his head.

HF-00137 reached down to swoop up Cyrus's limp body.

Cyrus awoke panicked in his large bedroom. The air felt thick as he brought his bandaged arms to wrap around his thin frame. Blue blood stained the folds of the gauze taped to his injection site.

"Welcome back, Cyrus." Pi said in a lightened tone. "No need to be alarmed, you're safe now."

Cyrus groaned, reaching up to press the palms of his hands into his eyes, rubbing away the enforced sleep from his groggy head. He had no idea just how long Pi had been standing in the corner of his room, waiting and watching his every move.

"Your father has been requesting a moment with you just as soon as you have awoken. Would you like to meet with him now?"

Cyrus sighed, analyzing the grand, orderly bedroom before him. His bedroom. Lying on the bed at his feet, his clothes had been restored; palace attire, fit for an heir. His clothing was consistently form-fitting; hugging his slim figure and always in shades of stony blue. A tight white, almost grey tunic was tucked underneath a slate-colored vest accompanied by a gold collared necklace. Slim pants to match, as every inch of fabric was smoothly pressed from wrinkles or imperfections. Much how his father tried to do to him.

"You're very smart, Pi. I'm sure you know my answer to that," he muttered, finally glancing up at him.

Pi's voice fell to a quiet tone, as he interlocked his steel fingers. "I'm afraid you haven't been given much of a choice..."

Cyrus was escorted out of his room by two A.I.'s with penny tinted skin-tones. They synchronized their steps behind him as they made their way to meet Hendricks.

Hendricks sat facing his window once more, looking out at the view he'd created for himself, with a glass of alcohol in his hand, which had become the norm.

Hendricks' artificial servants took a step back and left without a word, leaving Cyrus and Hendricks in competing silence.

"Everything I have done," Hendricks hissed amongst the tense quiet. "The lengths I've gone to, the dedication to my science, the power I put into the security of my Palace, and you thought you could breach the system."

Cyrus swallowed thickly. "I needed...!"

"NO!" Hendricks barked, standing up straight and glaring down at his son. "You needed nothing but to defy me!"

"But, father, listen to me!"

"You will visit with Ben tomorrow," Hendricks demanded.

"Please, not again," Cyrus pleaded.

"He's going to be taking samples of your blood."

"More samples? Haven't I given you enough?"

"Not another word, Cyrus!"

"Would you just try to understand! I know nothing except what's behind these walls! Why can't you see that? I've been trapped in this Palace my entire life. I'm lonely father!"

"Trapped?" Hendricks laughed, putting down his drink. "Trapped? I have built a world here for you. Do you forget about your mother? They're coming for you! You must understand that!" Hendricks spoke with a tinge of anxiety emitting from his voice.

Cyrus's breath hitched.

"You want to know what's beyond the Spheres? Your mother's killers, that's what! Starving, blood thirsty monsters waiting for their next moment to strike. They want *your* blood, Cyrus; they want your blood spilled to hurt me!"

"Is that why you're sending drones outside the Sphere? What's hiding out there?" Cyrus quizzed.

"Sphere3 is failing, Cyrus. We're running out of room; our population is growing. Our people are going to have to start moving outside the Spheres. My people's lives are at stake … my, *our*, people are in danger. I have to…I *must* protect them!" Hendricks pleaded for his son to understand what he was trying to tell him.

"In danger?" Cyrus questioned.

"Yes, I have built you a comfortable life, Cyrus. A safe, secure Palace, while children your age are being forced to move outside the Spheres."

"Still, why can't I see it? The outside. Maybe I could help our people."

"No!" Hendricks said. "Your place is inside the Palace, under my protective eyes. Safe from harm. I couldn't bear losing you too."

CHAPTER 43:
SKELETONS

AS HE WALKED OUT ONTO THE TERRACE that was connected to the living area, Hendricks carried a glass of brandy and a cigar. Selecting a chaise lounge in which to recline, he plopped down, clipped one end of the cigar, and lit the other end. As the smoke from the cigar wafted upwards, he watched as it swirled out into the atmosphere and disappeared. Outside the Sphere, he could see the stars gleaming through the light haze caused by the Sphere's material.

He was saddened by the moment. He and Antonetta had spent years on this terrace, enjoying the stars above and dreaming about their futures. Since that fateful night that she was murdered, he had barely used this terrace because the pain of remembering her was too great.

Hendricks sipped his brandy and contemplated why he had decided to come out to the terrace tonight. He was troubled. Troubled that, after all these years, he had been deceived by the one he thought was a loyal and obedient servant. A servant fortified by the injection of the blue serum. Not only had Silver James become a traitor, but he used the very creation that Hendricks had bought and paid for against him. His obsession with this disobedience had engulfed his mind and soul ever since.

If his hatred for Silver James and Tremont wasn't enough, he had become increasingly concerned and confused by what he determined was disobedience by his own flesh and blood. Cyrus and his rebellious behavior baffled him as a scientist. His son was a product of Blueblood birth. He was pure Blueblood. There should never be any behavior but total obedience to him. Still, there was a trend forming. A trend that he was also seeing from other children of Bluebloods. What was so concerning to him were not only the reports of these children, who were now growing into adulthood, but their parents had been reported to be displaying trends of disobedience also.

These trends reeked of rebellion, and he couldn't stomach the thought. Taking another draw of his cigar, Hendricks decided he needed to know just how and why. Picking up the phone, he called Ben Tolmie. When he answered the phone, Hendricks politely asked if Ben could join him tonight at the Palace.

Sensing that Hendricks was deeply troubled, Ben hung up the phone and headed directly for the Palace. Upon the announcement that Ben had arrived, Hendricks called out to him, motioning him to come outside. "Grab a glass, I brought the brandy out here. I'm anticipating drinking most of it this evening," Hendricks revealed with total honesty.

Choosing a chair adjacent to Hendrick's lounger, Ben accepted a pour of brandy into his glass. He could see the look of distress in his leader's face.

Never looking at Ben, and staring straight upwards towards the stars, Hendricks spoke. "Ben, you've remained allegiant to me. Even after discovering and knowing the truth, that I was Dolion Cozbi. Why do you believe that is?"

Ben laughed at the question. Then, in a matter-of-fact manner, he answered. "Because you engineered it to be true. Just like everybody who has taken the injection. Regardless, I am allegiant to you because I always believed in you, Hendricks. Unlike those that wouldn't believe in you as Cozbi, I have always believed in Hendricks Vesper, with or without the shot."

"Then why is it some have plotted to betray me? First, Silver James and Tremont, now I fear my own son has questions about my Sovereignty. I am troubled because my spies have told me that even the injected are having second thoughts about me. If they carry the same blood as you and me, why are my people transcending into this?" Hendricks asked, still never looking at Ben.

Ben couldn't help but recognize that Hendricks was drinking more and more lately. "Perhaps I should gather blood samples, starting with the children. My lab team could begin to analyze what, if anything, could be causing this sudden departure into insurgency," Ben offered, seeking to find favor from Hendricks.

Hendricks turned to stare directly at Ben for the first time since their conversation had begun. "That's why I know you are truly my friend."

"Always," Ben replied.

"I'd like you to start with blood samples from my son," Hendricks bluntly ordered.

"Sure, he'll be the first," Ben complied.

Leaving the Palace, Ben couldn't help but ponder that Hendricks hadn't divulged all his concerns to him. He shrugged it off as Hendricks being Hendricks. A man that has skeletons in his closet and will continue to gather them.

Pi woke Cyrus from his slumber. Feeling slightly annoyed that he had been awakened far before he wanted to rise, he bellowed a grumble at the synthetic being as he rolled out of bed.

Upon arriving at Ben Tolmie's lab, Cyrus walked in to find Ben discussing something with one of his lab assistants.

"Hey, Ben. I guess my father sent me here to have a tracking chip inserted in me so he can know every time I go pee!" Cyrus joked, although he wouldn't put it past his father to do just that.

"Yes, that's it. I have one, so you need one too!" Ben responded back with wit and humor. "Your father has nothing to do with your visit today. I'm taking blood samples from every natural born Blueblood. I'm concerned that since you and the other Blueblood children never had the injection, you might not carry the same levels of protection from radiation from the sun. Now that some have begun moving away from the Spheres, I need to know our people will be safe out there."

Shrugging, Cyrus pulled up his sleeve and pointed his right arm towards Ben. "Makes no difference to me. My father never lets me leave the protection of the Sphere so, either way, I'm safe."

"Most likely," Ben replied with a smile on his face as he readied the syringe to extract blood from Cyrus. After having collected enough to analyze the sample, he excused himself as having a lot of work to do, and Cyrus departed.

Ben couldn't wait to get the sample under the microscope. As he looked at the slide under different amplifications with low and then more intense light, he was astonished at what he was seeing. The blood sample from Cyrus showed all the characteristics of protection from radiation that would possibly be needed. What was absent in his blood was the cell formation of the mind control agent that the blood of all those, including himself, contained.

The sample from Cyrus was totally void of that feature. This told Ben that, possibly, natural born Bluebloods just might not be under the control of Hendricks. Startled by his phone ringing, Ben almost fumbled the vial that contained the blood sample he had taken from Cyrus. Picking up the receiver, the voice on the other end of the phone was Hendricks.

"Anything unusual?" Hendricks inquired, eagerly awaiting to hear about any monumental discovery by Ben.

"Not a thing. Nothing different at all." Ben expressed with surprising ease. Sticking a needle into his own vein, Ben extracted the blue blood from his own arm. He needed to look at it. Something had to be different in his own blood because, for the first time in over a decade, he had just told a lie to Hendricks Vesper.

CHAPTER 44:
ALLIES

PUTTING HIS TABLET DOWN and pushing it away from him, Cyrus knew he had studied enough of microbiology today. He hated science. When he studied art and literature, time seemed to pass very quickly. He wasn't like his father. There had been many times that he had wondered if he might be more like his mother. Her interests had become his. All he knew was that any more time spent studying what his father wanted from him wasn't going to happen.

Cyrus sat in the lower garden of the first floor of the Palace. A single, white, wrought iron chair was placed next to a matching table and served as the tranquil serenity that he sought when he was most depressed. Pulling out his notebook, he continued writing the poem he was working on. Glancing up from the notebook as he pondered the next stanza of the poem, he spied a young woman just outside the courtyard.

Her dark hair was pulled back into a ponytail that displayed her high cheekbones and enticing deep blue eyes. The woman was tall, but not particularly slender. Cyrus felt her body type was just right. Just what he liked. He had never seen her before. At least not on the Palace grounds. The woman held large pruning shears that she was busy using to sculpt the hedges that adorned the perimeter of the Palace.

Intrigued by her, Cyrus gained enough courage to approach and speak. "Hello, I'm Cyrus Vesper."

The young woman looked up at him, as she was busy pruning the hedges. She stopped just long enough to bluntly reply, "I know who you are."

He wasn't getting the sense that this woman was either impressed or cared who he was. "I don't think I've seen you on the Palace grounds before. Are you new here?" Cyrus responded, although he wasn't sure if he should even try and pursue the conversation.

The woman stopped trimming the hedges and stood upright. Turning towards Cyrus to address his question properly, and respectively, she responded, "I'm filling in for a couple of weeks for my father. He's Alonzo Contreras."

Cyrus smiled at her. He was intrigued by this woman. She infatuated him. Cyrus guessed they were close to the same age. "Is he sick?" Cyrus asked, wanting to tread lightly on this newfound friendship.

"Oh gosh, no. My dad is 'outside', working on building our home," she answered.

"Outside-outside?" Cyrus asked with an astounded look on his face.

For the first time since they had met, the woman smiled at Cyrus. "Yes, outside the spheres. We will be living outside," she responded.

Cyrus' interest had peaked at the explanation of her father's absence. "Have you been outside?"

"I live there now. We have temporary quarters. Dad's working with the team to build us more permanent housing."

Cyrus almost couldn't contain himself. He had a thousand questions to ask her, but he didn't want to scare her off by being too inquisitive. "What's it like? I mean, outside," He asked, hoping his question appeared simple and uninquisitive.

"It's…how should I explain it…bleak," The woman answered his question with complete honesty. "Still, I believe it will be nice someday. You know, not all of us follow your father like he is our God. Some seek freedom on the outside," She added reluctantly, knowing that she might have tread on sacred ground.

He was astonished by her statement. For the first time in his life, Cyrus learned that there was somebody else that felt the same way he did. His intoxication for this woman increased exponentially.

"You mean you've never been outside?" She inquired with some degree of intrigue about how he might answer.

"No, never. I'm hardly allowed outside these grounds, let alone these spheres," Cyrus reluctantly divulged.

"Well, I guess that's the price you pay for being the emperor's son," She giggled as she replied.

Cyrus found her laugh intoxicating. "Yep, I guess that's the price. How long will you be working for your father?"

"Maybe two weeks or so," she answered.

Cyrus was hoping she would be working on the grounds of the Palace for a lot longer. "Do you leave here each day? What I meant to ask is, do you go outside each day when your work is done?"

"Yep, each day. Maybe you should go with me one of these days," the woman replied not expecting that Cyrus would, or could, agree.

Cyrus thought for a moment about her offer. Deep down inside, he wouldn't put it past his father to plant a spy to entice his disobedience. "Hmm, and just how would I accomplish that feat? You probably just suggested that so you can run to my father and tell him what a rebel I am."

She laughed uncontrollably, surprising Cyrus.

"I can get you out of here. Trust me. Nobody pays attention to the clippings I haul out of here every day. You could easily hide inside the pile."

The look in her eyes told Cyrus her offer was in earnest. "Can I see you tomorrow? I want to consider your offer and discuss your plan some more," Cyrus asked.

"As long as you aren't going to turn on me and tattle to your father," She sheepishly responded.

Cyrus returned her previous laugh with equal vigor.

"Hey, what's your name?" Cyrus asked.

"I'm Violet, Violet Contreras."

"Nice to meet you, Violet Contreras," Cyrus responded like a boy at his first school dance.

Violet reached out with the hand that was free from holding pruning shears and touched Cyrus on his arm. The hair on his arm stood straight up and he felt a tingle that he had never experienced before. "Nice to meet you too, Cyrus," Violet replied with a smile that befitted the son of an emperor.

Electric lamps illuminated the campsite of Silver James. Venus had joined her brother, Dyce, Chip, and Blaze for the visit. Zenith and Dyce sat separately from the others who were playing their usual game with Primus. Dyce was whittling a piece of wood that served as kindling for an occasional fire when he addressed Zen with a question that came out of the blue.

"Do you remember your father at all, Zen?"

Glancing up from an ancient copy of Popular Mechanics magazine that Silver had brought with him to his cavern home, Zenith stared into the one green eye and one lavender eye of his friend. "I honestly don't remember him very well. Venus tells me stories about him all the time. She was older when he was killed. She seems to have more anger about his death than I do."

"I was just curious. As for me, I hate Vesper. I just can't seem to forgive him for the way he treats us. Like we're animals. I was wondering if you hated Vesper for what he did. I mean, what he did to your father," Dyce responded as he returned to his wood carving.

In another section of the campsite Zen could hear the laughter of Chip and Blaze as they once again were defeated in the game they played with Primus. Blaze, who was usually practicing combat moves with Tremont, was displaced by Venus tonight. She had discovered that Tremont could harmonize with her as she sang.

What had been a usual solo for his sister had turned into a duet with the bronze hulk. The funny thing about this unlikely duo was that Tremont seemed to enjoy it. Truth be told, his programming had enabled him to be a fairly good singer.

Silver had been sitting back enjoying the company of his visitors when he interrupted their activities to announce, "Cedric, I need to pull you from the fun and frolic to come here and help me."

Excusing himself from his friends, Chip walked over to where Silver was sitting. "What's up?" Chip asked.

"Can you encrypt this message center for me? I need to make sure nobody can track my messages in or out."

Chip scooted a chair next to Silver and replied with the confidence of a gambler with a sure bet. "Of course I can, Silver. All your message centers are encrypted. I'm the master of protection and at the same time the most magnificent hacker in human history!"

Silver chuckled at the comment.

A few moments later, Chip had installed an impregnable firewall on the specific message center. "There ya go, Silver. All safe. Why do you need this message center separate from the main one you use?"

"This center has two special contacts. I'll fill you all in later. For now, let's just say, it's my secret," Silver answered with an air of mystery.

Later that night, after Silver's guest had left for their camps, he sat down at his computer and typed in two message recipients and began typing a message.

I will attend the meeting next Tuesday.
I trust that the Outside location is secure?

Silver sat back in his chair and waited for a reply from Ben Tolmie and Alonzo Contreras.

CHAPTER 45: TASTE OF FREEDOM

FINISHING HIS MORNING MEAL, Cyrus hurriedly picked up his plate and glass to take them into the Palace kitchen to put them in the sink. Pi stood amazed at this display. He had never witnessed Cyrus lifting a finger to pick up or clean anything.

Grabbing his tablet and placing it under his arm, Cyrus moved quickly towards the stairway that would lead him out of the first floor and into the courtyard. "You don't need to follow me today, Pi. I need to concentrate on my studies alone. These are critical pieces to my upcoming tests."

"Very well, Cyrus. I admire your dedication to your studies. I understand that solitude can be a benefit to achieving maximum intellect," Pi responded in a manner that made Cyrus laugh.

Upon reaching the courtyard, Cyrus's heart skipped a beat at the sight of Violet standing over the flowers in the garden. Walking quietly over to her so as not to startle her, Cyrus gently placed a hand on her shoulder. She jumped despite his best efforts.

"I'm so sorry, Violet. I didn't mean to startle you," Cyrus exclaimed, feeling genuinely bad about how their rendezvous had begun.

Gaining her composure, Violet stood up and embraced him.

Her touch was like warm milk and honey.

"I wondered if you would be here today," Violet said.

Wanting to continue the embrace for an eternity and not wanting to push her away, Cyrus looked into her captivating blue eyes and gave her a slight kiss on her lips. "I wouldn't miss this for anything," Cyrus answered in a lovestruck tone.

Not having been annoyed by the display of affection that Cyrus showed, Violet smiled and cautiously asked, "You still a go for departure to the Outside today?"

"Sure am. Just remember, if we're caught, I want you to deny that you knew I was in the vehicle. Nobody will suspect you of knowing anything about my escape attempt. I've been caught before, so they will assume it's just because I'm bad at this escape business," Cyrus pleaded with her.

Not sure if he meant what he said as a joke, Violet gave a slight chuckle. "We had better not talk much longer, just in case the powers-to-be are watching you on camera."

"I wouldn't put it past my father," Cyrus agreed.

Crouching in a fetal position in the bed of Violet's utility cart, Cyrus watched as grass and hedge pruning's were thrown in over the top of him. "Should I throw some manure in on top of this just to discourage any investigation by the Sphere guards?" Violet jokingly asked.

Underneath the debris, Cyrus responded, "That's okay, I think I'll risk it."

"Hey, just trying to help since you're so bad at this escape stuff," Violet nonchalantly responded as she climbed into the driver seat and began the drive to the edge of the Sphere.

As the vehicle that carried Violet and a hidden Cyrus approached the guard station, she whispered their imminent approach to Cyrus. Stopping the cart at the edge of the area where vehicles departing the Sphere were allowed, two bronze guards approached the vehicle.

"Identify yourself and reason for exit," a guard commanded.

"Contreras 1026. Palace gardener. Taking landscape debris away from your lovely Sphere so your master doesn't have to look at it," Violet sarcastically responded.

Not being programmed to understand or engage in sarcasm, the guard responded with a stoic look on his face. "Contreras 1026. You have clearance to exit with the debris."

Violet was alarmed when the other guard that had not spoken began to shuffle his bronze hand among the debris that was covering Cyrus. "You want it? You can have it, big fella. Maybe you guys eat this stuff and I'm taking your midnight snack outside, away from you," Violet offered with even more sarcastic rhetoric than before.

The guard stopped moving his hand through the yard clippings and replied, "HF-2027 does not consume food."

"Suit yourself, big boy!" Violet exclaimed as she drove through the opening in the Sphere, giving Cyrus Vesper his first ever taste of true freedom.

Alonzo Contreras was pleased to see his daughter as the vehicle she was driving pulled up in front of a group of tents that served as dwellings for those that formed the first Bluebloods to venture outside. Climbing out of the vehicle she gave her father a hug.

"Everything go as planned?" Alonzo eagerly asked.

Pointing towards the yard debris in the bed of the vehicle, she motioned towards the pile that was beginning to move. "C'mon, Cyrus. It's safe now. You can come out." Poking his head out of the debris, Cyrus squinted at the brightness of the sun, even though it was nearing nightfall. "Daddy, I'd like you to meet Cyrus Vesper, the emperor's son," Violet offered the introduction like an announcer at a graduation.

Alonzo bounded quickly to the back of the vehicle and extended a hand to assist Cyrus out of the pile of debris. "Nice to meet you, young man. My daughter's told me a lot about you. I'm Alonzo."

Having no previous experience with greetings, Cyrus was unsure just how to respond. "Hello. You knew I was coming?" Cyrus inquired with an element of surprise.

"Heck, boy, it was my idea. Violet told me just how miserable you were living like a prisoner in the Palace." Stunned at the response coming from a Blueblood, Cyrus attempted a slight smile. "You're welcome here, Cyrus. Welcome to the Outside community. And most importantly, welcome to freedom," Alonzo added.

Violet came over to where her father and Cyrus had been talking and took Cyrus by the hand. "C'mon, let's get you cleaned up, it's almost time for supper."

Cyrus stopped Violet from pulling him along and with concern asked, "My father will put everything together and find out you helped me to escape. You can't return to the Palace! I mean it, Violet! What will happen to you now if you get exiled from the Sphere?"

With a gentle touch, Violet placed her hand on Cyrus' cheek. "Don't worry, my father has this all figured out. We won't be returning to the Spheres. We won't have to. Like I told you, not everybody worships your father. Inside or outside."

Cyrus looked deep into her blue eyes. For the first time in his life, he had found something that he could believe in. "Hey, I almost forgot to thank you. What you did at the guard station was amazing."

"That? That was easy. My father told me we're descendants of an entertainer that performed illusions. Apparently, it's in my blood to make people disappear," Violet laughed.

Cyrus had no idea what an illusion was, but he didn't care. The outside invigorated him. He could breathe. With every intake of oxygen he took, he knew that this breath didn't belong to his father.

CHAPTER 46: MISSING

HENDRICKS ENTERED THE LIVING QUARTERS upon returning from his office at the large building that was formerly Spheretech. Looking around the area, he found it eerily quiet. "Pi...Cyrus..." He called out like a master seeking for his dog to come.

Pi entered the room to meet him. "Welcome home, Hendricks," Pi responded.

"Hello, Pi, where is Cyrus?"

"Cyrus is studying in the garden courtyard. He asked not to be disturbed so that he could concentrate on his studies. Shall I go and bring him to you?" Pi obediently asked.

"No, I'll go get him myself." Hendricks answered as he left the living area to go and seek his son. Arriving in the courtyard, he found no sign of his son. Hendricks walked the grounds immediately connected to the courtyard only to discover Cyrus was nowhere to be found. With an air of being perturbed by the absence of his son, Hendricks climbed back up the stairs to confront Pi.

"He's not where you said he would be, Pi. It's your responsibility to know his location!" Hendricks addressed Pi as an angry parent would.

"I understand you're upset, Hendricks. It's also my orders to obey a Vesper, and young Cyrus commanded me to not disturb him today," Pi responded to Hendricks outburst.

Frustrated, Hendricks retrieved his hand-held radio from the table that he had set it upon, and called out to the sentries that guarded the Palace to search for Cyrus. Quickly the guards went into search mode and spread throughout the Palace and the connected grounds.

After an extensive search, they determined that Cyrus was not on the Palace grounds. Hendricks addressed HF-76 who was his Hendricks Force commander to review the camera footage that constantly surveilled the Palace and the grounds.

A short time later, the commander requested Hendricks attendance at the viewing terminal. Watching the displayed footage several times, Hendricks knew exactly where his son had disappeared to.

"Who is this woman?" Hendricks excitedly demanded.

"Contreras 1026," the bronze commander answered.

"Is she an Outsider?" Hendricks asked, despite knowing what the answer would be.

"Confirmed, sir," HF-76 replied.

Hendricks went into a rage.

Angrily pushing the radio to another frequency, Hendricks screamed into the radio for the Sphere force to mobilize for a full-scale deployment to the outside to retrieve his disobedient son and this woman who had deceived him into following her.

CHAPTER 47: APPEARANCES

CYRUS FELT A PEACE with these Bluebloods he had joined on the Outside that he had never felt before. The meal he enjoyed with them was filled with laughter. They genuinely liked being around each other and this was a foreign event to him. Violet gently touched his arm, motioning him to follow her. Her touch always evoked a feeling deep inside him. It was a feeling that he was trying to understand but it was also foreign in his life.

"Come, Cyrus, we're going to a meeting. A meeting of like-minded people," she said, never letting go of his hand as she directed Cyrus away from the supper table and leading him towards the vehicle that had enabled him to escape a future he didn't want any part of.

As they drove away from the Contreras camp, Cyrus was obsessed with what she had just said to him. "What did you mean by your statement of 'like-minded people'?"

"You'll see," she giggled, not revealing any information to her companion. The couple had traveled approximately three miles when they came to an old housing development with several homes, all looking just the same, lined up next to each other and abandoned. These dwellings were commonplace in the area surrounding the Spheres. Violet often wondered what life was like for the people that used to live here. She was curious if some of the Sphere inhabitants, that were now Blueblood, might have lived there. Cyrus was fascinated by the scene. This was beyond his wildest imagination. Violet pulled the vehicle onto a concrete pad that led to an attached space of one of the dwellings.

Cyrus climbed out of the vehicle and slowly turned, taking in all the sights his eyes could absorb. "What is this place?" Cyrus asked in a bewildered manner.

"Dad said it was called a track housing development. Families would occupy these dwellings. Each family had an individual dwelling, but they still called themselves a community," Violet answered.

"Sounds magnificent," was the only way Cyrus could express what he was seeing.

Several vehicles pulled up alongside where Violet had parked with several of the other Outside residents exiting their vehicles. One of the drivers was Alonzo Contreras. "Come on, Cyrus. Join us. You're about to get a history lesson that your father never taught you," Alonzo expressed earnestly while placing his arm on Cyrus's shoulder, directing him towards the dwelling in front of them.

Once inside, Cyrus marveled at the interior. It was almost like several smaller boxes that were inside a larger one. "This was called a home. Inside each home were separate areas where a family lived. Each room had a purpose. One for eating, one for sleeping, etc." Alonzo continued.

"Sort of like the Palace," Cyrus expressed in a matter-of-fact way.

Alonzo let out a big laugh. Patting Cyrus on the back in an affectionate manner, he responded, "Yes, just like your Palace, only smaller." The group that had joined them inside the dwelling gathered in the area that Alonzo called the living room. Cyrus estimated that there were approximately twenty people there, including Violet and himself.

Cyrus stood next to Violet who had placed his hand inside hers. Leaning in and whispering in her ear, Cyrus felt compelled to ask her a question. "Why'd we come all the way out here? I mean, it's a long way to go just to have a meeting. Couldn't we have all just met at the Outside camp?"

Violet looked intently into Cyrus's eyes. "We meet here, away from the camp, because many of us making our way on the Outside don't trust your father to not have spies. Sorry to tell you the truth, Cyrus."

He didn't respond, but what she had just said to him resonated like a drumbeat tapping the same rhythm over and over. Alonzo stepped to the front of the crowd and addressed them. Cyrus could clearly detect that Alonzo had become their leader.

"Thank you, my friends. Thank you for gathering with me tonight. First, I want to introduce you to a guest in our attendance tonight. I'd like you to meet Cyrus Vesper." There was an audible murmur that emitted from those gathered.

"Is it wise to have brought him here?" A voice from the crowd came forward.

Lowering the hand that was pointing towards Cyrus, Alonzo responded to the outcry. "My friends, please trust me. I invited Cyrus to join us here on the Outside, to join us here tonight. He is not our adversary. In fact, he is our ally. He wants the same thing we do. He wants to live in peace and independence. Free to live our own lives away from the control of Hendricks Vesper."

Just as more responses were voiced questioning the motives for having a Vesper join them, a hush came over the crowd. A new figure had joined them for this meeting. A large smile that revealed a silver cap over his front tooth was unmistakable. Accompanying the late arriving guest was a large bronze companion.

Cyrus had no idea who the new guests were, but he was certain that the bronze fellow was not recent issue from his father's home defense (HF) force.

CHAPTER 48:
A MEETING OF LIKE MINDS

PACING BACK AND FORTH in a frantic manner, Hendricks was alerted to the arrival of HF-76. "We have extensively searched the Palace and both Spheres. We haven't detected the whereabouts of Cyrus Vesper."

Hendricks angrily brought both hands to his head. Pulling on his hair, he cried out to the bronze commander, "Take a battalion of your soldiers. Go to the Outside camp immediately! That's where my insolent son will be! Find him! Find him now!"

"Level of force if we meet resistance, sir?" HF-76 asked.

"Kill anybody that stands in your way," Hendricks answered with no thought or concern.

Silver could feel the eyes of the gathered group upon him as he made his way to where Alonzo was standing. Even more than the curious eyes upon him, he sensed their uneasiness regarding the appearance of Tremont.

Alonzo let Silver address the gathered group."Hello, my friends. Many of you here know me. Some of you do not. My name is Silver James. I have been away from you for close to twenty years, but I haven't truly left you in my mind or heart. Truth is, I was forced to leave you and the

Spheres." A gasp echoed around the room. "I will clarify the word 'forced'. Much like all of you gathered here tonight, my conscience, my integrity, my blood, would no longer allow me to follow Hendricks Vesper. Since my decision to leave the Spheres, I have lived with, and among, the underground people that rebelled against forced compliance." Louder than the first communal gasp, the second was much louder.

A woman stepped forward to ask, "Then the underground rebels of Elijah Price live?"

"Not only do they live, but they are also thriving. They have found a different way for humans to exist in harmony and peace." Silver bared his soul to the group.

He watched as the eyes of the gathering darted from one to another in astonishment. A voice called out from behind the crowd, "Where are they living?" Alonzo immediately recognized that the question originated from his daughter, Violet. Silver smiled at the young woman. Recognition of Cyrus Vesper standing next to her delayed his answer.

"Let me just say that my people prefer to keep their sanctuary private for the time being. Perhaps one day they will reveal it to you and those that stand for freedom, Blueblood or not." Silver said knowing that the crowd gathered there had the same questions as Violet.

Alonzo felt the need to retake leadership of the meeting. "Folks, listen to me. Silver represents these people. It is their desire to assist us in our efforts to break free from Vesper. We can never accomplish that feat if we are dependent on the Spheres and Vesper! They can teach us to grow food, have fresh water, they have found a way to do all of this!" Alonzo emphatically appealed to the group.

"And what about this soldier? Where is its allegiance?" Cyrus asked as the murmur of the group hushed at his inquiry.

Silver wasn't shocked by the question. He had always been curious about just how much Cyrus remembered from that fateful night that his mother was killed by the artificial being standing next to him.

"Tremont is a member of my people. They have accepted him as such. He is allegiant to them and all those that are friends with his people. He is self-aware, and his allegiance is with them," Silver revealed as Tremont stared directly at his maker. It wasn't an adversarial stare, but one of acknowledgement that, finally, Silver believed that he had evolved.

Alonzo continued to speak to the crowd. "This is just one of the many meetings we will have to discuss how we, the people of Outside the Spheres, shall move forward."

Cyrus was unable to keep his mouth shut. Moving into the crowd, he slowly spun as he spoke to them. "He…my father…will never allow this. Don't you see? He will come for you with everything he has to stop this rebellion."

"This isn't a rebellion, Cyrus. Just like you, we want to live our own lives. Free from your father's rule," Alonzo interrupted Cyrus.

With a boisterous laugh, Cyrus replied, "Trust me, folks, you don't know my father like I do." As those words echoed around the group, a voice came over Silver's radio. With an excited tone, Silver recognized the voice as Ben Tolmie. "Soldiers on the move! A lot of soldiers! Going directly to the Outside camp! Get the asset out of there. They aren't going to stop until they find him!"

The group panicked and retreated to their vehicles to return to the Outside camp and their families. Violet looked directly at Cyrus with a look that revealed terror. Alonzo and Silver came to where Cyrus had been standing in the middle of the group.

"Cyrus, you need to trust us if you want to live the rest of your life in freedom from your father. You need to come with us now!" Silver spoke in a stern but honest manner.

"What about Violet? I won't leave without Violet!" Cyrus pleaded.

Before Silver could supply an alternative, Tremont grabbed Cyrus around his mid-section and carried him forcefully away from Violet who was left standing next to her father who had grabbed her arm. Violet reached out towards Cyrus but to no avail. Unable to resist the strength of Tremont, Cyrus was tossed into a vehicle driven by Silver. Where they were going, he hadn't a clue.

CHAPTER 49:
TARGET

UNABLE TO REMAIN STANDING UP due to being drunk, Hendricks fell into a chair and poured himself another drink. He was beside himself with fear. Fear of losing his son, fear of losing control, and, mostly, fear that his life was about to change. Perhaps change for the worse.

As the liquor flowed freely into his body, he waited impatiently for word about the discovery and retrieval of his son. Deep down, Hendricks believed this mission would not end well. He sensed that rebellion had begun, not from those he had forsaken so many years ago, but from the same people he had saved from certain doom.

Zenith walked the distance from his camp to where his mother had planted and cultivated this year's corn crop. It was a healthy distance to walk but it also gave him time to think. Several events had occurred that caused him to feel troubled. Troubled and curious. When he had reached the edge of the corn field, he called out for his mother's location.

"I'm over here, Zenith!" Lark loudly announced her location.

"Oh, there you are, mom," Zenith replied and walked to where Lark was working in the field.

"You walked a long way, honey," Lark said as she laid down a cultivation tool that Klous had made for her.

"It's not that far to walk. I enjoy the time to be by myself and think," Zenith responded.

Touching her hand to his cheek, Lark smiled and couldn't resist saying, "You are so much like your father."

Zenith had heard her say that so many times before and it never got old. "The corn's looking good."

"It's doing well. I was definitely worried about how corn would do in this growing environment, so I'm pleasantly pleased. But I don't think checking on my crop is why you came here."

Zenith could never lie to his mother. She was too sharp to not see right through him. "No, mom, it's not to check on the corn. Have you seen Silver or Tremont lately? Me and Venus have been to their camp several times and we can't find them anywhere. We're just concerned about them because they do go out often."

Lark pondered if she should reveal to her son what she knew about the whereabouts of Silver and Tremont.

"Where Silver and Tremont are should be none of your concern, dear. Let's just say that they're doing the work of the Cavern people, just like you and your sister should be doing." Lark answered with a stern but loving tone in her voice.

"Okay, mom. I do need to check on the UV towers. Some of our people have reported that some of the bulbs don't seem to light as they go for their light therapy."

"Thanks, honey. I love you. Give your sister a hug for me when you see her." Lark replied as she picked up the cultivation tool to begin tending to her crop.

"Ewww!" Zenith responded to his mother's request to hug his sister as he began the walk back to his camp. As he walked, his mind was still troubled. He couldn't shake the feeling that something was about to happen.

Tremont zigged-zagged the vehicle that carried Silver, Cyrus, and himself away from the meeting house. He was being extremely cautious and evasive to not leave a trail that could be easily followed.

"So, I have been freed from my father only to be held as a pawn for the enemies of my father. Is that the truth I'm now coming to realize?" Cyrus loudly called out to Silver.

"No, Cyrus! Not our intention. Never our intention! Sure, we want you on our side. We need you to be on our side. We need you to be an obstacle, in the way of what your father could do," Silver answered doing his best to diffuse the anger being shown by Cyrus.

"And what about Violet? Was she part of getting me to you, to be an 'obstacle'?" Cyrus eagerly waited for Silver to answer.

Before revealing an answer to Cyrus, Silver's eyes darted back and forth, searching the surrounding terrain, seeking any signs that would indicate that they were being followed. "No, son, I believe she genuinely likes you. None of us expected Hendricks to react with this much anger. Not against his own people."

Alonzo stopped the vehicle that carried him and his daughter back towards the Outside camp. Off in the distance he could see flashes of light. Flashes that could not be mistaken for anything other than weapons being fired by Hendricks' soldiers. He glanced over at his daughter to see tears streaming down her face and a look of terror in her eyes.

"Hector? Hector? Do you copy?" A voice on the hand-help radio excitedly called out.

Hector pushed the talk button on his radio and replied, "Hector copies. Go ahead."

"Get your defense troops to the Cavern entrance! All hell has broken loose and we're coming in hot! No idea if we were followed," Silver announced with high anxiety.

"Is the asset in tow?" Hector inquired.

"Yes!" Silver answered.

Hector, with a high degree of anticipation, had already assembled his Cavern protection force. He had that uncanny ability to foresee any emergency coming. Grabbing their weapons, he led the force to the Cavern entrance. Lark stood at her camp, which was the closest to the entrance, holding onto Venus and knowing that life was about to change for everybody. She instructed Venus to stay at the camp and as soon as the last of the protection force had passed her, she followed them to the entrance.

Skidding to a stop that propelled the vehicle sideways, Tremont hurriedly exited the vehicle.

"What's going on, Tremont? We're still a mile from the Cavern!" Silver asked as he jumped out of the vehicle with Cyrus following. Scanning the horizon and the skies above them, Tremont would not answer him due to every inch of him being on high alert. A bluff stood before them and Silver escorted Cyrus to crouch down just in front of the slope.

Tremont's blue glowing eyes continued to move back and forth. He pulled his weapon and pointed it directly at Cyrus. *This is the same creature that had killed his mother and now, he was certain, this thing was going to complete its ultimate mission and end his life*, Cyrus thought as he closed his eyes in anticipation of the blast from Tremont's weapon hitting its mark.

Without seeing Tremont readjust the aim of his weapon upwards towards the summit of the bluff, Cyrus heard it fire. He was shocked that he felt no pain. In fact, the blast of the weapon failed to even hit him. Slowly opening his eyes, and with his arms folded over his head, Cyrus witnessed the debris of a large drone falling to the ground.

Tremont's aim had not been intended to produce the death of Cyrus Vesper. The aim had been to bring down a drone. As the drone burned from the blast, Tremont gathered his companions to return to the vehicle. "We must hurry! Vesper will know we were here. We must get to the Cavern!" Tremont commanded.

CHAPTER 50: DELIVERANCE

FEARING FOR HIS FAMILY, but not wishing to endanger Violet, all Alonzo could do was to keep his daughter a safe distance away from the Outside camp. In what seemed like an eternity to him, he waited for the attack from Vesper's force to subside. Once he was certain that the onslaught had ended, he slowly drove the vehicle towards the camp.

Upon arriving at the camp, he and Violet were greeted with cries of pain. He witnessed several of his fellow Bluebloods lying on the ground writhing in pain, or worse, possibly dead. He wondered just how a man he once respected and followed to the ends of the earth, which is where they now lived, could do this. Alonzo felt remorse that his plan had produced this.

Violet ran through the smoke created by the fires that had been started from the blasts of the soldiers' weapons to embrace her mother. Teja Contreras would not let her daughter go. Sobbing, she looked to see Alonzo approaching them. Mother, father, and daughter came together to embrace each other and rejoice that they had survived.

"Where is Tony?" Violet exasperatingly called out.

"Your brother is fine. He's with your aunt," Teja answered. Alonzo breathed a sigh of relief upon hearing this news.

"What about Cyrus? Did the soldiers find you at the meeting place?" Teja asked with concern and curiosity.

"Our person inside the Spheres tipped us off about the soldiers coming. Cyrus was placed in the hands of our allies at the meeting. They have far better ability to protect him than we do," Alonzo answered.

"Price's rebels?" Teja questioned. Alonzo nodded.

The bronze commander of Hendrick's force marched into the room where Hendricks reclined, half panicked and fully inebriated.

"Report!" Hendricks demanded with spittle spewing from his mouth, intermixed with his words.

"No sign of Cyrus, sir."

Hendricks angrily attempted to stumble to his feet although it was a futile effort. He was in no condition to stand. "My people? Were they resistant to the search?"

"Seventeen dead. Many more injured," HF-76 replied.

Hendricks sank further into the chair that had harbored his labored existence. The sheer fact that those that had gone outside the Spheres resisted at all told him that his science had begun to fail. At this moment, his thoughts couldn't help but turn towards Ben Tolmie and the fact that, perhaps, his only ally had betrayed him.

His anger over the events of the evening began to subside and his cunning, plotting personality returned. "Well then, HF-76, I suggest you do whatever is necessary to find my son alive and return him to me or I will retire you to never-never land."

Not having a clue where never-never land might be, HF-76 ignored that outburst from his leader and spoke, "Our drones picked up several vehicles departing an area several miles from the Outside camp just prior to our invasion. All the vehicles moved towards the camp, with the exception of one."

Hendricks suddenly had a moment of clarity from the alcohol-induced stupor he was in. "Did a drone follow that vehicle?"

"Yes, sir. Our drone followed that vehicle for several miles until it stopped."

"And..." Hendricks pleaded.

Producing a small tablet from a compartment in his artificial body, HF-76 pushed the button that allowed camera footage from the drone to play. Hendricks focused intently on the video playing on the screen. His expression turned from extreme focus to despair. Shortly before the video went dark, Hendricks' worst nightmare had come true. The drone captured three figures as it scanned the area. The traitor Tremont, Silver James, and his son, Cyrus.

"Where was this taken?" Hendricks angrily demanded.

"It was taken near the excavation holes created for the underground housing of those that refused the injection, sir. You ordered those holes to be abandoned many years ago with no additional housing built." HF-76 answered in a true soldier's tone.

"You don't need to remind me! I know what I ordered!" Hendricks blurted out at the A.I.

Hendricks paused.

"Find me one of my people that worked that excavation. Bring him to me," Hendricks commanded.

HF-76 turned from Hendricks and retreated from the room to go and carry out his orders. Hendricks slouched and poured himself another drink. As the liquor did its job, his buzz returned. "So, Mr. Price. Your rebellion from so many years ago continues! Now you have my son. Well, you might have taken my beloved Antonetta, but taking my son will be the last thing you will do. I will find you, and all your traitors will pay!"

Zenith stood with Venus as Tremont, Silver James, Cyrus, and his mother walked by them. He had no idea who the new person was that had been brought into their home and sanctuary.

"Who is that?" Zenith quizzed his sister.

"I have no idea," she answered in earnest.

As Blaze, Cedrick (Chip), and Dyce joined them, Hector strode by just ahead of his defense force. It bothered Zenith that Hector was shaking his head in disapproval of what was occurring. Zenith needed to know exactly what was happening. He hoped his mother would divulge the roots of all this chaos. The group of friends retreated to the Price camp to impatiently wait for Lark to come home and provide some answers.

Hendricks, who had fallen into an alcohol-induced sleep, was fitfully awoken by HF-76. "I have brought you the person you requested." With drool running down the side of his mouth, Hendricks looked up to find HF-76 standing at attention with a short, disheveled character.

Perturbed by the sudden appearance of his commander and the man, Hendricks screamed for Pi. Arriving on the scene, Pi joined the group.

"How is it that you let people into my home without alerting me, Pi?" Hendricks addressed his servant with indignity.

"I requested that your soldier wait until I alerted you, sir. He pushed me to the side and repugnantly ignored my request."

Hendricks glared at his commander with a look that HF-76 was unaccustomed to. "In the future HF-76, you will obey Pi's requests of you. He is more of a soldier than you can ever hope to be!"

"Copy that, sir," HF-76 complied, despite processing an order that was not pleasant to him.

Turning his attention towards the man that HF-76 had brought to him, Hendricks attempted to regain his composure. "Hello, friend, what is your name?"

The short man with long, stringy hair, answered, "My name is Brett, sir."

"Well, Brett, am I to understand you were part of the excavation crew that dug the holes we were going to place the housing tubes into years ago?"

Hesitantly, the man replied, "Yes, sir. In fact, I was the lead man."

"Excellent, Brett! Excellent! So, my friend, tell me what you recall about those holes. I mean...like was there anything unusual or different about them?" Hendricks asked as if they were long-lost friends.

Brett could not look Hendricks in the eyes. He was intimidated by him. He finally developed the courage to reply to the question. "Well...hole number sixteen...when we were excavating it, we came upon a rock formation that had been buried. It appeared to have a cave-like entrance. I was going to report it as a potential problem to investigate, but then the placement of the housing tubes was cancelled. I just let it be."

Hendricks smiled an eerie smile. If Brett hadn't already been uncomfortable from this meeting, that smile would have certainly made him feel that way.

"Well, Brett, I'm glad you remembered where you encountered this, as you called it, this cave. HF-76, you can depart from us now. I'd like to pour Brett here a drink and thank him for coming." With that command, HF-76 left the room. Hendricks requested Brett to take a seat while he went and fetched another glass for his visitor.

Brett sat and looked around the room admiring its opulence. He smiled at Hendricks as he returned to the room, but his smile quickly turned to fear. Hendricks didn't return with a glass for his companion. Instead, Hendricks raised his right arm and pointed a 9-millimeter pistol directly at his head. With a flash emitting from the barrel of the gun, Brett wouldn't be returning to his family ever again.

CHAPTER 51:
LIKE FATHER, LIKE SON

NOT MANY WORDS WERE SHARED between Zenith, Venus, and their friends as they sat solemnly waiting for Lark to return to the camp. After what seemed like an eternity, Lark finally appeared back home. Eager to learn all the details about their new visitor, Lark quickly diffused their curiosity and sent Chip, Dyce, and Blaze back to their respective camps.

Reluctantly, the three boys departed and left Lark and her children alone. "C'mon, mom, you need to tell us just who this Blueblood is," Venus pleaded. Lark stared sympathetically at her daughter but wouldn't answer her.

Zenith decided not to press his mother about the events of the day. Having recognized this trait as being the same as Elijah would use, Lark came to him when he was alone. "When I wouldn't answer your sister earlier, you didn't drill me like she did. My dearest Zenith, I'm curious why not?"

Staring out beyond the confines of their camp, Zenith answered his mother's question. "I'll find out eventually, mom. Secrets inside these cavern walls don't stay secret very long."

Lark looked down at the cavern floor of their camp and hesitated for a moment. "He's Cyrus Vesper. Son of Hendricks."

Showing no emotion at his mother's revelation, Zenith replied, "So then, have we taken him prisoner? Will he be used as leverage for the future?"

"He isn't a prisoner, Zen. He is a human being just like you and me. We have offered him sanctuary. We don't believe he has any more love for his father than we do," Lark passionately explained.

Zenith turned to face his mother for the first time since they had started this conversation. "He is a Vesper, mom. He is Blueblood. In my book, that is two strikes against his character," Zen replied with the full extent of his feelings being exposed. "Where are we keeping him?" Zenith questioned.

"At Silver's camp. Tremont is standing watch," Lark revealed.

"I guess I'll go to bed now, mom." Kissing his mother on her cheek, Zenith left to go to his bunk. Sleep wouldn't come. He had never really known his father, but Venus had. Crawling from his bunk, he gingerly walked towards where Venus slept so as not to wake his mother. Zen was surprised to see his sister was still awake.

"I see you can't sleep either," Venus said.

"Did you know Hendricks Vesper has a son?" Zenith inquired.

"Nope, and I don't care," Venus responded with an air of seeming upset.

Zenith was troubled by his sister's comment. "What exactly do you mean by that statement, dear sister?"

With no emotion at all, Venus answered her brother's question. "A Vesper, is a Vesper, is a Vesper. In my opinion, the only good Vesper, is a dead Vesper." It became apparent to Zenith that he and his sister were on the same side.

HF-76 acknowledged the command he received. He was to lead a battalion of his soldiers to the coordinates he was given. His mission was to arrive at excavation hole number 16, surround the location, find the cave entrance, and destroy whoever, or whatever, was inside it. They were not to harm Cyrus Vesper, instead, they were to extract him and return him to the Palace.

With that command, HF-76 looked out over the battalion of bronze soldiers that were gathered. Standing in perfect rows, ready to march to their destination, the commander transmitted the orders to each of his soldiers. A large gap in the Sphere was opened and Hendrick's Force marched out of the Sphere in perfect synchronization.

Zenith could not rest and after sneaking out of his camp and quietly waking up his friend, Dyce, they went to do the same for Chip and Blaze. Without realizing that they were being followed, they made their way to Silver James' camp. Stopping just out of earshot, they gathered near the cavern lake that was close to where Silver had made his camp.

"I just can't make sense of why they brought him here. It just makes no sense," Blaze kept repeating over and over. Zenith crouched near the lake shore and tossed a small pebble into the water. His friends could tell he was deep in thought. Chip almost gave away the impromptu meeting of the group when he screamed from being startled by the sudden appearance of a figure.

"Venus? What the heck are you doing here?" Zenith scolded her.

"Since when do you sneak out of the camp and not invite me, brother?"

Glancing around their immediate position to see if anybody had been alerted to their presence, Zenith was satisfied that Chip's outburst had not summoned anyone to check out the noise. "We need to be extremely quiet if we're going to approach Silver's camp. We need to know what's going on with this Vesper that has invaded our sanctuary."

Venus stepped forward, suggesting that she had the best chance to gain some intelligence on the situation and could report back to the boys. "I'm the nimblest. All you guys are clumsy, and Chip will probably just scream again if he gets startled."

Zenith couldn't help but give a short chuckle at her statement. "Okay, sis. You go up there, but don't linger. Just get a lay of the land and come back here." With the group all agreeing to this plan, Venus began her short trek from the lake to Silver's camp. Stealthily, she practically crawled on all fours. Inside the camp, she could see several men gathered around conversing about the arrival of their guest.

Suddenly, the talking stopped amongst the men gathered there. She caught a glimpse of Cyrus when he stood up. All eyes in the camp had turned to focus on Tremont. With blue eyes glowing, they were listening intently to a radio message being broadcast. It was unexpected by Hendricks Vesper that since Tremont was the original soldier created, he would still possess the ability to intercept all commands relayed to Hendricks' current soldiers.

The men, including Cyrus Vesper, stood in disbelief of the orders being broadcast. Realizing that their location had been discovered and Hendricks had ordered all hell to reign down on the Cavern people, Silver said with exasperation, "This isn't what we wanted!"

Hector, who was in attendance, motioned at Tremont. "You ready, big guy? We're going to need your firepower if we're going to survive this onslaught."

Tremont, in his usual stoic manner, replied, "The rest of you can stay home and go to bed. I got this!" Not being a good time for humor, a trait that Tremont had only just acquired, his statement still seemed to bring a sense of relief to everybody gathered. Silver called out to the men who had gathered at his camp to make haste and follow him and Hector to assemble the rest of the Cavern defense force.

"What about me?" Cyrus questioned.

Silver looked at him as though he were a long-lost brother and answered, "Please, just stay here. I'm going to let Lark know what's going on. She'll come and get you and take you to a safe place." Cyrus reluctantly agreed, although he didn't have much choice. It seemed the same, whether here in the Cavern or back in his father's control.

Venus was beside herself with all she had just seen and heard. Frantically retreating to where her companions eagerly awaited news about what she had learned, she met the boys back at the shore of the lake. She had a difficult time explaining what she knew. Zenith had to tell her to stop and take a deep breath.

At last, she was able to slow her speech well enough to fill the boys in on the situation. "I wonder what Silver meant by mom would come and move him to a safe place?" Zenith expressed to his companions with a look of confusion on his face.

"Have any of us ever seen how deep this cavern goes?" Dyce asked.

Dumbfounded by his question, none of them could answer. "No matter how far she could take him into the cavern, if Hendricks' soldiers breach our home, they will eventually find him and the rest of us will probably all be dead," Zenith replied with an honesty that none of them could deny.

"Perhaps we should take him. Take him somewhere that Vesper won't find him. Use him as bait to stop any attack," Venus offered.

"You mean like leverage?" Zenith said, remembering the very words he had spoken earlier to his mother. "But where and how?"

Dyce stepped forward to assist his best friend. "I think I know of such a place!"

"Here in the cavern? What good will that do?" Zenith asked.

Dyce smiled a broad smile as he responded, "Oh, it's not here in the cavern. But it will do just fine," he answered with a sinister appeal in his voice.

CHAPTER 52:
THE CHAMBER

CYRUS PACED AROUND SILVER'S CAMP. He couldn't help but wonder about Violet. Was she safe, or did his father eliminate her just as he had done with so many of what he called 'traitors'? He longed to see her again. She was better at conflict than he was, and he needed her, to give him a plan to relieve the tension he was so desperately experiencing.

He didn't want to sit, but fatigue was beginning to overtake him. It had been a long and arduous day. He closed his eyes for a moment, leaning his head back and resting it on the crest of the chair. Without warning, he found an arm wrapped tightly around his neck. Struggling for a moment, he decided that it only exacerbated his ability to draw breaths of oxygen into his lungs.

"Somebody grab his legs!" Blaze yelled out to the group that had intruded into Silver's camp. Dyce quickly secured Cyrus' legs and after drawing a rope that was hung on his arm, he began to tie and secure Cyrus. Venus took some electrical wire that Silver had left lying near Primus and began securing Cyrus' arms and hands behind his back.

This is how it ends for me, was the only thought that would enter Cyrus's mind. With only a dim amount of light, Cyrus could only see shadows cast by his assailants. The tallest of the group stood in front of him demanding, "Is he secure?"

Venus answered, "He ain't goin' nowhere."

"Okay, let's pick him up and get him into Silver's vehicle. Put the blindfold on him!" Zenith commanded.

Hector surveyed the excavation hole outside the Cavern entrance. "I need fifteen launchers on the ridge! All the automatic rifles positioned on the bluff above the opening. Tremont, you go where you believe it's the best position for you!" Hector yelled his commands. Silver was busy on a secure radio frequency speaking with Ben Tolmie. Ben's voice chirped over the radio's speaker.

"They'll be there soon. Is everything ready?" Ben excitedly inquired.

"I hope so, Ben. I would've liked to test Tremont's new weapon, but we're going to find out if it works soon enough."

"Keep this line open. I'm laying low right now. I believe Hendricks is suspicious of me. I'll do my best to keep you posted," Ben's voice echoed with a degree of distress.

Unaware that a vehicle that carried Zenith, Venus, Chip, Blaze, and Dyce, along with their kidnapped victim, Cyrus, had slipped by him, Silver retreated to the Cavern to set Lark's part in the impending battle into motion.

"I think we got out unnoticed. With all the commotion, I don't think anybody saw us," Dyce offered to the group.

Blaze pointed just due north from their current location. "It should be about a mile straight ahead."

"I've never been there. I hope you're right, Dyce, and this will be a secure place to hold our leverage," Zenith acknowledged. After a short time, the vehicle came to a stop at a rusted outcrop of a building. Stepping out of the vehicle, Zenith was astonished to see at least fifty of these same buildings scattered and jutting out from the barren landscape. "What are these?" Zenith half whispered to himself and half wanting his companions to hear him.

"These are the entrances to the underground city. Each of these is a portal to an underground chamber that used to house our parents. These chambers were the epitome of Hendricks' hatred for our parents," Dyce explained with a degree of disgust.

"Into one of these chambers, is that where we're taking him?" Venus reluctantly asked.

"Sure, what place would be more befitting for a child of Vesper. He held our parents captive in this squalor," Blaze added his two-cents worth in reply.

Cyrus could feel his heart beating very fast. Whatever intentions these kidnappers might have for him, he understood that they held no value for his life. *Perhaps father was right. All they desire is my blood to be spilled,* he thought to himself.

Dyce pointed at the building directly in front of them. "This one. This is where we're going. The chamber below is where my parents used to live. Dad showed it to me once and I come here every now and then. When I need time to think and be alone."

Pushing Cyrus, whose legs had now been freed, Blaze grabbed the handle on the rusted door that would allow them to enter the stairway and descend to the hallway that would lead to the living chamber. Thanks to Venus's quick thinking, they held flashlights she had grabbed from Silver's camp during the kidnapping. With light beaming directly ahead of them, there was an eerie feeling among the group.

A musty and unpleasant smell permeated their nostrils. Even though Dyce had visited this chamber often, he hadn't spent any time doing housekeeping. "Holy cow, Dyce, this place is disgusting!" Venus offered her opinion without reserve.

"Hang on, it gets worse," Dyce laughed. Fumbling to direct the beam of his flashlight into what used to serve as the chamber kitchen, Dyce found a fuse box. Switching on the main power, lights inside the chamber began to flicker. "Chip connected the power to some of the solar panels that weren't taken from here for the Cavern, and so, voila, power."

"Yeah, and I promised I would never come back here again and, voila, here I am again," Chip admitted to the group. His attempt at humor was able to cut the tension in the room.

Cyrus struggled through the blindness and disorientation, and finally opened his mouth to speak. "Is this where you're going to murder me?" He could hear Zenith's footsteps follow his voice. "Just how you killed my mother. Your kind only wishes for blood."

Zenith grabbed Cyrus by the shirt. Towering over him, he dragged him to a dust-infested chair, making him sit. He leaned over Cyrus; the feeling of Zenith's presence and his hot breath made him gulp.

"No," Zenith said with a power filled smirk radiating off him, Cyrus could hear it in his voice. "No, Cyrus Vesper, unlike dear ol' dad, your blood is too valuable to spill."

Cyrus took in a shaky breath. In an attempt to keep his composure, he refrained from returning a comment. "If you want to stay alive," Zenith commented while backing away, "Your father is going to have to make a decision."

"What's the plan now, Zenith?" Venus questioned her brother.

Chip interrupted Zenith's answer. "I managed to link the camera to all the screens in Sphere1 & 2. In about 15 minutes, pretty boy here is going to go *live*."

Cyrus had a burning curiosity about what they were going to force him to say. *Should he resist them?* The question burrowed deep inside his thoughts. He couldn't reconcile if his father would truly sacrifice his power for him.

Silver was beside himself. He fumbled among his personal belongings to try and discover exactly what had been taken. "Where would Cyrus go? He hasn't any idea how to navigate this cavern!" Lark interjected.

Primus, who had sat quietly until this moment, spoke. "Vesper did not leave on his own accord."

Astounded by what the talking head had just said, Silver and Lark moved closer to Primus to interrogate him. "Tell us, Primus, what do you know about where Cyrus has gone?" Silver drilled his creation for information.

With his eyes clicking in animated motion, Primus answered the inquiry. "The young ones. Your offspring, Zenith, and his sister, along with the others, have taken the young Vesper." Lark stood in disbelief at the revelation.

"Did they say where they were taking him?" Silver excitedly prodded the talking head for information. "They bound him, took a video camera, flashlights and your laptop, Silver. Where they were taking him, they didn't reveal." Primus answered.

Quickly running to the outside of his camp, Silver realized his vehicle was gone.

Lark joined him.

"I don't think they're in the cavern any longer," Silver said.

Memories of Elijah Price invaded Lark's mind. She recognized what was happening. Her son, Zenith, carried the same traits as her beloved husband. The need to lead, to take control without including her in his thoughts or plans, had come to fruition. Deep down she always knew this day would come. She mourned the moment. She could not bear to lose him, or his sister, and fear engulfed every inch of her body.

Hendricks sat reviewing the multiple camera views of his force marching upon what had been the mysterious stronghold of those who hadn't subjugated themselves to him and his genius. He reached for the bottle to pour himself a drink. With his hand grasping the bottle, he slowly released it without lifting it from the table.

Years of anguish and grief were about to come to an end. He would be reunited with Cyrus and this time it would be different. He would be a better father now that his darling Antonetta had been avenged. He needed his wits about him, and the alcohol would only get in the way.

Just a half mile south of the underground city, the battalion of artificial soldiers moved towards the Cavern. In the chamber below, Zenith and his companions hurried to prepare their own plan. A plan that would hopefully destroy the man that they could never follow.

CHAPTER 53:
RECONNING

As Chip finished the last elements that would allow the kidnappers to take control of the Sphere's video system, Venus stood in front of Cyrus intently studying him, bending at her torso to get a closer look. "Not much to look at, is he?" Venus said to the group, not clarifying if it was a statement or a question.

Cyrus could detect that one of his assailants was female. The others' voices were distinctly male, but this voice was distinctly female. He refused to let himself slip to her level and chose not to respond to the derogatory statement.

"We close, Chip?" Zenith questioned.

"Five more minutes, Zen." Chip answered.

Needing to decide just what action he would take, Cyrus needed to know exactly what these would-be rebels had planned. Or worse, what they were capable of. He decided that the voice, the one they called Zen, was the leader. "What do you hope to accomplish by broadcasting to my people?" Cyrus blurted out in the direction of Zenith.

Laughing at his question, Zenith determined there would be no harm done by answering Cyrus.

"What we hope to accomplish? Well, let me tell you, Vesper. Your dear ol' dad needs to back off and let us non-Bluebloods live our lives in peace. He agrees to do that, deactivates his bronze army, he gets his beloved son back!"

Cyrus was amused at just how naïve Zenith was. "What makes you believe he will honor that agreement, even if your plan works?" Cyrus responded like a lawyer cross examining a witness on the stand.

It took a few minutes for Zenith to say anything. Before he could answer Cyrus's question, Venus interrupted, "We don't. Or at least I don't. Your father never honored anything that doesn't serve his only reason for living, his power."

Cyrus pondered Venus's words. He would never admit it to her, but he believed that what she had just said was the truth. "Then why do this? I know you'll never listen to me, but maybe we aren't that far apart on what we both want," Cyrus professed.

"What we both want?" Venus expressed her question with a heavy dose of anger. "What I want is to put a bullet in the brain of Hendricks Vesper. An eye for an eye. Your father killed my dad. I want to end the life of Hendricks Vesper!"

Zenith stepped into the conversation between Cyrus and his sister. "Enough, Venus! Trying to reason with a Vesper is a futile effort."

"And just how do you plan on ever getting close enough to my father to kill him?" Cyrus asked in earnest.

Zenith pulled the back of Cyrus's hair in a jerking action forcing the front two legs of the chair that Cyrus was sitting on to raise slightly off the ground. The action frightened Cyrus into believing that violence against him was not off the table with any of these people. "I don't know, Vesper. Instead of trying to kill him in his Palace, we'll force him away from his protection. I don't know...like maybe here!" Zenith callously replied.

Letting go of Cyrus's hair, the chair returned to a stable position with a thud. "You rebels tried to kill my father in his Palace once before. I was there. It was a long time ago, but I still have some memories of it. I think it would be wise on your part to try another plan. That plan, long ago, lead to the death of my mother and the rebel leader," Cyrus spoke with a calmness that he hoped would defuse the anger that was prevalent in this underground jail.

His words didn't help.

"That rebel leader was my father, Elijah Price," Zenith exposed the truth to his prisoner.

"Mine too," Venus piped in.

It now made some sense. Two of his kidnappers were the children of Elijah Price. This was revenge against his father. Pure and simple, revenge. Cyrus remained quiet upon the revelation. Zenith returned to face a blindfolded Cyrus. Reaching around the back of Cyrus's head, he removed the blindfold. Even though the room was dimly lit, Cyrus struggled to have his eyesight return to normal. Squinting, he couldn't help but glance around the chamber that he was being held captive in.

Cyrus could make out five blurry figures. Immediately, he knew the tallest of the figures was Zenith. "We're ready to go with the video, Zen," Chip announced.

"Okay, get our boy here in focus for the camera. We will hack the system in two minutes," Zen proclaimed.

Cyrus's eyes began to focus. With his sight returning, he could make out the features of his captors. It startled Cyrus to have so many different colors of eyes staring intently at him. None of those piercing eyes were blue.

He felt the need to try and reach out to his captors, stop their misguided plan to stop his father. "You know, it was your father that fired the first shot," Cyrus said.

Ignoring that statement by Cyrus, Zenith called out to the others, "One minute-one minute to showtime."

Venus stepped up to Zenith and placed one palm on her brother's chest. "Just what did he mean by that?" she asked with curiosity.

"What difference does it make, Venus?" Zen responded with a slight degree of irritation that she had interrupted his thoughts.

"It makes a difference to me. What does he know?" Venus answered.

Cyrus determined that if he was going to try and avert their plans, now was the time. "It was the artificials! Tremont killed my mother. Our servant, Pi, killed your father." Looking past Venus, Zenith's and Cyrus' eyes met.

"It changes nothing." Grabbing Venus by her shoulders to lightly push her out of the way, Zenith walked directly over to where Cyrus was sitting. "Your father is still a murderer. No matter who fired the first shot." Zenith pointed directly at his friend Blaze. "I suppose your father told all of you Bluebloods that his father, along with a gang from the underground city, started all of this a long time ago."

Pi had told Cyrus exactly that story. He understood his father lied about many things, to many people. He also understood that sometimes leaders must lie to protect their people. "If you are considered evil, evil is what you eventually become," Cyrus muttered.

"False!" Zenith shot back, his neck turning towards Cyrus. "You are here with us tonight because I considered you an accomplice to murder. Just like your father, maybe you didn't pull the trigger, but you stood silent against the one who ordered it."

Cyrus lowered his chin towards the floor. He wasn't sure why, at this moment, he pondered just how disgusting this place was that he was being held captive. The musty smell was akin to the time Pi had taken him on an excursion to the underground tunnels beneath the Spheres. "Perhaps my father wanted to be a savior. All your kind wanted was his head on a silver platter," Cyrus blurted out. He gulped knowing that his remark had struck a bad chord with his captor.

Zenith didn't immediately react as Cyrus believed he would. Instead, Zenith turned his back to him and instructed Chip to get ready to hack the Sphere video broadcast system. Then he responded with a statement without turning to face Cyrus.

"It's a matter of perspective," Zen proclaimed.

Chip motioned Dyce to prepare the camera to focus on Zenith's face before eventually turning it towards Cyrus to expose to Hendricks that his son was, indeed, being held captive. "We are going live in ten seconds-ten-nine-eight-," suddenly, the handheld radio that Venus had carried with her from the beginning of this impromptu mission began to chirp. A slightly garbled female voice came over the speaker of the radio.

Zen, Venus, are you there? Answer me, please, it's your mother!"

Lark held the radio tightly and once again pressed the speak button repeating her command, pleading for her children to answer. On the other end, Venus looked questioningly at her brother. "What should I do?" she asked, seeking guidance.

Stopping the countdown, Zenith called out to his sister, "Answer her."

"Mom, this is Venus."

"Venus! Thank God! Where are you?" Lark pleaded.

"We're safe, mom. I can't tell you where we are."

"Is Zenith there?"

"Yes, he's here."

"Hand him the radio, I must speak with him," Lark pleaded. Venus walked over to Zenith and handed him the radio. He held it like it contained a disease. Bringing the radio to his mouth, he pressed the button to speak, "Mom, this is Zen."

Lark closed her eyes as she prepared to deliver her only shot at stopping whatever plan her son and daughter had cooked up. "Listen, son. I know you have Cyrus Vesper. I know you, son. You are your father's son, but whatever you have decided to do today, stop! You need to trust me. Cyrus Vesper is on our side. He wants our freedom. Not only for us, but for the Bluebloods also. Nothing good will come out of what you have planned. We have this under control! Soon, this will all be over."

The group took turns glancing at each other upon hearing Lark's statement. Zenith looked over at Cyrus who sat quietly and stoically. "Okay, mom, we'll stand down. I need to know what's going to happen." Zenith demanded. Waiting for his mom to answer his question, the radio echoed with what Zenith detected was a rapid succession of explosions. No response came from his mother's radio as the musty smelling chamber grew deathly silent.

CHAPTER 54:
COMMON GROUND

LARK PICKED HERSELF UP OFF THE GROUND of the campsite. The percussion of the explosions had shaken the cavern, knocking her off her feet. She frantically searched for where the radio had landed after she had lost her grip on it. She found it lying under a chair that sat next to her personal library shelves. The antenna had broken off and the power indicator wasn't lit to show it was operational. Lark could only hope her plea to Zenith would be honored.

Her mind could not help conjuring the memories of just how much her beloved husband would often ignore her pleas. This caused her much angst knowing just how much Zenith was like his father.

"They're approaching the edge of the excavation! The first wave will be visible any time now!" One of the cavern commanders screamed out to the defense that was positioned around the perimeter of the area. If successfully breached, Vesper's army would have a straight shot to the cavern entrance and freedom for the Cavern dwellers would be over.

Silver frantically moved in front of Tremont and cried out," "This is it, my friend. Now or never! You don't have to do this. You don't have to fire your weapon upon your own kind." Silver offered *the out*, knowing full well he needed his creation to choose to save his home and the homes of the humans that inhabited the Cavern.

Without taking his artificial eyes off the horizon of the excavation rim, Tremont began marching forward towards the rim. Turning his upper torso back to face Silver, he responded to the option he had been offered. "These soldiers that approach our cathedral are not *my* kind. They answer to an authority I do not. I am an aware being. I answer only to myself."

Silver smiled at Tremont's words.

"Take care of that annoying head you keep in your quarters. He is my friend and needs protection," Tremont requested as he continued his march towards his destiny as an aware being. Silver witnessed a weapon that was produced from Tremont's right arm. It glowed with an iridescent blue color.

It wasn't as large of a weapon as it might have been for the power it was thought to possess, but if all his research and the contributions provided by his friends, Elijah Price and Ben Tolmie were correct, Silver believed that the reign of Hendricks Vesper might be over.

Lark sat down in the chair she had discovered the radio under. She was tired and she was scared, just like the night that she and Elijah had met, when he had come to her rescue. It had been many years now without him. She longed for him to come and rescue her now, to take over and let her rest. She tilted her head back to relieve the tension in her neck. A stream of tears had formed in her eyes and were running down her cheeks.

She reached her hand up to wipe the tears from her eyes when she noticed a small, leather-bound book lying on the floor. Recognizing it as Elijah's journal, which she had placed on her library shelf, she realized it must have fallen during the barrage of explosives fired by Vesper's army.

She picked up the journal which had landed open. Caressing the pages as if they might somehow speak to her, Lark read the passage that appeared on the open page.

OBSERVATION: Having witnessed the failure of the last series of panels at the site of Sphere3, it has become a suspicion of mine what might be causing these failures. The temperature setting on the cold extrusion is correct at 33 degrees, but more likely the failures of these panels occur when they reach the outside. I'm not sure what might be causing this, and I will consult with Silver James in the morning.

My thoughts are that the outside temperatures are beginning to cool ever so slightly. Once the panels are exposed to the outside temperature, they must heat up to 117 degrees Fahrenheit to grow and bond. I don't believe the outside temperatures are hitting that high, thus, the panels are failing.

Lark had never bothered to read her husband's journal before. This notation could possibly explain why no other spheres had been constructed. It wasn't hot enough anymore! She laughed. "Well, well, Hendricks Vesper. The mighty genius behind the Sphere technology and the blue injection, that locked my husband out and sentenced our people to extinction. All along, Elijah had the answer. A simple extrusion specialist had *your* answer!"

Tremont walked up and reached the rim of the excavation hole that contained the cavern entrance inside it. Scanning the area, he used his advanced eyesight to recognize that three columns of bronze soldiers were approaching less than one hundred yards away. With blaster weapons raised and poised to administer more ballistic power than could possibly be defended, he raised the arm with the glowing blue weapon upward and extended the weapon outward.

Zenith looked puzzled as he turned to face Dyce and Venus, who was now standing next to Dyce and reacting to her brother's confused gaze. "What do we do now? Mom was emphatic that we stop whatever we were planning," Venus pleaded.

"I don't know. I'm as confused as all of you by my mom's statement that 'we have this under control'." Zenith replied. "What do they have under control?" The thought echoed in Zenith's mind over and over.

Chip chimed in to advise everybody that they had hacked into the Sphere's video system. "Not sure how long we can remain inside the system before they recognize we've gained access. If we're going to do something, we'd better do it soon!" Just then, the monitor began to display a flickering motion. A few seconds later, an image appeared on the monitor, displaying the face of none other than Hendricks Vesper.

With an eerie smile, Hendricks began to calmly speak. "Greetings to you, my un-loyal subjects. I admire your courageous efforts to infiltrate my video system. Although quite naïve of you to discount our security systems and our ability to thwart your attempt," Hendricks spoke with an arrogance that was part of his typical persona.

"Truth be told, and I'm all about telling the truth, I let you in to my system to make it easier to get a message to you, my precious rebels."

Zen had to let out a slight smirk at Hendricks' statement. "He wouldn't know the truth if it stabbed him in the neck," he mumbled quietly.

Hendricks continued the impromptu meeting, "First, I wish to see the face of my adversary. I assume you have a camera system that will allow that," Hendricks arrogantly inquired. Zenith signaled the approval to his friend, Dyce, to turn on the camera and point it at his face.

Hendricks gasped!

It was like seeing a ghost. It had been several years since he last saw Elijah Price and it was almost like he was looking at him now. "Forgive me for my silence. I'm a bit taken aback by what I'm seeing. There is a strong resemblance to an old friend of mine."

"He was no friend of yours, Vesper," Zenith offered in defiance.

"Perhaps you are correct, young man. Would you do me the honor of introducing yourself?" Hendricks responded.

"I'm Zenith Price."

A guarded smile crept onto Hendricks face but quickly disappeared. His mind raced upon hearing the face on the other end of the video conference announce himself. "So, the vermin managed to procreate. Humans, even at their lowest form, managed to continue," Hendricks thought to himself. "Well, then, Mr. Price, I am pleased to see Elijah's legacy continue."

Zenith immediately knew he was lying.

"Get to the point, Vesper!" Zen urged without patience.

"Ah, just like your father, I see. Stubborn and impatient. Perhaps you are correct. Maybe it is time to get to the point. My forces have discovered your lair. In a matter of minutes, you and your kind will have surrendered to my dynasty and can begin the transition to joining us by taking the injection," Hendricks nonchalantly professed.

"And if we refuse to surrender and take the shot," Zenith's question toyed with Hendricks' emotions.

"Then you die. The human race will be rid of your infection and ignorance forever."

"And what is to become of your son?" Zenith decided it was time to pull the card he had hidden up his sleeve.

Hendricks facial expression turned from one of calm, to agitation. "I am aware that you hold my son, Cyrus, hostage. By now, he must understand just how bloodthirsty your kind are. Soon, my forces will discover his location and whatever pawn you believe you possess will be for naught."

It was then that Zenith and his friends realized that Hendricks didn't know where Cyrus was. They still had that ace up their sleeve.

"Look, Price, I have grown impatient with your little game," Hendricks barked. Turning the camera away from him, it focused on a woman that was bound and gagged with tears flowing from her face, pleading for help. "This is Violet Contreras, one of the many Blueblood rebels that had joined with your kind to overthrow me. Foolish as this girl was, I have decided to use her to barter the release of my son."

Cyrus could hear everything his father was saying. Springing from his chair, unabated by any of the kidnappers, he sprang to view the screen that displayed the woman he loved. Wanting to rebuke his father's actions, he was restrained by Blaze and his mouth cupped by Blaze's forceful hand before he could identify that he was there with Zenith.

"I'm certain you know where the gallows are at the underground city. Bring my son there. In what is my benevolent nature, I will swap this young rebel lady for my son. She can live out what time she has left with you and learn what a mistake she has made. Should you decide not to accept my offer, well then, these beautiful gallows will once again be put to use," Hendricks spoke with assertion and no doubt the truth.

Dyce once again turned the camera to project Zenith's face onto the screen. "When will this exchange happen? I need time to fetch your boy!"

"Tomorrow night at dusk. I don't want you and your friends to get sunburned!" Hendricks commented with total disrespect. Before Zenith could respond, the screen went dark, and Chip announced they were no longer joined in the system.

For the first time since taking Cyrus into captivity, he could clearly see that Cyrus was sweating. Not only was he sweating, but he was also frantic. He became aware that the girl that Hendricks was holding captive on his end meant something to Cyrus.

"A friend of yours?" Zen inquired.

Dyce let go of Cyrus. "Sorry, Vesper. I couldn't let dear ol' daddy know you were here," Dyce said.

"Yes! She is a friend of mine! She's a friend of yours, too! Her father has joined up with your mother and Silver James. They've been freed from my father's spell and wish to live outside the tyranny he forces upon them. Now do you understand, you poor dumb bastard! I'm not your enemy!" Cyrus collapsed in a chair close to him with his chest heaving up and down.

Venus moved over to where Cyrus was sitting. Her female instinct in these matters was much keener than Zenith or any of the men present could ever understand. Placing her hand on Cyrus's shoulder, he looked up at her with swollen eyes. "You love her, don't you?" Venus softly remarked. He shook his head in an affirmative manner.

Grabbing the radio in her hand, Venus pressed the speak button and began repeating, "Silver, Mom, are you there?" Silver answered the call.

CHAPTER 55: COOLER

THE ADVANCING COLUMNS OF VESPER'S ARMY that were rapidly approaching the rim of the excavation hole began firing their ballistic weapons at the small defense force of the Cavern people. Their aggression was halted about fifty yards from the rim of the hole. Commander HF-76 was analyzing the potential threat from the one-lone soldier that stood at the rim with his weapon drawn and pointed towards them.

"Odd, this soldier appears to be one of us. Why then is he pointing his weapon at us, and where did he come from?" HF-76 processed the information before him.

From the blue iridescent weapon came a spray that was not ballistic in nature. It coated the front soldiers in the columns like they were getting sprayed with a water hose.

Hf-76 was puzzled.

Lifting the weapon to a higher trajectory, Tremont began to discharge the spray deeper into the columns of soldiers, coating them. HF-76 determined that this spray had done no damage to his soldiers, but he was still confused by the nature and purpose of the weapon. He would have to have it removed from the bronze soldier upon his destruction and analyzed for his own curiosity.

Commanding his soldiers to return to their advance, they began to move once again with blue eyes glowing in compliance. Suddenly, just like somebody turning out a light switch, the soldiers that were positioned on the front line froze. Their glowing eyes grew dim and eventually went totally black. With their weapons still ready to fire, they no longer did.

The next wave of soldiers followed suit. Soon, the advance of Vesper's soldiers was over, and a calmness fell over the landscape. At the entrance to the Cavern stood Silver James. He started the chant of whooping and hollering that soon engulfed and included the entire defense force. He knew his belief in neutralizing these beings was valid. His research was correct. His silver tooth could be seen from miles away emitting a gleam like the first star of the night from his smile.

With one last blast of the weapon from Tremont's extended bronze arm, a blast that had been calculated and its projection confirmed, the stream fell over HF-76 like an afternoon thunderstorm. His sensors sent an alarm, but still trying to process the event that had befallen his soldiers, he was unable to contact Hendricks Vesper in time. He had failed in his mission and would certainly be destroyed.

With that last thought being transmitted through his circuits, HF-76 went dark.

Silver reached for his radio and spoke. "It worked, Ben. The threat has been neutralized."

"Hallelujah, Silver. Price's intuition was right. You don't need to blow these things up. They just can't function when it's cold outside. They weren't built to operate in cooler temperatures! Everything about this technology working was based on temperatures getting warmer. Even us, we got minds of our own after things got cooler!" Ben excitedly explained.

"I know, Ben, I built these things!" Silver laughed as he answered. Silver's other radio began to chirp. He knew immediately that it was Venus calling out… "Silver, Mom, are you there?"

He answered her call. In less than thirty minutes, Venus, her brother, and their newfound ally, Cyrus, drove over the rim, skidding to a stop at the cavern entrance. Off in the distance, Tremont picked up the frozen statue that used to be HF-76. Placing it on the ground, he began to drag it towards the excavation hole and cavern entrance.

As he approached the entrance, Silver stopped his bronze friend, "Why did you drag that here?"

"Because my friend needs a body. This will make a good one for Primus," Tremont answered as he continued to drag the body of HF-76 into the cavern.

Silver smiled at the action, "He truly has become his own being!" With the immediate threat of Vesper's army over, Zenith and his sister found the waiting arms of their mother, Lark.

In an action that surprised even Zenith, he cupped his outreached hand around Cyrus's neck and said, "C'mon, friend. Let's plan just how we're going to get your girlfriend back and put an end to this madness."

Cyrus glanced at Venus who had produced a big smile on her face.

CHAPTER 56:
ULTIMATE BETRAYAL

HENDRICKS WAS CERTAIN that something had gone wrong with the onslaught of his troops as they descended upon the Cavern of the rebels. The Cavern that had eluded him ever since the murder of his beloved, Antonetta. He questioned Pi regarding whether he had received any new reports from the Palace guard.

"No, Hendricks. The reports are the same. All communication with the Commander, HF-76, have gone silent," Pi commented.

"What are your thoughts, Pi?" Hendricks asked.

"I've had discussions with Dr. Tolmie. I tend to agree with his evaluation that the rebels have discovered a way to bring down communication between the army and the Palace. He said they were obviously very clever since they found a way to hack into our video system," Pi expressed his opinion.

"Perhaps. They might think they're clever, but I'm always one step ahead of them," Hendricks responded.

"Maybe you shouldn't proceed with taking the Blueblood woman to the underground city. At least until we can confirm that the rebels have been defeated and Cyrus has been found," Pi suggested.

Hendricks pondered his servant's idea. "Either way there won't be an exchange. This girl has caused me nothing but problems since she came onto my property and into my son's life. She will hang either way."

"That won't bring you reconciliation with Cyrus," Pi stated.

"He'll get over her. It's best he doesn't have anybody to preoccupy his time when he takes over for me. Love caused me too many distractions."

Pi simply nodded his affirmation of what his master had just proclaimed. He hadn't any concept of the emotion of love. Only submission and loyalty. "Dr. Tolmie is accompanying me tonight, correct?" Hendricks asked again, even though he had confirmed it several times before.

"Yes, Hendricks. You and Dr. Tolmie will travel together. The woman will be towed in a cage on a trailer behind a vehicle that carries twelve of your Palace guards," Pi reiterated.

With no affirmation of what Pi had just told him, Hendricks left to prepare for their departure. Later, Hendricks appeared in what Pi's databanks described as military fatigues. He had never seen these before in Hendricks' wardrobe. "I'm departing with Dr. Tolmie now. If you get any communication from my assault force, let me know immediately."

In keeping with the outfit that Hendricks was wearing, Pi decided a salute was appropriate.

Stopping in front of Ben Tolmie's laboratory, Hendricks put the ATV into park as Ben climbed in. "You brought several injections?" Hendricks questioned.

Ben looked behind the ATV at the vehicle that carried the Palace guard and a caged Violet. "Yes, I have several blue vials. We'll be able to inject several of the Cavern people on site that wish to conform."

"Good. We'll be saving them from extinction," Hendricks nodded.

"A little extreme, don't you think? Having the girl caged up like a dangerous animal," Ben asked.

"Dangerous animals need to be put down," Hendricks answered with no hesitation. Placing the ATV into drive, Hendricks and Ben moved down the path that would allow their departure from the Sphere and onto the road to the underground city. As they drove, Ben placed his hand of the one lone vial that had been separated from the rest. He gently patted it with his palm, not desiring to be too forceful or to bring suspicion since this injection was already in a syringe with a needle, ready for insertion.

Zenith gently placed the restraints on the wrists of Cyrus who had put his arms behind him. "Test them. You should be able to pull them loose with a slight tug on one of your wrists. This is just for show for your father."

Cyrus gave a slight pull to the restraint immediately allowing his arm to be set free. "Yep, it's good." Off in the distance and directly north of their position, Cyrus could see dust being churned up into the air. He felt his anxiety begin to heighten.

Zenith spoke loud enough for everybody who was attending the exchange to hear. "Showtime everybody." Silver, Hector, Tremont, Dyce and Cyrus all acknowledged Zen's attempt at humor. Cyrus glanced around the compound and was stricken by the sight of the gallows. His disdain for this apparatus of pain and death sealed the deal that his father must be removed from power.

As the ATV that carried Hendricks and Ben pulled up and parked some distance away from where his son stood, Cyrus' focus wasn't on his father. He could clearly see the way Violet was being treated and it repulsed him. The soldiers disembarked from their vehicle and two of them marched back to the cage that held Violet.

Cyrus could see she had been crying and this caused his anxiety to increase. He firmly resolved to end this tonight. Still, he had to play the game, or this whole thing could go wrong very quickly. Hendricks stood with his feet spread and postured himself in a way that would make him seem to be in control of the situation. Ben walked in front of the ATV and joined Hendricks, standing by his side.

"Good to see you, son. I trust they've treated you fairly," Hendricks said.

Wanting to respond with anger and run to physically attack his father, he held back with all the restraint he could manage. "Yes, father. They have treated me fairly."

Turning his attention to Zenith and Silver, Hendricks spoke with arrogance towards them as he walked up to face Zenith. Looking directly into his eyes, Hendricks studied him for a moment. "My-oh-my, you certainly are your father's son. Quite the resemblance. It's amazing that your kind found a way to procreate. So nice of you to agree to my terms and join me tonight. I do hope my soldiers are treating your mother well, now that we have found your lair."

Zenith bit his lip. If his eyes had been a weapon, they certainly would have fired upon Hendricks. The fierceness of Zen's look certainly provoked one of the bronze soldiers to prepare his weapon. "No need for animosity," Silver extended his arm with his palm outward towards the soldier. "We are here to get this over with and move on."

Hendricks moved and now was standing before Silver. Leaning in towards Silver's ear, he whispered, "I can't wait to study you. There must be a reason some of my subjects chose to rebel against me. You'll be one of the first I probe."

Motioning to the soldiers to bring Violet forward, Hendricks proclaimed, "Yes, we are here to get this over with. Ben, go and fetch my son. Once we have him with us, I will release the traitor."

Zen raised his hand in defiance. "Not so fast, Vesper. My man will come and take control of the girl. Once she has moved away from your soldiers, your man can have your son." Hendricks pondered the proposal.

"Gutsy! For someone without a position to make demands. I have many soldiers here. What do you expect this abomination here with you to do against my force? Nevertheless, come and get her."

Tremont remembered this man that used to control him. He didn't care for him then, and he didn't care for him now. His senses told him it wasn't wise to expose the fact that twelve soldiers wouldn't be difficult for him to handle due to the fact that he had vanquished an entire battalion of Vesper's army.

Hector placed his arm around Violet and began to move her away from the soldiers. At the same moment, Ben placed his arm around Cyrus, placing a syringe and needle into the hand that had been freed from the loose restraints. He leaned in to hug Cyrus and whispered softly in his ear, "Remember, put the needle directly into his neck."

Hendricks found Ben's display of affection for his son heartwarming. It meant much to him coming from his loyal friend from all these years. He considered that his suspicion that his long-time associate had turned against him had been unfounded. Smiling, he motioned for Ben to bring his son to him. Reaching out with open arms, his father's embrace repulsed Cyrus. "Now, we will begin anew. First, your captors will get a little display on why not to defy me. This young woman hanging from a rope will cement that notion."

Cyrus pushed back from his father's embrace upon hearing these words. He brought the syringe and needle up and forced it into his father's neck and released the contents into Hendricks' bloodstream.

Shocked by the action his son had just taken, but probably more shocked by his son's betrayal, Hendricks stumbled backwards with the needle still stuck in his neck. With a violent command for his soldiers to fire upon those that had defied him, Hendricks collapsed to the ground from the effects of the injection.

The soldiers raised their weapons upon Hendrick's command, but it was already too late. Tremont's weapon had already been discharged. The last vision that Hendricks had before losing consciousness was seeing the glowing blue eyes of his force turn dark.

Cyrus ran over to Violet and hugged her like he would never let her go. "You're safe now, Violet. We are all safe."

As Violet kissed her hero, he hoped he would never again have to taste her salty tears. Tears that had been born of pain and fear. Ben embraced Silver and Zenith. It was difficult to return the embrace for Zenith, but he had learned very recently that help comes from the most unexpected people and becoming a leader meant you must know when to accept that help.

CHAPTER 57:
LEADER

LARK STROKED VENUS'S HAIR with the brush that had been fashioned from the plant fibers that she had cultivated from her gardens. Violet looked on as Lark motioned her to come and sit for her turn. Violet was in no hurry to leave the comfort of the Caverns and the people that lived there. She found it a little cold, but that was to be expected since she was a Blueblood.

Violet was still euphoric from the shower she had taken in the waterfall springs that fed the lake. The water was fresh, untreated, and clean. It made her hair soft, and the natural lavender shampoo gave off a fragrance she had never experienced before in her young life.

Everything about the Spheres seemed to be so...she struggled for the word before it finally came to her... unnatural. She could have certainly brushed her own hair without Lark's assistance, but the loving touch of Lark's fingers, as she gently stroked her wet hair while pulling the brush through it, brought a sense of peace to her soul.

She could never remember a moment like this with her own mother. Her mother was a strong and determined woman, just like Lark, but tenderness wasn't an emotion she could recall her ever displaying. She chalked it up to the clinical environment in which they lived, inside the Spheres.

Venus began to sing and the delight she found in Lark brushing her hair was magnified. Violet had never heard

Venus sing. In fact, she had never heard anybody sing. Apparently music wasn't a priority in the world of the Bluebloods. All she knew was that Venus's singing brought a higher understanding. An understanding that these people, who rebelled against Hendrick's Vesper from the very beginning, hadn't been deprived of anything.

In fact, their resilience and development of a culture that was all their own was remarkable. She rejoiced in the lyrics as Venus sang her song.

So far away
Doesn't anybody stay in one place anymore
It would be so nice to see your face at my door
But you're so far away

She stopped listening to the lyrics to ask Lark a question that had been on her mind ever since the reign of Hendricks Vesper had come to an end. "Do you ever worry about how life will be different, not only for you, but for the people of the Spheres, now that they don't have a leader?"

Lark deeply pondered the question she had just been asked. Looking up as she continued to brush Violet's hair, she delved deep for insight on how to answer the question. Stopping brushing Violet's hair, she answered with all the honesty she could conjure. "Violet, I know that is what Cyrus, Zenith, Silver, and Tremont are discussing with your father at this very moment."

"Cyrus doesn't want to lead the Blueblood people. He senses that there are many who don't trust him, being a Vesper and all," Violet offered.

"I can certainly understand how some people could feel that way. Your father, Alonzo, is the likely choice. He has the respect of the Blueblood's living inside and outside the Spheres," Lark replied.

Venus had finished singing the last stanza of the chorus and replied to Lark and Violet, "The rumor that I hear is that my brother should be the leader."

Lark and Violet shot a gaze of astonishment at Venus. "Why are you looking at me like that? I only said it was a rumor," Venus held her hands upward with arms extended.

Violet responded with a sly smile on her lips, "I don't believe we were questioning that Zenith could be the leader, we were just wondering how you could be singing and still listening to our conversation at the same time!"

The three women laughed long at hard at Violet's revelation. When the laughter had finally subsided, Dyce poked his head around the canvas covering of the Price's camp site. With a shyness that was uncharacteristic of Zen's right-hand man, he bashfully said, "I was just passing by and heard Venus singing. It was really good, Venus."

With a slight redness to her cheeks, Venus responded, "Thanks, Dyce. Glad you liked it." After a few short interchanges of conversation with Lark and the girls, Dyce excused himself to head back to his camp site. As he departed, Lark and Violet stared at Venus with looks that had the appearance of knowing a secret.

"What? What are you looking at?" Venus protested their unusual stares with her question.

Lark walked up to her daughter and placed her arm around her shoulder. "Can't you see it?"

"See what, mom?" Venus replied.

"That boy is smitten with you," Lark responded.

"So smitten," Violet chimed in.

Cyrus shook hands with Alonzo Contreras as their meeting was adjourned. All the men and women that formed the committee that would steer the futures of both the Cavern and Sphere peoples had agreed that Alonzo would be the leader. He reluctantly agreed, but expected both Cyrus and Zenith to take strong roles in bringing what was left of humanity together.

Zen started his walk back to the ATV they had driven to the meeting when Cyrus approached him. "Hey Zen, I need to go to the Palace. I need to check on our A.I. servant, Pi. He's probably confused that his master, my father, hasn't returned to him and he's no longer receiving any communication from the soldiers of the force. I need to talk to him and let him know the truth."

"I understand, but when Ben Tolmie hit the kill switch on what was left of your father's force, that didn't shut down your servant also?" Zen asked.

"No. Pi was a different *breed* so to speak. I don't believe he's dangerous. Well, at least not to me, I'm a Vesper."

"You need me to go with you, Cyrus?"

"Not tonight. It would only confuse him. I'll be fine." Cyrus and Zenith gave each other a guarded hug. This had become a relationship forged out of struggle and strife. It was in its infancy, but it was evident that these men were on that journey of mutual respect and, hopefully, trust for each other.

Cyrus found Pi standing at attention in the Palace living area. His posture showed that he had no other knowledge of what to do and had been standing in the same spot for a long time. Upon seeing Cyrus walk into the room, Pi's eyes clearly showed relief and, in a way, happiness that Cyrus had arrived. "Hello, Pi," Cyrus greeted him.

"Master Cyrus, I am relieved to see you. Please, let me fix you some sustenance or perhaps get you liquid refreshment," Pi gleefully offered.

"I'm fine, Pi. I don't need you to wait on me. I'm here to bring you knowledge of current affairs," Cyrus spoke in a manner that would make sense to Pi.

"Should we wait for Hendricks to arrive so he can be part of our discussion?" Pi inquired.

Cyrus paused as he considered just how he would answer this question. He decided the best way was to be honest and straightforward, "Pi, Hendricks will not be coming home."

Unable to show any emotion, Pi responded to the news Cyrus told him in the only way he knew how, "Has Hendricks ceased to function?"

"In a way, Pi. It's sort of like that."

"I am here to serve the house of Vesper. Now I'm allegiant to you, Cyrus.

Not confident this conversation had gone the way he had hoped, all Cyrus could offer was to be affirmative to Pi until Silver could intervene and give him advice on how to handle him. "Thank you, Pi. As for right now, I want you to go shut down for a while. I will be fine, and in the morning, you can make me some breakfast."

Pi reluctantly obeyed his master. He was anxious to discover more information about Hendricks but was programmed to comply with orders. Cyrus could see Pi's glowing aqua blue eyes begin to dim, which meant that his servant had gone into dormant mode. Grabbing his hand-held radio, Cyrus moved the frequency dial to connect directly with Violet. She answered his call.

"Hi, Vi, how're you doing?" Cyrus asked.

"I'm good. Actually, I'm great. I'm having a wonderful time with my new friends. Where are you? I was wondering, since Zenith came back without you," Violet curiously responded.

Cyrus had walked out onto the terrace where his father had sat so many times before. It felt odd and unnatural for him to be there looking out on the terrain of Sphere2, just like his father. "I'm at the Palace. I came to check on my servant, Pi. He's the A.I. I told you about. I'm worried about him. He isn't military and doesn't operate like my father's force, so Ben can't just shut him down remotely. I'm going to stay here until the morning."

With obvious sadness in her voice, Violet replied. "Okay, my love, but I will worry about you. Is the A.I. any threat to you?"

Cyrus chuckled. "No, he's gentle. Confused and curious, but gentle. I'm going to take him with me to visit my father in the morning. He needs to see where my father is and why he won't be serving him any longer."

"Is that a wise thing to do? I mean, your father could command him to attack you and try to escape," Cyrus could hear the alarm in her voice.

"Don't worry, Violet. I'm taking Tremont with me too. Father's afraid of Tremont. He won't try anything with him around."

"Does Zen know you're going to see your father?" she inquired.

"Not yet, but he's my next call."

"Where are we going this morning?" Pi quizzed Cyrus.

"You know of the underground city, don't you, Pi?" Cyrus responded.

"Yes, it was the desolate city for those rebels that refused to follow Hendricks. It has long been abandoned. Since the rebel leader, Elijah Price, was destroyed and the rebellion and the first war ended," Pi answered, knowing full well that he had been the one that ended the life of Elijah Price.

Cyrus didn't respond to Pi's acknowledgement and understanding of the underground city. As the ATV that carried them to the city eclipsed the distance from the Spheres, Cyrus's attention was suddenly distracted by something in the sky, spread out and covering what must have been a large area. The object was white, with a grey underbelly. It had no uniform structure and appeared to be moving very slowly.

Cyrus had never seen anything like it.

"Pi, are you seeing the structure before us? Up there in the sky?" Cyrus quizzed his companion.

"Yes, Cyrus. I have been analyzing my data banks for some time now to see if they contained any information as to what it is."

"Did you find anything?" Cyrus pleaded as he almost ran the ATV off the road due to keeping his focus on the object.

"I discovered one possibility that would explain the object, Cyrus." Pi answered. After a short delay in the conversation due to Pi finishing his scan, he finally delivered the results of his research. "I believe it is called a 'cloud'. It is an atmospheric occurrence that, many years ago, would form and carry and release water onto the earth from above."

Cyrus did his best to keep the ATV on the road despite the object that Pi called a *cloud* beginning to display a deeper and darker gray color to its underbelly.

CHAPTER 58:
HEALING

THE METAL DOOR FLUNG OPEN, startling Hendricks. Standing in the doorway to his underground confinement stood an ominous Tremont. Not wanting to acknowledge his bronze jailer, Hendricks reclined back into the ratty couch that served as the only furniture in his disgusting prison.

Coming out from behind Tremont, Hendricks felt elated at the appearance of his son, Cyrus, and his servant, Pi. His first thought was that they had come to rescue him and take him away from this miserable place. "Oh, thank God," Hendricks proclaimed with glee as he quickly sprang from the couch to seek the arms of his son.

Tremont abruptly stopped the approach of Hendricks by extending his formidable bronze arm. Realizing those arms of welcome weren't going to happen, Hendricks knew he had no ability to contend against such a foe as Tremont. Recognizing that his joy was short lived, he relaxed.

Cyrus casually spoke to his father, "Can't say you're looking well."

Pi had no programming or understanding of how to deal with what was happening before him. "Cat got your tongue, Pi? Can't believe what they've done to your friend, can you?" Hendricks pointed his question directly at Pi.

"No, Hendricks, I have no resource to draw upon," Pi replied as he continued to scan the environment.

"Well, let me help you to understand. Your companion here is a traitor. He has decided that he would rather be vermin than a prince."

"I don't understand, Hendricks. Cyrus is not a rodent. He is a Vesper," Pi responded in a matter-of-fact manner.

Hendricks turned away from his visitors to recline on the dusty and torn couch. Turning his attention to a tear in the upholstery, Hendricks spoke, attempting to display a regalness he was no longer in a position to show. "This man is no longer a Vesper, Pi. He will lead humankind to ruin. He is nothing to me. He is dead to me."

Cyrus refused to show any disgust for the man who had been his father. "I can only hope that you can learn from this, father. To serve out your remaining years in the same chamber where Elijah Price was made to live, perhaps you can learn what humanity truly is."

Hendricks peeled the wrapping of a nutrient bar that had been provided for him for his sustenance. He used every source of his mind and soul to not gag while he ate it. "Elijah Price and his kind were well provided for. I will be just fine living this life of luxury, thank you very much."

"My reason for coming here today is not to have a battle of insults with you, father. I only came here today so Pi could learn that this is where you live now. He is no longer your servant. He is no longer my servant. He can now begin his journey to self-awareness."

Hendricks smirked as pieces of the nutrient bar flew from his mouth. "Self-awareness? This is what you expect Pi to achieve. You believe just like the rest of humanity! Oh yes, we will all find our way," Hendricks mocked his son.

Cyrus had grown tired of this meeting. He dropped a pack that he had been carrying on his back onto the floor. Turning to depart from his father's underground cell, he pointed towards the pack lying on the floor. "There, father, I brought you some notebooks and pencils. I know just how important keeping a journal was to you in your former life, Dolion."

As Pi, Cyrus and Tremont closed the metal door to begin their ascent to the surface, Cyrus could almost feel the pain his father was feeling, knowing that his son now knew the truth. The truth was that his father's life had been nothing but deceit and lies. No matter what had begun with earnest intent, power had taken control of the man his father had been…and changed him.

Zenith sat on the bluff above the Cavern entrance. The same bluff to which he had always retreated, ever since he was a young boy. The stars had not yet appeared in the evening sky. It wasn't quite dark enough for them to show their brilliant shine. Tonight would not be a night to focus on the stars. Instead, the object he witnessed, that appeared in the sky directly above him, had captured every moment of his current attention. He hadn't seen anything like it before.

Lark appeared with Venus to interrupt his solitude. "It's called a rain cloud," Lark offered without being asked. "They were very commonplace here in what used to be called Colorado. That was back before the madness of the warming that turned where we lived into a desert."

Zen sat up with his elbows on the ground, lifting his upper torso. "What is rain, mother?" Zen quizzed.

"A miracle that you are about to feel!" Lark answered. A short time later, Zenith and his family retreated to the shelter of the Cavern after getting soaked by water that fell from the sky. Zen watched with amazement as the rain continued to fall and the ground outside the Cavern entrance began to swell as it greeted a long-lost friend.

Six Months Later

Zenith walked over to the field where his mother was cultivating the garden. A vegetable garden that she could only have dreamed of a short time ago. This garden was on the surface, and it was thriving due to rain and irrigation from the ponds that were formed in the excavation holes that once were intended to offer humans that had not taken the injection a place to live in buried concrete tubes.

He felt it was quite ironic. These same holes now provided receptacles to store water above ground. These same humans once had to live underground and depend on a madman for their very existence.

It was still odd to see Primus with a body. He loved working with Lark in the garden and he was a constant companion as she taught both Bluebloods and Cavern people alike the knowledge of how to grow food. His head was very similar to the one that used to sit upon Silver James' table, but with the improvement in A.I. technology and the surrogate body of HF-76, which Tremont had provided for him, Primus had achieved the desires of his existence.

Lark waved at her son as he approached her. She placed her hands on her hips as she called out to him, "Need something, sweetheart?"

"No, just checking on you. It's still hot out here, mom."

"Not too hot for me. Plus, it's getting cooler every day," Lark replied as she looked up into the morning sky adorned with clouds forming. Zenith wasn't about to tell his mother to come inside from the surface. He knew how being able to spend time on the surface made her feel. The sun no longer caused irreparable harm to humans that had not taken the Blueblood injection, as long as they limited their exposure to just a few hours per day.

The earth had begun to heal itself. Somehow, no matter what Hendricks Vesper believed or could comprehend, he hadn't taken into consideration that the earth could heal itself. Whatever had started the destruction of the ozone, whether it be human ignorance or whatever, those things were gone, and the planet and humans were healing themselves.

Lark waved at her son in a way that told him that she needed to get back to work. Zenith obliged, knowing that he had to get to a meeting with Cyrus to discuss additional security for the underground chamber that held Hendricks Vesper. As he drove off to attend the meeting with Cyrus, Lark had a vision of someone or something standing a short distance from her.

She knew that it wasn't Primus because he was the only companion close to her before Zenith arrived. For a moment, Lark considered that she was feeling the effects of the heat just as her son had warned about. Then, her vision became clearer. It was her beloved, Elijah, standing a short distance from her in the garden. Without words he spoke to her, "At last, my love, you have found the surface. Your cherished earth is now accessible to your touch once again."

Be it a ghost or a vision produced from her heart, Lark didn't care. The specter's appearance gave her joy as it disappeared as quickly as it came.

Pi had gone missing. It worried Cyrus, as the A.I. had begun to act very strangely shortly before he disappeared. He couldn't explain why, and neither could Ben Tolmie or Silver.

They both considered that what was causing Pi's erratic behavior was the same thing that had happened to the mind controlling substance in the Blueblood serum. Hendricks had never considered that the earth's temperature wouldn't continue to rise. In fact, it had begun to cool as the ozone started to repair itself.

With time, and the gradual cooling, the people that received the injection were no longer compliant to Hendricks Vesper. That same element came into effect with the failure of the Sphere panels for the construction of Sphere3 and now, the decay of the existing Spheres.

As rain began to fall once again, large holes in Spheres1 and 2 had begun to form. Ben Tolmie predicted that eventually the Spheres would deteriorate and dissolve, just like moisture dissolved cotton candy.

Both Cyrus and Zenith sat quietly staring at the snow that had formed on the mountain peaks jutting high into the western sky.

"I wonder what snow is like?" Cyrus remarked.

"Mom says that the tallest mountain used to be called Long's Peak. I guess it was named after somebody who must have been famous. Someday we'll have to go there. Just to see what snow is like," Zen acknowledged.

"I don't think we'll ever name one of those mountains 'Hendricks Peak'," Cyrus nonchalantly said.

The two men laughed uncontrollably at Cyrus's joke. After the laughter had ended and solitude and a mutual and natural silence had returned to their communion, Cyrus and Zenith marveled to see two cottontail rabbits frolicking just a short distance from them.

EPILOGUE

My first and only journal entry in captivity
Hendricks Vesper, Unknown month, 2698

I STRUGGLED AGAINST WRITING anything down since I'm held prisoner by the very people I saved from extinction. After resisting the temptation of recording my thoughts in this journal, I succumbed to the notion that should I never see the surface again and die in this, for lack of a better description, tomb, then I must leave a record of my defense. I must defend myself. For those that will find it and what's left of me.

This record will explain that my entire existence, my whole reason for living, was to give this biological species that is called human, a chance to survive. History will try and display me as evil and demented. It might even try and paint a picture that I was insane. Out of my mind! Perhaps they were correct in that perception.

My life was devoted to science and the proliferation of the human species. If wanting our species to survive a fate that humans were too ignorant to recognize as being imminent, I'm guilty as charged. I used my genius to ensure our survival. If that is the definition of insane, then that is the legacy I leave.

Even my own flesh and blood has forsaken me. I suppose I shouldn't have been surprised. Instead, I became complacent because I developed a way to convert the very DNA of humans, so they could survive in an unhospitable world. Adding a mind-altering element to that injection that would alter their DNA, that would cause them to follow my every command, without questioning, was necessary. I was naïve to not foresee that the offspring of those who received my blue injection wouldn't be naturally allegiant and loyal to me. Including my own child.

This is where I made my biggest mistake.

Now I understand that, and it has led me here, held against my will, left to live out my life in squalor and desolation. In a previous life, I had just given up. I had no hope for intelligent life to continue its reign on this, our planet. So, I ended that life. Well, at least in my own mind I ended that life, and I let the ocean of my mind determine the fate of that soul. What that sea yielded was my resurrection, as Hendricks Vesper.

I was unable to exterminate the ignorance that still existed in our world. I have no doubt that, like a plague, those that refused my genius and now hold me in contempt will inherit this planet and they will ultimately lead it to the destruction of our species.

Perhaps the creatures that discover my journal will learn that Dolion Cozbi and Hendricks Vesper were not evil or degenerate. Neither were they insane. Should my remains be gone, know that I have been resurrected before. Maybe, just maybe, I have been resurrected again. Perhaps those creatures will search for me and the truth. If they find the man that used to be Dolion Cozbi and Hendricks Vesper, they will understand that man is to be followed and revered. They will seek him out to save their souls.

Hendricks Vesper put down his pencil, folded the notebook that held the prophecy of the man that created the Bluebloods. He did not know his ultimate fate. That fate was in the hands of time and the deep blue sea of his mind.

www.ingramcontent.com/pod-product-compliance
Lightning Source LLC
Chambersburg PA
CBHW072123020726
47501CB00003B/953

* 9 7 8 1 6 3 8 6 8 1 5 4 0 *